To the growers of flowers and tenders of bees, thank you all.

Emma Davies

The House at Hope Corner

bookouture

Published by Bookouture in 2019

An imprint of StoryFire Ltd.

Carmelite House
50 Victoria Embankment
London EC4Y 0DZ

www.bookouture.com

ISBN: 978-1-78681-843-0
eBook ISBN: 978-1-78681-842-3

Prologue

'Are we completely mad?' asked Flora, snuggling down into the sleeping bag. 'Or only partially?'

'Well that depends,' answered Ned, picking his way across the dimly lit roof garden with a mug in each hand. 'On how mad we were to start with, and how much this may have tipped us over the edge.'

Flora giggled. 'Then I declare us to be a lost cause,' she said. 'Come on, get the drinks over here, I'm freezing.'

Ned grinned, stumbling as he tripped over his foot. He took two tumbling steps before his legs caught up with the rest of him, but somehow still managed to keep hold of the mugs and their contents.

'We ought to be drinking champagne really.'

'Why,' asked Flora, 'when hot chocolate tastes about a million times better? Especially when it's got a drop of brandy in it.'

She waited until Ned had nearly reached her before snaking a hand out from beneath the covers to take the drinks. A blast of cold air filled the gap and she gasped as he began to climb in next to her. Even with her fleecy pyjamas, jumper and woolly hat on she was only just warm enough, but she didn't care, because right now she couldn't think of a nicer place to be.

Ned wriggled up against her before taking his mug.

'We should raise a toast,' he said.

'What to?'

'How about living happily ever after?' he replied. 'Us getting married, you selling your shop and your flat. It's a brand new start, isn't it? For both of us.' His face grew sombre for a moment. 'And are you happy, Flora? Honestly?'

'I am,' she replied without a moment's hesitation. 'I've never been more sure of anything in my life.'

He beamed at her. 'Which is fortunate really because I find myself quite convincingly and utterly in love with you. It shouldn't even be possible given the short amount of time I've known you. But it's true, and I cannot wait to take you home and marry you.'

'But why me?' queried Flora. She had asked the question a dozen times since he had proposed, but she never tired of hearing the answer. 'Why not a farmer's daughter with a face full of freckles like yours...? Someone who knows one end of a cow from another and has big sturdy hips to bear you lots of children?'

'You know why,' teased Ned. 'Because all the farmer's daughters I know think I'm soppy. And, whereas *I* think lying on my back on a freezing cold December night to watch a meteor shower is a great idea, they don't.'

'But it *is* a great idea.'

'See?' Ned laughed. 'But now I want to know why you would even consider the offer, what with my two left feet and hands the size of dinner plates? Marrying me is a big step. It will take you away from everything you know, out of the city and into the middle of nowhere, which at this time of year is basically full of mud.'

Flora gazed up at Ned's face as she sipped her hot chocolate. She thought of her flat below them and her shop below that, full of flowers, even in the middle of winter. She thought of all the reasons why she shouldn't be doing this, how it was throwing common sense out of the window and taking the biggest leap of faith in her life, but despite it all, nothing in her life had ever felt this right. And, after all, it really couldn't have come at a better time. She had to make this work, for her sister's sake if nothing else. She would never forgive herself for what she had done, but perhaps this might be a way to atone for some of it, at least.

'Because you knew that inviting me to look at the stars was far more magical than being wined and dined in some fancy restaurant. No one else has ever got that about me…' She frowned slightly. 'Or maybe they did, but they never had it within themselves…'

She swallowed the last of her chocolate, putting down the mug so that she could snuggle deeper under the covers and closer to Ned. She was about to add something else when a sudden spark lit the sky.

'Oh, look…!' She sighed. 'Isn't that beautiful?'

Ned pulled her close. 'Promise me we can always do this, even when we're old and grey?'

'Especially when we're old and grey,' replied Flora. 'Are the stars really beautiful where you live?'

Ned nodded. 'The sky seems to go on forever when you look down the valley. And there's no light pollution. It's utterly black. Some nights I swear you can see the swirls of the Milky Way itself.'

Flora pulled herself up into a more upright position so that she could look at Ned's face. 'Tell me again why it's called Hope Corner Farm,' she said.

'No one really knows for sure,' he answered. 'But the story has it that the first farmer who settled there came from Worcester, driven out by some feudal disagreement over land, so he took off, with literally just the clothes on his back and a handful of cattle which he drove along the roads. He was headed further north but, starving, thirsty and exhausted, and with his cattle on the point of collapse, he realised he could go no further and stopped there to let them drink from the stream. As night fell, he made a rough shelter and, when morning came, he couldn't believe his eyes. He awoke to find that his cattle had all crossed the stream and were grazing out in a pasture of the greenest grass he'd ever seen. Taking it as a good omen, he decided to stay and the rest, as they say, is history. Somewhere along the line, because the farmer always said that this was where his fate changed and he found hope, the bend in the road where he turned off became known as Hope Corner. The farm took its name from that point forward.'

Flora sighed happily. 'And it will be all right, Ned, won't it? Your mum and dad *will* like me?'

'Of course it will, they're going to *love* you…'

Chapter 1

Was it excitement, or was it nerves? Flora wasn't entirely sure which, but something had woken her. Ned had left their bed hours ago, kissing her on the nose before getting up to milk the cows, and she had rolled into the warm spot he had left, relishing his scent and the memory of him. She had fallen back asleep almost immediately, but now, though, she was wide awake. She wriggled her toes experimentally, feeling the weight of the old eiderdown that covered the huge brass-framed bed, and contemplated the day ahead of her.

They hadn't arrived at the farm until yesterday evening, and though the house had been a shining beacon of welcoming light, the gardens, the fields, barns, and whatever else surrounded it had been hidden from view in the all-encompassing darkness outside. It was only her second visit but, as the pile of suitcases in the boot of the car attested, this time she wasn't just visiting, this time she was staying for good, as the future Mrs Ned Jamieson.

The first time she had met Ned's parents had been every bit as awkward as she had expected. But then, having their son bring home a complete stranger, telling them he was going to marry her, must have come as a huge shock. In fairness, back then, Flora had still been trying to get used to the idea of their engagement herself, so she couldn't begin to imagine how Hannah and Fraser must have felt. Flora wasn't absolutely sure that his mum had liked her choice of bright yellow tights either, despite what she'd said.

Yesterday, though, Ned's parents both seemed more enthusiastic in their welcome and her nerves had finally begun to settle. This was her home now, they had told her, and today she had every intention of exploring it.

She flung the cover back from the bed, wincing at the chill that greeted her, and swung her legs over the side of the mattress. Even so, her feet still dangled several inches from the old oak floorboards beneath her and she had to shuffle forward just to put her feet flat on the floor. She regretted it the minute they made contact with the icy cold surface, and snatched them back up again, staring balefully at the huge expanse of wood around her, not a rug in sight. She lunged for her clothes which, discarded last night, were still hooked around the bedpost, and dragged them into the centre of the bed where she pulled them on hurriedly. She lay on her back and kicked her legs in the air to hitch up her tights, bright orange this time, and then wriggled her dress back down again. The sooner she got up and moving, the better. Slipping an extra pair of thick stripy socks on before her boots, she wasted no more time in the bedroom and headed down the stairs. She was starving.

The farmhouse kitchen was almost as big as her old flat. Back in Birmingham she'd only had a small galley and a tiny adjoining sitting room, but the glass that ran the whole length of one wall afforded a fabulous view over the city where Flora could sit and watch the twinkling lights and dream her dreams. To be fair, before she'd met Ned, those dreams had usually involved her being whisked away to a remote Scottish castle by a dashing Highlander in a kilt rather than by a burly red-headed farmer to an isolated farm in a Shropshire valley, but it was close enough. Flora was thirty-five, by her own admission a little bit weird, and not hugely enamoured by the prospect of being left on the shelf.

Apart from when the fire was lit in the main sitting room, the kitchen was the warmest room in the farmhouse by far. If you weren't sitting at the enormous well-scrubbed pine table, then you were sprawled on the threadbare sofa which faced the window. A huge dark blue range cooker dominated the middle of one wall, and radiated heat around the room. An elderly chocolate Labrador named Brodie seldom moved from beside it and he thumped a lazy tail at her now as she crossed the room to scratch the top of his head on her way to fill up the kettle.

Tea was normally always the first thing on her agenda, but this morning her attention was caught by the view from the window and, totally distracted, she abandoned her task, the kettle only half full. Stopping only to grab a weather-beaten oilskin from a row of hooks in the scullery, Flora headed out the back door and into the garden.

The view took her breath away; staring down a valley, a sweep of dips and rises on either side stretched into the distance, and the colours – lime, olive, ochre, chestnut, heather, and something approaching teal – all leaped out at her. It was the middle of winter for goodness' sake, where did all the colour come from? Closer to her, within the confines of the garden, were shades of ruby, verdigris, plum and honey… everywhere she looked, tiny patches of colour glowing in the morning sun. She turned back to look at the house, a solid red-brick building of jumbled rooflines, windows and chimneys. It was like stepping into a scene from a painting. Except it wasn't, because, instead, this was now her home.

A gust of wind billowed Flora's dress around her and she clutched the coat tighter, feeling the wild air tug at her hair. A sudden shiver of excitement rippled through her and she dashed back inside the house, letting the door crash behind her as her thoughts tumbled through her head. What did she need to do first? Eat? No, drink… put on some more clothes, grab her sketchbook, or her camera, although both would probably be useful. She gripped the back of one of the kitchen chairs and grinned at Brodie.

'You didn't tell me it was *this* gorgeous,' she said, impulsively rushing over to throw her arms around the dog.

'Does anyone ever take you for walks?' she asked, cocking her head to one side. 'Or maybe that's supposed to be me? I don't know… what do you think, Brodie?'

The dog gave her hand a tentative lick and got to his feet, tail swaying gently as he padded across the floor to the door.

'Ah, so you *do* want to go out,' she said, looking down at her clothes. She shrugged off the oilskin and deposited it on the table. 'Back in a sec,' she added.

She ran back up the stairs and into their room, grabbing one of her suitcases and heaving it onto the bed. Inside was an assortment of clothes, jumpers mainly, and Flora pulled several out before finding the one she wanted. It was bright red with pom-poms around the bottom edge and, most importantly, it was warm, which was all Flora really cared about. She pulled it over her head and down to where it reached almost to her knees, and looked around for her coat and hat. Both were slung over a chair in the corner, and she picked them up before leaving the room again, grabbing her phone at the last minute as she passed the dressing table. She looked at her reflection in the mirror for a moment – spiralling black hair, startling green eyes and rosebud mouth – and she grinned. It was definitely excitement, not nerves.

Brodie was back beside the range once more, his eyes following her as she began to systematically open cupboard doors.

'So there must be some glasses, mugs or something, somewhere,' she said out loud. 'Ah ha ha! Found them,' she added, taking down a glass. 'And if I could just find something to eat as well then we're in business, Brodie…'

She continued her search, stopping when she noticed a round tin on the counter top. She pulled it towards her and cranked off the lid, smiling at the sight of a large round fruitcake nestled within. She checked her watch. 'What do you reckon?' she asked. 'Too early for cake?' She grinned at the dog's silent face. 'Nah… that's what I thought too.' A further search elicited a plate and a knife and, moments later, Flora was chewing thoughtfully.

She should probably start exploring the house first, but with all that was waiting outside she really didn't think she would be able to. She had all day, after all; there was plenty of time to see the house later. There was bound to be a huge number of things to do – everyone knew that farmers' wives were always busy – but Ned had muttered for her to have fun as he had left their bed at the crack of dawn, and in Flora's world that didn't equate to spending the day inside dusting… Plenty of time for all that.

There was a carton of orange juice in the fridge and she hesitated for a moment before opening it, carrying it over to stand it beside the plate that held her now half-eaten slice of cake. Presumably the task of buying their groceries would now fall to her, so it surely couldn't matter if she had some of the juice. Why put it in the fridge if it wasn't for drinking? She stared at it for a moment longer before decisively wrestling off the top and pouring herself a large glass, which she drank almost straight down before glancing back out the window.

She would take some photos first, she decided; the process would be much quicker that way, and she could still capture some pretty good ones using her phone. The flowers and trees weren't going anywhere, after all; she could always go back and take some more tomorrow if she needed to. She smiled to herself. She could go any time…

'Right then, Brodie, let's go and see what we can find… Are you coming, or what?' She tipped her head at the dog. 'I've no idea if you've been out yet, but it's a beautiful morning.' She waited until Brodie had got to his feet before pulling on her coat and, tucking her hair behind her ears, she jammed her red beret over her wild curls. They didn't always stay put, but it was better than nothing.

Back outside, she stood still for a few seconds getting her bearings. To her left were more buildings and the pale open space of what must be the yard. They had driven past the house when they arrived yesterday and parked in some sort of barn, open on three sides. The road would probably lead on into the yard, she surmised, but for now the buildings could wait. The technicalities of how the farm worked would be something to get to grips with later. At the moment it was the garden and what lay behind that was drawing her forward.

There were no discernible edges to the sides of the garden; it circled the entire house, stretching out in front of her, firstly in a series of paved areas and planted beds, then on to trees, rougher grass, bigger trees and on into the yard which served the farm. The main garden where she was now standing was separated from the fields beyond by a fence at the bottom and it was this view that she had already marvelled at, the valley sloping away in front of her.

Her eye was drawn to a burgeoning holly bush a little distance away, deep darkest green and covered in bright clusters of berries. She pulled her phone from her pocket and, with a glance back at Brodie, made her way a little closer. The dog was busy sniffing the grass, and she reminded herself that he knew perfectly well where he was. It was *she* who was seeing the garden for the first time. She had only caught a few glimpses of it on her first visit to the farm just before Christmas and had been far too nervous then to ask if she could have a proper look around.

The holly bush must be ancient – she couldn't even see the main branch at its heart – but she touched a finger to one of the glossy leaves, tracing its spine to the prickly tip, before looking up and around her. For there to be berries on this bush there must be male plants close by and, sure enough, she spied several, simply resplendent in their shiny green coats. She moved around the bush until she found a branch with the perfect combination of leaf and berry. Zooming in with her phone, she took several photos, all from slightly different angles.

A cluster of crocuses under a nearby tree drew her on, and she smiled at the sight of the aconites and cyclamens that had also been planted there. Behind her a perfectly manicured bed was bright with heather and skimmias and, up against a small shed, the intense fragrance from a flowering daphne bush was unmistakeable. Without even knowing she was doing it, she let the sing-song Latin names of each plant run through her head as she moved from each new discovery to the next. Moments later, she dropped to her knees as the delicate beauty of some hellebores caught her eye. They were one of her favourite late winter flowers and she had drawn them many times. To find them here, and so many of them, was a wonderful surprise. She'd never even considered that such a beautiful garden was something her new life would bring. It made the pain of leaving her beloved shop behind just that little bit easier.

Was this what had made Ned fall in love with her so quickly? she wondered. As their eyes first met across the counter, her arms full of hydrangea blooms, had she unwittingly reminded him of home, with her flowery apron over a dress covered in bright red tulips? On that dark rainy day in October when they'd met, he'd told her she was like a burst of sunlight on a stormy day. She blushed now, and couldn't remember half of the things he'd said afterwards, but she did remember every flower in the bouquet she'd made up for him. And the one she'd made the day after, his 'It was a good excuse to come and see you' bouquet.

It was two days after that, as she'd sat poring over her accounts in the little back room of her shop, that she'd finally admitted to herself that her business was on its knees. Despite what she'd done, in the end it had made no difference. 'Daisy Doolittles', the florist's shop she had owned and run for over ten years, had served her well, but the pedestrianisation of the street on which it stood had been the beginning of the end for her. Her landlord had hiked up the rent, and then a well-known convenience store opened on the corner and she lost all her passing trade to the lure of a cheap bunch of cellophane-wrapped flowers.

Ned's phone call two weeks later had been *her* burst of sunlight on a stormy day. After a whirlwind romance conducted largely on the phone to one another late at night, Flora had been shocked by his proposal, but delighted – despite what Rowena had said. It wasn't too soon, or too convenient, although she could understand perfectly why her sister might think that. It was perfect and Flora, who lived her life largely according to her intuition, was determined not to look back. And wasn't today evidence of just how right she had been? How many other places had a garden like this, full of flowers, even in winter, full of everything that made Flora's heart sing? She turned her face to the sky and walked on into the morning.

Flora had no real sense of time passing but, after a while, she became aware that the scudding clouds above her had grown darker and, looking around for Brodie, realised that the dog was no longer following her. The wild hedgerows had yielded some interesting finds and she had moved from one spot to the next without thinking. She was in the middle of the field now, her feet damp and cold, her hair tangled. With a sigh she glanced at her watch and began to retrace her steps. Well over an hour had gone by.

By now the house was quite some distance from her, but ten minutes' determined walking brought her back into the more formal gardens where she spied Brodie lying patiently on the patio. He got to his feet when he saw her, giving a half-hearted wag of his tail, but she could tell by the way he moved that he'd had enough of being outside.

'What's the matter, boy?' she asked. 'Are your old bones protesting, eh?' She bent down to run her fingers through his fur. 'Come on then, back in the warm for you.' He trotted by her side as she let them both back in through the door, sitting wearily in the scullery while she stopped to take off her coat and hang it up. She had one hand on the kitchen door when she suddenly stopped, her smile freezing on her face; she could hear the chatter of voices inside.

Before she could work out whose, Brodie nosed open the door and, as it swung inwards, the voices ceased abruptly, leaving an awkward silence. Seated at the kitchen table were Ned's mother and father, Ned himself and, beside him, a blonde woman Flora had never seen before.

'Goodness, Flora,' said Hannah, putting down her fork with a clatter and getting to her feet. 'We wondered if you'd run away. Wherever have you been?'

Chapter 2

'Come and sit down while I get your breakfast,' continued Hannah. 'And you haven't met Caroline yet, have you? Ned can introduce you...'

Flora stared helplessly at Ned as he struggled to stand, but his chair leg caught on the tiled floor and, after a few seconds, he gave it a shove which caused a hideous screeching noise to reverberate around the room. He rolled his eyes.

'Yes, come and sit down, Flora. This is Caroline, from the farm next door. She's a friend... of the family.'

The woman got smoothly to her feet and came around the table to meet Flora, her hand extended in greeting.

'Oh, I've heard so much about you!' She laughed. 'Well, not that much actually under the circumstances, but you're here now. Come and tell us everything about yourself. Hannah was just saying how nice it will be to get to know you properly.'

Flora took her hand and returned the smile, a slight frown hovering around the edges of her eyes. Under *what* circumstances? *She* hadn't heard a thing about Caroline – was she supposed to have? And although her greeting was friendly, Flora wasn't quite sure how to react to this assured-looking blonde who was wearing skin-tight cream jodhpurs and a pale pink shirt. Her hand went to her head, pulling her hat from it as she wondered what kind of state *her* hair was in.

Flora faltered, unsure what to do next, and looked at Ned for reassurance, relieved to see he was now smiling, his mad freckles stretched taut across his face. He moved forward to stand beside Caroline and took Flora's arm, guiding her to the table.

'There you go,' he said, pulling out a chair for her. She took her seat slowly, thinking how she would have much preferred to sit next to Ned instead of at the head of table where she felt exposed, but Caroline had already resumed her place in front of a hearty plate of food. Flora plucked at her jumper, suddenly feeling a flush of heat, heart sinking when she saw what Caroline was eating.

'Here you are,' said Hannah, returning to the table. 'Still warm, so no harm done.' She put a heaped plate of food in front of her and Flora stared at it in horror. She swallowed. Three thick strips of fatty bacon were stacked beside two sausages, a fried egg and a large mushroom on top of two slices of toast. Flora's stomach heaved as she spied a slice of black pudding hiding beneath the blanket of egg and she gave a weak smile.

'Is everything okay, Flora?'

She looked up at Caroline's smiling face, with her perfect blonde hair falling in glossy waves halfway down her shoulders.

'Yes… It's just…' She swallowed again and turned to her future mother-in-law. 'I'm so sorry,' she said. 'I didn't think to mention it before, I wasn't expecting this, you see, but…' She gestured towards her plate. 'I'm a, a vegetarian…'

A strange noise that sounded suspiciously like a strangled snort came from Ned's direction. He coughed.

'Oh, Ned… you could have said! Honestly…' Hannah tutted loudly, throwing her son an exasperated look. 'The poor girl…'

Ned clapped a hand over his mouth, obviously trying to stop himself from laughing, and he ducked as Hannah sought to clip the back of his head in passing. He threw up his hands.

'I didn't know, okay?' He grinned.

Flora stared at Caroline, whose mouth was also twitching. It really wasn't funny. Flora felt mortified.

Her plate was whipped away at high speed and carried to the sink, much to Ned's father's alarm.

'Hey, wait a minute. Don't let it go to waste, I'll have her sausage…'

Hannah clucked her tongue, looking at Fraser fondly. 'What are you like?' she said, returning to the table and handing him Flora's food.

'How could you not know something like that, Ned?' she added. 'You're marrying the girl for goodness' sake.' She shook her head at him and then smiled at Flora. 'I do apologise for my son's lack of communication,' she said. 'Honestly, he's that daft at times. Now then, dear, what can I get you instead?'

Flora shook her head. 'No, honestly, I'm fine… I—' She stopped as her eyes flicked to the cake tin on the counter… which was no longer there. Nor was her plate, or her knife, or the glass she had poured juice into and drunk, leaving it empty on the side.

'Perhaps I could just have a cup of tea?'

'I can do you a kipper?'

'Thank you, but, well, I don't eat fish either…'

'Some toast then?'

Flora smiled again, jumping as she felt Ned's hand slide onto her knee. 'Honestly, tea will be just fine.'

Hannah brought the teapot to the table, and sat down with it in front of her. She smoothed down her greying bob and pushed her glasses back up her nose, composing herself. Then she poured strong tea into a mug which matched the plates and passed it to Caroline, who passed it down to Flora.

'So, what do you do, Flora?' asked Caroline politely.

She was about to answer when Ned got there first. 'Flora had her own business,' he said. 'The most amazing florist's shop,' he added. 'The colours, the smells, I'd never seen anything quite like it. And of course, there in the middle of it all was Flora. It was love at first sight.'

Flora blushed and slipped her hand under the table to take Ned's fingers. She gave them a squeeze.

'*Had* your own business?' asked Caroline. 'Oh dear, did something happen?'

'Well, yes it…' Flora stopped suddenly, staring down the table at Caroline, sitting next to Ned with a sympathetic expression on her face, at Hannah, who was sitting bolt upright and still looking faintly disapproving, and at Fraser, who was busy devouring his food and didn't seem to be listening anyway. She lifted her chin a little.

'It was sold. My shop was in Birmingham you see, Caroline, and whichever way you look at it, that's rather a long commute.' There was no way she was about to admit what had really happened. 'I could hardly keep the shop on now that I will be helping here on the farm.'

Caroline smiled. 'Gosh no, that would be nigh on impossible, wouldn't it, Hannah? There's so much to do here, it really is a full-time job all on its own. How lovely for you though' – she reached over to pat Hannah's hand – 'to have some help. I mean – you've kept everything running perfectly for all these years, you deserve to have some time to yourself.'

Hannah laid her hand briefly over Caroline's. 'Why thank you, dear. There's a lot to learn of course, but I'm sure that Flora will do just fine. The flowers that Ned bought me were utterly gorgeous. He has good taste.' She smiled at Flora, who narrowed her eyes at Hannah's words. Did she just imagine that, or was Caroline's wrist just verbally slapped?

'But tell them about your art too, Flora,' urged Ned, seemingly unaware of the undercurrents eddying around them.

Flora wasn't sure she wanted to. She had a strong feeling that unless she painted horses Caroline wouldn't be in the least bit interested, although she wasn't sure why that should bother her. She looked up to see an expectant expression on her face – at least she was pretending to be intrigued. Fraser flashed her a glance but carried on eating.

'I make prints,' she began. 'Botanical ones, from things I find, so they're very seasonal. I've just taken some beautiful photos this morning as it happens. That's where I was, earlier…' She pressed her tongue against the roof of her mouth in consternation. *For goodness' sake, Flora, why do you always feel the need to justify yourself?*

'Oh, photography?' said Hannah. 'I thought you said she was a painter, Ned?'

'Well, yes, I do paint,' added Flora quickly. 'I make sketches first, either directly or from photographs I've taken, and then I make a watercolour of my design before I go on to cut the block which will produce my prints.'

Ned nodded, beaming at her. 'You should see them, Mum…'

'It sounds like an awful lot of work to me,' Hannah replied. 'I don't have a creative bone in my body, dear, but if you enjoy it, then that's lovely. And what do you do with these prints when they're finished?'

'I sell them,' she said. 'On Etsy.'

Flora looked at the blank faces around her. Even Caroline, who looked to be roughly the same age as her, showed not a flicker of comprehension.

'It's an online shop,' she went on to explain. 'I add my designs when they're ready and then people can buy them if they want to.'

'And people do that, do they?'

'Oh yes. It can be quite lucrative.'

Caroline placed her knife and fork together on her plate. 'Well, that makes sense,' she said. 'I was admiring your dress when you came in. All those colours, it's very… arty. Of course I don't think I could wear it, I'd be completely overwhelmed by it, but it suits you. How lovely to be so quirky.'

Ned's grin widened even further, but Flora wasn't so sure it was a compliment. She took a mouthful of tea to hide her feelings.

Hannah got to her feet again. 'It's a shame we have so many pictures up around the house already,' she said. 'But I'm sure we'll get to see what you do at some point.' She picked up her plate. 'Now, have you men finished? Come on, let's have you out of my kitchen, Flora and I have lots to do.'

Flora's head swivelled.

Within seconds Ned and his father had both jumped up, Ned collecting the plates and taking them over to the sink. He came back to kiss Flora full on the lips. 'I'll see *you* later,' he said, with a twinkle in his eye, before turning back. 'Dad, you ready?'

Fraser nodded, and for the first time looked straight at Flora. He was slightly shorter than Ned, but years of hard physical work had given him a build that matched the farmhouse's solid oak front door. Father and son also shared the same pale colouring, and Flora envisaged Fraser's hair had been the same bright copper as Ned's at one time, but now it had faded to a sandy thatch.

'Don't take any nonsense, Flora,' said Fraser, and with a slight wave of his hand, picked up his jacket and followed Ned out of the door.

Flora swallowed the last of her tea and pushed her chair away from the table. 'I'll wash up, shall I?' she volunteered.

Hannah exchanged a look with Caroline. 'I'll show you where everything is,' she said. 'I don't suppose you've had much of an opportunity to find out yourself.'

Flora had no idea what time Caroline had arrived at the house, but Hannah at least would be very well aware that Flora had found her way around several things that morning, namely the cake tin and the fridge. Someone had washed up her things from earlier and Flora doubted it was Caroline.

She smiled her assent. 'Thank you, just as long as I'm not holding you up?'

'In doing what, dear? Goodness me, no. You won't be holding me up, you'll be helping me. I said to Ned last night that I would make sure that by the end of the day you knew exactly what was expected. It will take you a while to get used to it all, I don't doubt, but the sooner you get going, the sooner it will all become second nature.'

'Well, that's very kind, but I'm sure I'll be okay on my own. You must have other things you'd like to do?'

Caroline gave a tinkly laugh. 'Oh, you are sweet,' she said, coming across the room to give Flora's arm a light rub. 'Ned hasn't told you a thing, has he? But you really are in very capable hands, so I will leave Hannah to show you the ropes, but if you need anything else then you must give me a call. In fact, do that anyway, it will be wonderful to get to know you better.' She turned back to Hannah. 'Breakfast was lovely as always, thank you so much.'

'It's a pleasure,' replied Hannah. 'I expect we'll see you tomorrow anyway, but give my love to your parents, dear.'

And then there were just the two of them, her and Hannah, standing in the kitchen looking at one another. Hannah pushed up her sleeves.

'Well, thank heavens for that,' she said. 'Lovely girl, but honestly, sometimes I think she spends more time at our house than she does her own… Now, how about another nice cup of tea before we make a start, what do you think?'

'Lovely…' muttered Flora weakly, wishing it wasn't so early so she could have something stronger.

*

The frying pan looked like it had already done a lifetime of service, and Flora scrubbed at it one more time before passing it to Hannah to dry. It was the last of the things to be washed up and Flora pulled the plug from the sink in relief. She had never seen so much congealed fat, and the smell of it would take some getting used to.

During the last ten minutes she had learned that breakfast was at ten. Well, the proper big breakfast, that was; Ned would have porridge and toast when he got up at about five in the morning. Lunch was at one o'clock (soup and sandwiches) and then tea was at six (a hearty meal obviously) with supper following at nine. Nothing fancy, said Hannah, usually just cake or crumpets, although at the times of year when the men were very busy, they wouldn't get back until around eleven, so supper was often foregone.

Flora found her head bobbing up and down like a nodding dog's as Hannah imparted information to her in a never-ending rapid-fire monologue, and it left her feeling like the new girl on her first day at work; woefully inept and massively out of her depth. She tried to listen, but her head kept saying other things to her; rebellious thoughts that had no place in the new life that Hannah had envisaged for her. It certainly wasn't Flora's idea of how life as a model farmer's wife should be.

Apart from the very obvious question of where all the food came from, and who would be buying it, was the equally pressing one of who would be cooking it. Flora was an okay cook, she was even pretty good at some things, but she certainly wasn't used to cooking around the clock like this, or in such quantity. How did people eat so much food? She was used to eating when she was hungry, nibbling here and there between serving customers in her shop. Here mealtimes were clearly an integral part of a regimen that she would be expected to follow. She couldn't help but wonder what would happen if she didn't...

Picking up the dishcloth once more, Flora gave the sink a final wipe and then went to dry her hands on the towel which hung over the Aga's rail. She was aware of Hannah checking her watch and she hastily finished what she was doing, turning around and mustering a bright smile.

'Right, what's next?' she said.

Hannah led her over to the door beside the Aga.

'In here is the pantry, where I keep all the tinned and dry goods, together with my stock of jams and relishes, jellies and chutneys. We're fortunate that the farm has a good stock of fruit trees and our hedgerows provide a plentiful bounty too, so I use whatever is available seasonally.'

Flora gazed at the rows and rows of jars that lined the shelves, all neatly labelled.

'It's just how I imagined Brambly Hedge to be,' said Flora. 'I didn't realise people still did this...'

Hannah frowned. 'Brambly Hedge?'

'Yes, the books... you know the children's stories...?'

Hannah shook her head.

'They're mice… who live in the hollows of trees and…' Flora trailed off when she saw Hannah's expression. 'Sorry… they're just lovely stories, beautiful illustrations…' She cleared her throat. 'This is lovely,' she finished lamely.

'Yes, well, we don't have money to buy inferior-quality shop-bought goods. We use as much of our own produce as we can…'

Flora nodded. 'It makes much more sense…'

Hannah's lips were still pursed. 'Anyway, I have already made the bread for today as I wasn't sure we would have the time this morning. You do make bread, don't you?'

'Oh yes,' lied Flora. 'All the time.'

'Good. Well, I start it off first thing, once Fraser and Ned have gone out, and then I leave it to prove as I'm preparing breakfast. That way, I can pop it into the oven to cook as I'm washing up and it's ready in time for lunch. The soup doesn't take long either. Although, we might have to rethink certain things, as you're vegetarian.'

'Yes, I'm sorry about that. I hope it doesn't make things awkward.'

Hannah regarded her over the top of her glasses. 'So you don't eat meat *at all*…? Not even chicken?' She didn't wait for a reply, which was fortunate, because Flora really wasn't sure what she would have said.

'Right, well, we have a bit of time now before we need to prepare the soup, so why don't I take you upstairs and I can show you where I've put all your clothes…'

*

'Honestly, Ned, it was awful…'

Flora was lying flat on her back, spread-eagled across the bed. 'And my feet are killing me!' She sighed dramatically.

Around her, on the floor, on the bed, hanging over the back of a chair – but mostly on the floor – were all her clothes. Flora had flung them there in a fury about an hour ago but now hadn't the energy or the inclination to pick them up.

It was ten o'clock at night and she hadn't long been 'released' from Hannah's day-long course on how to run the house. It was well meant, she knew that, but that hadn't stopped her jaw beginning to ache furiously from faking a smile with each new chore added to her list.

She took a deep breath. It wasn't that bad, was it? She was tired and being melodramatic and, she admitted to herself, suffering from a huge amount of irritation that the day she had planned out for herself had fallen so spectacularly by the wayside, but she was already beginning to feel suffocated by Hannah's ferocious domesticity. Breakfast was bad enough, but finding out that, while she had been having such a lovely time out in the fields, Hannah had not only unpacked her suitcases but put away *all* her clothes, had rather set the tone for the rest of the afternoon.

Ned, who had just emerged from the shower, leaned over and kissed the end of her nose, his tousled red hair curling around the nape of his neck. Flora would have loved to twine the ends in her fingers and then let them take a walk south, but Ned's parents were sleeping just down the hallway and, well, she was very ticklish and Ned knew just where to tickle her…

He propped himself up on his arm. 'So, come on then,' he said. 'What was so awful?'

Flora gave him a wayward glance. 'Well breakfast for starters, I mean, how embarrassing was that? It didn't even occur to me that you wouldn't know I was a vegetarian. It looked like we were on a blind date or something.'

But Ned just grinned. 'I thought it was hysterical, actually. Did you see Mum's face? I thought she was going to faint.'

'Ned, it's not funny! She probably hates me even more now. You're farmers for goodness' sake, what kind of daughter-in-law am I going to be if I don't eat meat?'

'Do you want to eat meat?'

Flora shuddered. 'No… And I'm not going to, but that's not the point.'

Ned watched her for a minute, his pale grey eyes roaming her face. 'It is, you know. It's exactly the point. Because you're absolutely perfect just as you are, and don't let anyone say otherwise. More importantly, don't you dare change… I'd go off you if you did… And besides, Mum doesn't hate you…'

He was trying to cheer her up, but the day had been too wearing to give in just like that.

'She does… I stick out like a sore thumb here. She's so organised and I only have to look at stuff and it makes a mess. She's a domestic goddess who can cook nineteen different types of pastry without having to look up the recipe, and I had to lie about making bread, which I've never done in my life, but don't you dare tell her… and… and…' She lifted one leg off the bed. 'The whole day was just a very long list of all the things that Hannah does, at which I am spectacularly useless, but which are all vital to the smooth and efficient running of the household. In fact, I think that might have been a direct quote.'

'I don't believe my mother called you spectacularly useless…'

Flora slapped his arm. 'Not that! The smooth and efficient running bit…'

Ned was smiling but he was also watching her closely. He tilted his head to one side. 'There is another way of looking at it…' he said.

Flora raised her eyebrows.

'I think my mum is finding it quite difficult too. She's been looking after Dad and the farm for thirty-odd years, and then of course me once I came along. She's never done anything else, and although this is quite a tight-knit community and she knows pretty much everyone, she doesn't have many proper friends… I think she's every bit as nervous as you are, and just as desperate to make a good impression.'

Flora stared at him. She hadn't really thought about what it must be like for Hannah to have a stranger land in her domain but Ned's words made perfect sense. She was the proverbial cuckoo in the nest and, even though Flora had no intention of usurping Hannah's role in the household, her future mother-in-law could well be feeling incredibly threatened.

She bit her lip. 'So, how am I going to fit in?'

'By just being you, and very soon everyone will love you anyway, just the way I do. What's not to love, Flora? You're funny, kind, beautiful, talented… but more than anything, you have this spark inside of you that, even when you don't realise it, comes tumbling out. You never take anything at face value, you challenge perceptions, are brave and adventurous, quirky, non-conformist, and…'

Flora held the back of her hand up to her brow in a mock swoon. 'Oh, don't stop…' she giggled.

'Bloody fantastic in bed…'

A loud snort echoed around the room, which Flora quickly stifled. 'Shhh,' she whispered, thumping Ned's arm. 'Don't start me off, you know what I'm like!'

'Oh I do,' he replied, nuzzling the side of her neck. 'That's what I was banking on…'

Chapter 3

Flora was out of bed like a shot the following morning. Well, not quite at four thirty like Ned was, but it was a very long time since she'd last seen six o'clock in the morning! She didn't know how Ned did it; they hadn't got an awful lot of sleep…

She hopped across the bedroom floor, wincing at the cold, and over to where her clothes still lay abandoned from yesterday. Grabbing a random selection, she got dressed as quickly as she could. No doubt she would be docked points for leaving their room in a mess but—

Flora Dunbar, stop right there… She stared at herself in the mirror. *You are never going to fit in if you carry on like that. This is Hannah and Fraser's home and, for the moment, whether you like it or not, you're the newcomer and you can't expect everything to be like it was before. Which is exactly what you hoped for, remember? Your old life wasn't so great and you've always wanted to live in the country, so quit moaning and just get on with it. And while you're at it, remember that a little tact and diplomacy wouldn't go amiss.*

She tucked her hair behind her ears and gave a stern nod at her reflection, hitched up her tights, straightened her skirt, and went downstairs.

One thing she had learned yesterday was that the kettle was always warm in the farm kitchen and, as such, could be induced to boil in pretty short order. Rule number one, always keep it filled with water. Flora took it to the sink, her eyes automatically drawn to the view outside. It was so tempting to slip outside again and lose herself for an hour or so, but she knew that wouldn't help the situation at all, although… She glanced at her watch. Maybe there was time enough to gather some flowers for the table. There were several clumps of early narcissus growing around the side of the house, and they were so lovely and cheerful.

For the second time in as many days, the kettle was abandoned by the side of the sink as Flora was enticed into the garden. It only took a few moments to pick enough flowers to fill a vase and, spying a forsythia bush a little distance away, Flora cut some long stems of the bright yellow flowers to accompany the other blooms. She was just about to turn back towards the house when she heard her name being called, and was surprised to see Hannah coming across the garden to meet her. As she drew closer she could see that Hannah was holding a round wicker basket. To her relief she was also smiling.

'Good morning!' Hannah called. 'Did you sleep well?'

Flora, who had hardly slept at all, didn't know quite what to say. She scrutinised Hannah's face. Was that what she was implying, or had her greeting been a simple enquiry? She decided that it was and replied accordingly, suddenly spotting what was in the basket Hannah was carrying.

'Oh, eggs! Does that mean you have chickens?'

Hannah's smile was warm. 'We do, only seven now, but they're good layers. Would you like to see them?'

Flora nodded. 'I've always wanted chickens, ever since I was a little girl.'

'But you don't eat eggs?'

'No… but not because I'm a vegetarian. I don't actually like them. It's the texture of them, I think.' She gave an involuntary shudder.

'So you would eat them if you liked them?'

Flora nodded.

'But yet you don't eat the chicken itself?'

'No, but I like cats and dogs and I don't eat them either!'

For a moment Flora thought that Hannah's face was going to be pulled into a frown but then, to her relief, she burst out laughing.

'It's a bit like that old joke,' she said. 'I like children… But I couldn't eat a whole one.'

Flora smiled, shielding her eyes from the low slanting sun. It wasn't really like that at all, but she wasn't about to contradict her. Hannah was trying to be friendly and, in view of her conversation with Ned last night, voicing her opinions on eating meat now would very probably lead to her packing her bags and returning to the remnants of her old life with her tail between her legs.

'It must seem a bit odd to you, me being a vegetarian?'

Hannah regarded her for a moment. 'I don't know any farmers' wives who are,' she replied. 'Well, cattle farmers anyway, but…' And she shrugged.

The words 'there's a first time for everything' dangled unspoken. Flora already knew from her conversations with Hannah yesterday how little she liked things to change. Instead, Flora turned the subject onto safer ground.

'So do you feed the chickens every morning?'

'I do,' said Hannah. 'Pellets and fresh water in the morning, and then grain of an afternoon. The eggs need collecting every day too. The village shop takes what I can't use, but it varies.' She held out the basket for inspection. 'Today's a full house.' There were indeed seven pale brown eggs nestled inside.

Flora took one, holding it gently in her palm. 'Oh, it's still warm!'

There was another smile. 'I still marvel at it,' said Hannah. 'One of nature's little miracles.'

'I know I don't like them, but even I can see that if you do, having them fresh like this must be the nicest thing,' said Flora, hesitating for a moment. 'I was wondering whether it would help you if I took over feeding them? I'm not sure how difficult it is, but if you showed me where everything was, and how to do it… It would be one less thing for you to think about?'

Hannah nodded. 'I was actually thinking that too,' she replied. 'I can show you now if you like, but would you like to go and put the flowers in some water first? No point picking them if they're going to be half dead by the time we get back. I'll wait here.'

Dismissed, Flora hurried back inside and hastily filled the scullery sink, leaving the flowers to soak before retracing her steps back outside. Hannah led the way, walking around the side of the house and through a gate into a yard that stood at its front. From there the yard opened out onto a service road which connected with the lane and the outside world to her left, and the rest of the farm to the right. It was here that Flora could see a long straggle of traditional buildings, including the milking parlour, and she followed Hannah to the first of them.

It was a dark, almost black, timber-framed shed which stood beside a small path that led into another area of garden divided from the first by a long low hedge. The grass was rougher here, and right in the centre was the chicken coop, three tawny hens pecking in the exposed soil.

'Lucy, Mabel and Polly if I'm not much mistaken,' said Hannah.

Flora gave her a sideways glance. 'Blimey, how do you tell them apart?' she asked. 'They all look the same to me.'

'That they do,' Hannah replied, tapping the side of her nose and smiling. 'But there are subtle differences once you get to know them and what you don't yet know is that Lucy, Mabel and Polly are the greediest three of the lot. So you can bet that when they've just been fed, those are the ladies still eating twenty minutes later.'

Hannah unclipped the catch on the side of the coop and ducked inside, motioning for Flora to follow her. 'You can leave the door open now if you like, so they can stretch their legs.' She pointed to a low trough on the ground. 'A good layer of pellets in there is all you need first thing, and then each of the drinking containers need swilling out and fresh water added. There's a tap over there.' She pointed to a pipe which poked from the ground by the hedgerow. 'Then that's it until later in the afternoon, when I usually put out the grain. A few handfuls scattered out in the grass and they'll all come running.'

Flora nodded. 'That all seems pretty straightforward.'

'The pellets and grain are in the shed. It's never locked. Then just collect the eggs from the nest box and you're done.'

Another nod as Hannah checked her watch, again. It was something of a habit Flora had noticed and usually preceded another task.

'Okay, I've got that,' she said with as much confidence as she could muster. 'And what about at night? Do you need to do anything then?'

Hannah gave her an amused look. 'Just one thing,' she replied, as she strode back out through the coop door. 'Make sure the hens have all gone to bed and that you close this at dusk, otherwise come morning you'll have a pile of dead chickens and a very fat fox…'

'Oh…' Flora could have kicked herself. Hannah had very kindly managed to keep the scathing tone from her voice, but Flora was sure it had been a struggle. Everybody knew about chickens and foxes, didn't they? She followed Hannah back across the garden, trying to think of some way to redeem herself.

'I'm sure it won't take me long to get the hang of it,' she said. 'And then, before you know it, I'll be helping to milk the cows.'

Hannah gave her a sideways look. 'I don't think so, dear.' She took in a long breath. 'Now, we'll have some tea first, I think,' she said, as she walked, but then fell silent herself. Whatever was coming next was obviously going to remain a mystery for now.

Quarter of an hour later, with mugs of tea in front of them, and a digestive biscuit each, Hannah cleared her throat.

'I've been thinking,' she began.

Flora braced herself.

'And I want to apologise also,' she added. 'What must you have thought of us yesterday? I didn't stop talking at you the whole day…' She paused, breaking her biscuit in half. 'I was a little nervous…'

'You and me both,' said Flora, dunking her biscuit in her tea and only just managing to get it to her mouth in one piece. But then she grinned. 'I was probably hugely insensitive too, so I'm sorry if I was a pain. I didn't think what it must feel like to have me come barging in as if I owned the place, scattering stuff left, right and centre. I'm not a very tidy person, I'm afraid…'

'But I had no right to go around clearing up after you either. You must have felt very unwelcome. And as for putting all your things away, I really didn't think… I've always done it, you see.'

Flora flinched, inwardly praying that Hannah hadn't been in their bedroom this morning and seen all her previously carefully folded clothes now strewn around the room. She made a non-committal noise in her throat.

'You have some lovely things though…' added Hannah.

Surprised, Flora looked up.

'I've never had the confidence to wear things like that, all those colours clashing together. Even when I was your age and had the chance to wear things that were a little more… modern, I didn't really. Not much cause for it on the farm, I suppose.' She ran her eye over what Flora was wearing. 'It's not at all conventional, is it? But somehow it suits you.'

'Thank you.' Flora blushed at Hannah's unexpected words. 'They're probably completely impractical for life on a farm, but I've worn things like this for so long now, I'm not sure I'd be comfortable wearing anything different.'

It was the first time Flora had even considered what Hannah wore. For the most part they were practical clothes, designed to be warm and comfortable, but now that she thought about it, they hid Hannah's shape and personality like a blanket. She had no idea how old Hannah was, but the dark drab colours and unflattering cut of the things in her wardrobe probably added ten years to her age. Maybe at some point in the future there might be an occasion when Flora could suggest some changes – if Hannah wanted to, that was.

The two women smiled at one another, their tentative start at friendship settling between them. Flora drank a mouthful of tea and this time she was the one who looked at her watch.

'Right,' she said. 'What can I help you with first?'

Hannah looked a little nervous. 'Actually, I wondered if I might ask you a favour?' she replied. 'I really do need to go into town to pick up a few things I can't get locally and it's a visit I've been putting off, never quite being able to justify the time to do it. So I wondered if you'd be all right here by yourself? There's the bread to make, and the men will need their breakfast, but I'm sure you're very capable of doing that, and I'd be back in time to help serve lunch…'

Flora's head was already nodding. 'Of course, you must go, I'll be absolutely fine.'

'And I thought it might be quite nice for you to have the run of the house,' added Hannah. 'Without me standing over you telling you what to do.'

'Well, I think I need a bit of standing over,' replied Flora. 'I've got a lot to learn, but thank you, that's a very kind thought. And if it helps you out too, then so much the better.'

Hannah opened her mouth to reply, but then hesitated and instead, with a shake of her head, got to her feet. She gave a warm smile.

'In that case, I'll just go and powder my nose,' she said.

Flora watched as Hannah carried her mug over to the sink, patted her hips as if checking her pockets for something, and then turned to walk from the room. She had almost got to the door, when she half-turned, tutting, before turning back.

'Is everything okay?' asked Flora.

'I just wondered… well, before I go…'

'Yes?'

'I told you where everything was, didn't I?'

Flora made a show of thinking for a minute. 'Yes, you did…' She paused, looking about the kitchen. And then, 'Yes, I'm sure you did. But don't worry, I'll do exactly what you did yesterday, so go and enjoy yourself. And take your time, there's no need to hurry back.'

A final nod of the head and Hannah was gone.

Flora sat at the table for a few minutes more, watching the play of sunlight across the floor. The morning hadn't turned out the way she had expected at all, and she acknowledged how difficult it must have been for Hannah to relinquish her kitchen to her. Whether the trip to town was really necessary or not didn't matter, it was a kind thing to do, and Flora felt heartened by the turn of events. Whatever happened now, she mustn't let Hannah down.

She got to her feet and refilled the kettle, quickly washing up both mugs and leaving them to drain. Then she pulled open the pantry door and stood looking at the array of stored ingredients with pursed lips. First on the list of jobs to do was make the bread, which sounded easy enough, except she had absolutely no idea how to do it…

*

Swearing didn't seem to help, and neither did pulling all the dough off her fingers and looking at it, but Flora tried both of these things, several times. The sticky mess she had made was either in the bowl or all over her and nothing she tried seemed to make any difference. She eyed the bowl sternly and, with a deep intake of breath, began to turn out the mixture onto the floured table top. The instructions she had looked at on the Internet told her that the dough required a thorough kneading so perhaps this was the key. She'd give it one last go, but this time she'd show it who was boss.

Five minutes later and all that had happened was that the goo was now spread in a wide uneven circle on the table. Flora gave a frustrated groan and banged her hand on the table, raising a cloud of white around her. She caught Brodie's eye as he watched her balefully from beside the Aga.

'Don't look at me like that,' she said. 'I thought this was supposed to be easy. I don't suppose you have any tips for me, do you?' She tipped her head to one side. 'No, I thought not… Well, you're no use at all…' She rubbed at an itch on the side of her nose with the back of her hand. 'I've a good mind to throw the whole bloody lot in the bin; they can have shop-bought bread for a change, it won't kill them…'

'Oh dear, that doesn't sound too good.'

Flora whirled around to see Caroline standing just inside the back door. How long she had been there, she didn't know, and she blushed bright red.

Caroline was looking as fresh as a daisy; jodhpurs again today, but a pale blue shirt instead of the pink. Cornflower blue, thought Flora, as she rearranged her face into a smile.

'Oh, hello, I didn't know you were coming over today.'

Caroline broke into a broad smile as she came into the room. 'Oh, don't mind me, I sort of have a standing invitation.'

There was a gentle woof and Brodie thumped his tail lazily against the floor. Traitor, thought Flora.

'Is the coast clear?' asked Caroline, coming to stand beside her. 'I wasn't sure if Hannah would actually go.'

Flora gave her a puzzled look. 'I'm sorry, I'm not sure I follow.'

'I had a devil of a job to persuade her to go out today,' replied Caroline. 'But I didn't think you'd be able to stand another day like yesterday, with Hannah looking over your shoulder every five minutes. She means well, I know, but I couldn't let you suffer that again. You'd be packing your bags by the end of the week.' She gave a conspiratorial smile. 'Shall I put the kettle on?' she added with a wink.

Flora stared at her. 'But I thought…' She broke off, not quite sure what to say. She'd had no idea that Caroline had intervened on her behalf and, while she was grateful, she couldn't help wondering how on earth Hannah had felt about the suggestion.

'I love Hannah to bits,' said Caroline, her back to Flora while she filled the kettle. 'She's like a second mother to me, I suppose, and has a heart of pure gold. But…' She leaned heavily into the word, '*but*… she lives, eats, breathes this place. She hardly ever goes out. It's not healthy. I know it, Ned knows it, Fraser knows it, but there's no telling

Hannah. Consequently, the only time she feels comfortable is when everything is just so… Over the years we've all just fallen in with it and try to make sure it stays that way.'

'Oh…'

Caroline turned at the tone in her voice.

'Shit, I'm sorry, that just all rather poured out, didn't it? I didn't mean it to.' She smiled at Flora's shocked face. 'I really do love Hannah, and I'm not being disloyal, honestly. I can just see how difficult it must be for you coming into a strange house. I grew up with Ned and I've never seen him so happy as he is now. He finally meets the love of his life and if we're not careful Hannah will chase her off again. You won't leave, will you?'

Flora blushed again, taken aback by Caroline's words. Today was turning out to be full of surprises.

'Well, I wasn't planning to… but I admit, yesterday was a little tough. It can't be easy for Hannah, though, having a strange woman arrive in your house.'

'And Hannah knows that, really she does. Which is testament to how lovely a person she is. She doesn't want to make things difficult for you, so whatever she said to you this morning would have been absolutely genuine but, nonetheless, she's going to need a little… encouragement, shall we say, to embrace the change. I've known her all my life so I can say these things, whereas you can't, and I told her that Ned's future happiness depends on you being here. Therefore, if she wants to ensure that continues, she's going to have to adjust, however hard.' She turned back to the kettle. 'Do you have sugar in your tea?'

'Er, no. No thank you, just milk.' Flora stared at Caroline's face, looking for any trace of subterfuge, but it was entirely without guile. 'It must have been a bit of a shock for you all though,' she added. 'Me suddenly coming along, I mean.'

'I suppose it was, a little. But that's Ned all over for you. He's always kept things rather close to his chest, even as a child, so the fact he was hiding a girlfriend was a surprise, yes, but not unusual. Anyway, now that you're here, I think it's the best thing that's happened in a long time.'

Caroline came to stand beside the table, where she stared down at the mess Flora had made.

'And while homemade bread is lovely, I really don't see why occasionally Hannah can't unchain herself from the kitchen and let everyone eat shop-bought bread instead. The village store sells it wonderfully fresh from a local bakery.'

Flora stared at her hands. 'I seem to have made a bit of a dog's dinner of it,' she said. 'I rather foolishly said I knew how to make bread yesterday, which was rather rash seeing as how everyone is going to expect to be eating it today.'

'No problem,' replied Caroline. 'I'll finish it if you like. No one will ever know it wasn't you that made it. And I'm certainly not about to tell them…'

Flora didn't know what to say. It was an extraordinarily generous thing to do. 'It might be beyond repair. I've been faffing with it for quite a while.'

Caroline grinned and peered at the dough. 'Do you want to finish off making the tea and I'll give it a go? I doubt it's ruined; I just don't think you've kneaded it enough. That's why it's so sticky.'

Flora didn't need to be asked twice, escaping to the sink and finally pulling off the bits of dough from her fingers that had begun to harden around them like concrete.

'I really can't thank you enough,' Flora said, once her hands were clean and she'd brought the mugs of tea over to the table. She watched as Caroline expertly scooped up the mess she had made and somehow pulled it all together into a ball, whereupon she began to knead it so fast it was almost a blur. Within a few moments Flora could see that it was changing consistency.

'This is what you get for living in the country,' said Caroline, continuing the motion. 'While everyone my age in the city knows the ingredients and exact measurements for the perfect cosmopolitan, all I learnt was how to make bread and suet puddings. Oh, and ride of course, that goes without saying.'

Flora giggled. 'I've never even *been* on horse,' she said.

Caroline stared at her. 'No, really? You've never been on a horse before? Well, we'll have to change all that.' She cocked her head to one side. 'I tell you what, why don't you come over and meet Samson soon. He's an absolute darling and Hannah would love it if you were able to ride. Everyone around here does.'

'Samson?' echoed Flora. 'He doesn't sound like a darling…'

'The name's ironic, I promise you. He's a big softy really, and he'll take good care of you.' She looked down at the table. 'Now look at this wonderful loaf you've whipped up. Hannah will be *very* impressed…'

Chapter 4

The village shop, if Hannah were to be believed, was a treasure trove for local produce and, as such, frequently visited. This at least was something that Flora approved of and she was interested to explore it herself. Besides, it was high time she started to get out and about and an abundance of eggs gave her the perfect excuse.

To her delight, as soon as she mentioned her intention at lunchtime, Ned announced that he would accompany her. He had a couple of hours before the afternoon milking and he would enjoy showing her off in the village.

'There's someone I want you to meet,' he added, tapping the side of his nose and refusing to say any more.

'You've got work to do, lad,' said Fraser, gruffly, looking up. 'And it won't get done if you're off gallivanting around the village.'

Flora's heart sank and she was about to say that she would go by herself when Ned got up from the table.

'I'll be an hour and a half at most, Dad. There's nothing that I can't see to when I get back. And I want to show Flora around. She lives here now, it's important that she gets a feel for the place.'

There was a long pause. 'Aye, well don't make a habit of it. Sneaking off in the middle of the day. I know what you young ones are like.'

'Like I'm ever going to get the chance,' Ned retorted, holding out his hand to Flora. 'Come on. Let's get going. The sooner we go, the sooner I can get my nose back on the grindstone.' He was smiling, but Flora still felt distinctly uncomfortable.

It wasn't a particularly long walk into the village, but the day was fresh and, along with the cold, the thoughts whistling around Flora's head stirred her to walk faster and faster. Even so, Ned's stride was long and lolloping and she had a job to keep up with him. He slowed when he reached the place where the track from the farm met the bend in the road.

'Hope Corner,' he said, grinning. 'You'll never find a finer place.'

Flora looked across at him, his cheeks florid from the wind, his eyes shining. 'You really do mean that, don't you?'

Ned held his arms up in an expansive gesture. 'I know every inch of every field, lane, and hedgerow for miles around,' he said. 'Where the best place to see the first snowdrops is, the spot the sun never reaches and is always icy, and where the wild honeysuckle grows so vigorously you can smell it on the wind come the summer. And there' – he pointed to the sweep of fields away to their right – 'are our cows. Holstein Friesians, like ninety per cent of all the dairy cattle in the UK...' He grinned at her. 'The black and white ones?' he added. 'And I love every single one of them. They're all I've ever known, Flora. I can't even begin to think of a life without them in it, and now that you're here too, everything is perfect.'

Flora couldn't help pulling a face. 'I'm not sure your mum and dad think that way.'

He took hold of her hand. 'Don't take any notice of what my dad says, it's just bluff and bluster. He's soft as muck really.' He regarded her for a moment before dropping her hand and pulling her woolly hat down further over her ears, tucking her hair under it a little. 'Are you warm enough?' he asked.

She nodded and took hold of his hand again. 'Come on.'

It was good to be outside, though, and Flora enjoyed the feeling of the wind snatching at her hair and burnishing her cheeks. It wasn't just her head that was feeling cooped up, her muscles were too, and she picked up her pace even more, lengthening her stride as she rounded the bend of Hope Corner before turning and looking back towards the farmhouse. Despite Fraser's harsh words of earlier, she couldn't help but feel a flush of happiness. It was beautiful and she couldn't wait to see the seasons changing the landscape as spring deepened and turned to summer.

They followed the long slow hill up into the village, which left her panting slightly, before crossing into the main road. They were heading for the one and only shop which lay at the far end and, despite still looking very much like the house it obviously had once been, it apparently sold anything and everything. Ned pushed open the door for her and ushered her inside, the basket of eggs held in front of her.

The first thing Flora heard was a bright peal of laughter in the room away to her left, which was followed by a sunny-sounding voice. 'Oh, go on with you, Brian, you love being mollycoddled so don't pretend that you don't!'

She moved towards the sound, looking through the large square room towards the far end to see an elderly couple standing by a counter. It was laden with loaves of bread and enough bottles and jars to make their stash at home look paltry by comparison. Behind the counter stood a tall, willowy woman with softly curling grey hair that reached well past her shoulders. She wore pale jeans and a simple navy tee shirt that should have looked ordinary but instead added to the woman's elegant bearing. Her face was split into a wide smile. She nodded a welcome as she saw Flora and Ned enter the shop before continuing her conversation.

Flora glanced at Ned and took the opportunity to have a look around. At a guess, she would have said that she was standing in what would originally have been the main living room to the house. The period bay window with its deep sill provided an enticing space for display, but rather than cramming it full with goods, someone with an eye for detail had simply stood a huge blue jug there and filled it with twigs of hazel, cotoneaster, and bright glossy springs of holly. It set the tone for the whole shop which, now that Flora looked, was hung with bunches of herbs, wreaths of dried flowers and a garland of what looked like eucalyptus leaves. She moved closer to get a better look, intrigued by what she saw.

Lost in contemplation, it took a moment for her to realise that Ned was gently nudging her arm. The woman from behind the counter had come to stand beside them.

'You must be Flora,' she said, her hand outstretched.

'Oh…' Flora replied, startled. 'Sorry, I was miles away, but yes, I am…'

The woman grinned. 'And despite the fact that you're here with Ned, which is a bit of a giveaway, I feel as if I'd know you anywhere.'

Flora took the hand and shook it. 'Really?' she asked, looking down at her boots rather self-consciously.

'Oh yes,' came the reply. 'And don't worry, Hannah provided me with a perfect description of you.' She laughed, noticing the expression on Flora's face. 'Oh dear, I can see that's worried you even more. But fear not, Hannah had nothing but good words to say… although admittedly she was a little bemused by the range of coloured tights you wear, whereas I, on the other hand, think they're fantastic.'

Flora blushed. 'Thank you…' she managed, realising that today's choice, pink and orange stripes, were not exactly subtle.

Ned grinned. 'Flora, this is Grace,' he said. 'Who I have known all my life…'

Grace rolled her eyes. 'Yes, thank you, Ned, for reminding me just how old I am.' She looked at Flora. 'Welcome to the village and our humble little shop.'

'Hardly humble,' Flora replied. 'You look as if you sell everything in here. And I was looking at the decorations—'

'You approve?'

'Oh yes…' Flora didn't mind the interruption at all; she had a feeling she knew exactly who was responsible for them. 'Just lovely. Perfect in fact.' She smiled. 'I used to—'

'Be a florist,' said Grace, interrupting again. 'Yes, I know. And now you're an artist, I believe. Caroline told me that. Oh, and not horsey…' She gave a surreptitious look over her shoulder and then turned back to grin at Ned. 'Thank heavens for that,' she whispered.

Flora laughed. 'I can only imagine what Caroline said. I'm not sure she understood the whole artist thing, but then I can't see the attraction of riding. It looks frankly terrifying and I've been invited out on a ride soon… I'm honestly not sure how I'm going to cope with that,' she confided. 'Somehow I don't see Caroline and I ever becoming bosom buddies.'

'No?' Grace's face was a picture. 'Shame.' She smothered her grin. 'And you're right, Caroline won't understand you being an artist at all. She'll think you're weird, like me. But that's okay.'

Flora felt the slight tension in her shoulders beginning to ease and she pointed to the wall-hanging. 'So am I right in thinking that this is your handiwork?'

'Indeed it is, and all plants from my garden, which is my absolute pride and joy. I can't help it, I just find myself collecting stuff and then the next minute… well, that was one of the results. Fortunately for me, Bill doesn't mind my projects overflowing into the shop. He's the owner,' she added.

'I can't see why anyone would object,' replied Flora. 'I think they're beautiful.'

Grace cocked her head. 'So what do you do? Something colourful, obviously.'

'I make prints,' said Flora. 'Sketch first, then paint and then, if I like the painting, I go on to make a print. And you can use those on anything; cards, pictures, fabric, wallpaper…'

Grace's eyes lit up. 'Can you show me? We could sell them for you if you like. The adjoining room is full of local produce, everything from jam to baby blankets, runner beans – when they're in season, obviously – to Mrs Jessop's hideous homemade wine.' She cupped a hand around her mouth. 'But don't tell her I said that.' She looked at Flora expectantly.

Ned beamed at her. 'See, I told you,' he said.

Flora shoved a hand in her bag, fishing around for her phone. She hadn't realised that Grace meant she should show her right that minute. 'Hang on…'

'Here, let me,' said Grace, relieving her of the basket full of eggs.

Flora smiled her gratitude and after a moment removed her mobile with a flourish. 'Just a sec,' she said, as she waited for her Etsy page to load. 'It's a bit hard to tell with the pictures being so small, but you get the idea.' She passed the phone to Grace, who stared at it with wide eyes.

'Ah…' She sighed, turning the phone around. 'Stunning. I knew they would be.' She looked up at Flora. 'What's your Etsy shop called?' she asked. 'I'll have a proper look when I get home.'

'Daisy Doolittles,' she replied. 'Don't ask me why…'

'Oh, no… I think that's perfect.' She studied the pictures for a few moments more, scrolling through the images. 'I think, if you weren't a

Flora, that being a Daisy would suit you very well indeed.' She grinned, handing back the phone. 'Or at a push, a Poppy…' She looked down at the basket in her hands. 'Right, eggs,' she said. 'Let me just offload them and you can have the basket back. How many have you brought?'

'There's two dozen. Is that all right?'

Grace waved an airy hand as she walked back to the counter. 'They'll be gone before tomorrow,' she replied. 'Pension day, you see.' She plonked the basket down and lifted out the trays. 'Now, did you come in for anything else? You didn't need to, it's been lovely just meeting you, but I'm supposed to ask.' She rolled her eyes. 'Bill is ever hopeful he'll make a proper saleswoman out of me.'

'Just some honey please,' answered Ned.

Flora nodded. 'Oh, yes. I think there's one in particular that Hannah…' She broke off as Grace hoisted a jar aloft. 'Ah, I see you know which one. It's very nice. Is it local?'

Grace nodded. 'Hmm, not too far away. Do you just want one jar?'

'No, I'll take a couple please. I was planning on making a honey cake for supper. And I have to confess I like it lashed onto fresh bread just out the oven.'

'Nothing better,' said Grace. 'And don't worry about paying,' she added, seeing Flora fish in her bag again. 'I'll take the cost off what we pay Hannah for the eggs, same as usual.'

From the hallway came the sound of a tinkling bell as a new customer pushed open the door to the shop. Flora held out her hand for the basket. 'We should get going,' she said. 'But, thank you, Grace. It's been lovely meeting you.'

Grace beamed at her. 'You too. So, I'll see you again,' she replied. 'And next time, bring some of your prints in with you.'

Flora blushed again. 'I will,' she said, raising her hand in goodbye as she made way for the next customer, an excited buzz filling her head. 'Oh, I definitely will.'

Grace came around the counter to say goodbye.

'As for you, young man,' she said, a warm hand on Ned's arm. 'Take the greatest care of Flora, won't you?'

He grinned and pulled Flora in close. 'Oh, I intend to. Believe me.'

They were halfway home before Flora suddenly stopped, realising that she had walked the entire way without saying a word; her head was stuffing itself full of ideas again.

She turned to Ned ready to apologise for her silence only to find that he was already watching her, an amused expression on his face.

'You can't wait, can you?' he remarked. 'All those thoughts inside your head whizzing around. I can almost see them, just as if you'd spoken them out loud.'

'There's just so much inspiration here,' she replied. 'Everywhere you look.' Her face fell slightly. 'You won't let me get carried away though, will you? I'm not going to have time to be sitting around making prints all day, and you know what I'm like; I get engrossed and the day just goes.'

'So let yourself,' said Ned. 'It's a thing you do, Flora. And you shouldn't try to deny it. Besides, Grace will now expect a regular supply of things to sell and if you don't come up with the goods, she'll want to know why.'

'Is that okay, though? No one will mind?'

'Who's going to mind?' He gave her hand a squeeze. 'I think it's a brilliant idea.'

So did Flora. In fact, it could be the solution to more than one problem.

Chapter 5

Flora turned on her side and snaked an arm across Ned's chest. The clock showed it was past four o'clock and it would be time for him to get up soon.

'Are you awake?' she whispered.

Ned turned towards her slightly, murmuring, but he was still fast asleep, the blankets tucked under his chin. And so Flora lay quietly beside him, fizzing with excitement, until the alarm went off ten minutes later.

Adept at creeping from their bed and getting dressed in the dark, Ned nearly jumped out of his skin when Flora leaned over and turned on the bedside light.

'Blimey, Flora, you'll give me a heart attack!'

'Sorry.' She grinned. 'I've been awake for ages. I thought I might get up with you.'

He gave her a sideways glance. 'Are you mad? Why on earth do you want to get up when you can stay here where it's warm? I wouldn't be getting up if I didn't have to, believe me, but the cows won't milk themselves…'

Flora was already beginning to regret her decision now that Ned had left the bed and a blast of cold air shot underneath the blankets. 'Well, that's what I was thinking about actually. I wondered whether

I could come and help you today? Then it wouldn't take so long and you wouldn't have to get up so early.'

'Oh aye, trying to entice me back to bed so you can have your wicked way with me, are you?' He shot her a grin. 'Don't tempt me.' And with that he disappeared towards the bathroom.

Flora lay back for a moment, undecided as to what to do, but then she flung the bedclothes back and sat up. It wasn't a yes, but then it wasn't a no either. Hurriedly pulling on yesterday's clothes, she went downstairs to make them some tea.

'You weren't kidding, were you?' said Ned, fifteen minutes later as he came into the kitchen.

Flora was just pouring hot water into an enormous teapot.

'No, well I couldn't sleep so I thought it was about time I made myself useful. The toast is on.'

Ned came across the room to kiss her, nuzzling her neck. 'I could get used to this. Are you going to get up with me every morning?'

She pushed at him playfully as his still wet hair made her cheek damp. 'I haven't decided yet,' she replied.

He smiled but then his face grew more serious. 'So how come you couldn't sleep? I wasn't snoring again, was I?'

She shook her head. 'No, not this time, but…' She gave him a sheepish smile. 'Well, if you must know, I was too excited. There doesn't seem to be enough time in the day to do all the things I want to do.' She busied herself bringing butter and jam to the table.

'Aw, I think that's sweet…'

She blushed. 'Yes, but I feel a bit like a six-year-old.'

Ned put his hands on his hips, smirking. 'Believe me, you don't look like a six-year-old.' He grinned at her choice of outfit. 'Well, maybe… but you definitely don't act like a six-year-old… At least you certainly didn't last night…'

Flora looked over her shoulder. 'Shhh,' she said. 'You can't say things like that!'

'Why not?' He sidled up to her across the kitchen, pulling her close, with a wicked grin on his face.

'What does a man need to do around here to get a cup of tea…?' Flora sprang away from Ned as Fraser came into the room. She could feel herself blushing, and was about to apologise, when he chuckled.

'Go on with you, I was just joshing… Does a man good to see that kind of thing first thing in the morning.' He took a seat at the table. 'You're up early this morning, lass. Bed bugs bite, did they?'

Flora brought a rack of toast to the table and smiled. 'I just thought I might come and give you a hand this morning,' she said, brightly. 'I was awake anyway, so just stick me in a pair of wellies and tell me what to do.'

Fraser's hand paused on its way to claim a piece of toast. 'Oh, aye… Ned invite you, did he?' he said – somewhat carefully, thought Flora.

'I didn't think you meant to come out *milking*,' said Ned, coming to sit down himself. 'Just that you'd got up to make breakfast. Were you really thinking you would come out with us?'

Flora looked between the faces of the two men. 'Why? Isn't that a good idea?' she asked, watching Ned's reaction carefully. His face was open, but there was a definite flicker of something behind his eyes.

'No, it's a lovely idea, but it's bloody freezing out there, Flora. And dark, and it doesn't get much better the whole time we're milking.'

'You manage it though…'

'Because I'm used to it, but—' He stopped when he saw the expression on her face.

Flora stuck her tongue in her cheek. 'It's okay, I'm not going to give you a hard time.' She grinned. 'I know when I'm not wanted.' She hefted the teapot and began to pour tea into three mugs. 'And you're probably right. Whilst they look lovely in the fields, I reckon the cows would be terrifying up close. I'd probably run a mile if one looked at me a bit fierce.'

'Aye well, they can give you a right good thumping, lass, make no mistake.' Fraser sank his teeth into a slice of toast. 'Need a bit of respecting, do cows.' His expression was hard to fathom and Flora wasn't at all sure how he viewed her offer of help.

Ned picked up his mug and swallowed a mouthful of tea. 'It isn't that you're not wanted, Flora, not at all, but the farm isn't a place you can just turn up to and pitch in, not if you don't know what you're doing. It can be a dangerous place and we're… well, we're a bit under pressure at the moment.'

And there it was again, the slight flicker… Of what exactly? Flora couldn't quite put her finger on it.

'Maybe when it gets a bit quieter…'

'You're optimistic, lad, aren't you?' muttered Fraser. 'When is that likely to happen?' He rubbed at his arm and took a swig of tea to wash down his toast. 'Right then, you ready?'

Ned nodded and shoved a crust in his mouth as he rose from the table. 'Sorry, Flora,' he said. 'I'll catch you later.' He bent to give her a kiss.

She smiled. 'Ned, it's fine, honestly. Go on, off you go. I'll see you in a bit.'

And then she was on her own in the quiet kitchen surveying the remains of the hasty breakfast. It was, as Ned had said, pitch black outside, and a glance at the clock confirmed it had just gone five in the morning. What on earth was she going to do now?

She sat nursing her own cup of tea for quite some time, eating a piece of toast although she had no real hunger for it. It was far too early for food and, besides, so much was eaten later on when the men came back for their 'proper' breakfast that eating anything now was just silly.

What Ned had said made perfect sense and she hadn't even considered that the business end of the farm wasn't a safe place for her to be in until she knew what she was doing. The trouble was, of course, that she would never get to know unless someone showed her the ropes and that wasn't looking likely to happen any time soon. Cooking and keeping house was all very well, but she wanted to do more. She wanted to be by Ned's side physically as well as emotionally, working with him day by day, sharing the load, but that was something else she would have to learn, it seemed. She had thought that their life together would include an equal division of labour, but every time the subject came up, the dividing line came down to gender and it was a line she was clearly going to find difficult to cross.

Draining the last of her tea, she carried the mugs and plates over to the sink, leaving them there to wash later, and then she wandered back upstairs and into their bedroom. It was even too early to feed the hens, but so far she hadn't had the opportunity to properly unpack her art materials and, after her conversation with Grace yesterday, she was itching to use them again. When she'd been at the shop all day she always had her sketchbook and pencils with her at the very least and, once home, she would pick them up whenever inspiration or the inclination struck. She could often be found with a sandwich in one hand and a paintbrush in the other, but unless she found a way to make it work, that was never going to happen here. Still, with nothing else around the house that needed attending to straight away, now could be the perfect time. Ned certainly didn't have a problem with her print-making, and well, maybe everyone else would just have to get used to it. Apart from anything else, it might be the only way she could get any money together while she was here.

Carrying the first of her boxes downstairs, she set it down onto the dining room table before returning to fetch the second. She'd been mulling over an idea she'd had for a composition lino cut using the beautiful hellebores she'd seen in the garden on her first morning at the farm. Coupled with some forsythia stems, the contrast of flowers could work well, but she needed to play with some designs first. She placed her phone on the table and sat down.

The dining room seemed rarely used and it was freezing. By eight o'clock she could scarcely feel her fingers they were so cold, but she did, however, have three designs which she was happy with.

'You're not daft, are you, boy?' she said, wandering through into the kitchen to put the kettle on and looking at Brodie, who was in his usual position by the Aga. 'Budge over though, eh, I need to warm up too.'

She rested her bum against one of the doors, holding her hands a little distance from the hot metal. She would need to go and feed the hens in a few minutes and then make the bread for lunch, but she had also decided to go and investigate the woodpile. Hannah wouldn't be back until later that afternoon – a rare morning at the local WI apparently. Flora wasn't sure what she had planned for them for the rest of the day, but if she could, she wanted to continue with her art and for that she needed warmth of some sort. Sitting hunched up with cold was making her shoulders ache.

An hour and a half later she had the fireplace in the dining room ablaze, the warmth of the flame totally transforming the room, disguising the heaviness of the wooden furniture and dark soft furnishings and revealing their hidden colours. Flora looked around her. It was a peaceful room, she decided. Tucking her hair behind her ears, she picked up her lino cutter.

She wasn't even aware of the sound at first, or rather she wasn't aware of its significance; it was several minutes before she tuned in and realised that what she could hear was Ned and Fraser talking in the kitchen. Moments later, Ned's bulk filled the doorway beside her.

'Flora?' Ned's eyes fell on the table where she worked, now covered in tiny strips of spent lino cut away from the block she was using. She'd made quite a mess...

'I'll clear it up, don't worry,' she said. 'It's what you might call work in progress.'

He nodded and drew in a breath. 'It was more... well, I was wondering about breakfast... Fraser, you know, well he likes...'

Flora's head shot up in shock as she suddenly realised the time. Her hand flew to her mouth. 'Bugger! Ned, I'm so sorry, I got completely lost in what I was doing.' She began to get to her feet. 'I'm coming now, just give me ten minutes and I'll have something sorted.'

She was level with him now, but instead of the answering smile she expected to see, his face was anxious. He glanced at his watch. 'We're running a bit late,' he said.

The smile dropped from her face as she followed him down the hallway into the kitchen where Fraser was already sitting at the table.

'What would you like?' she asked him. 'I'll get the kettle going for starters and then, how about I make some more toast? Or there's plenty of cereal, at least I think there is...'

She busied herself at the tap, only turning back around when she realised that Fraser had not answered her.

'I'm really sorry, I lost track of time.' She gave an apologetic smile. 'Got stuck into making one of my prints and...' She trailed off as she caught the look on his face. 'Are you all right?' she asked. 'You look a bit pale.'

Fraser swallowed. 'I came in for my breakfast,' he said. 'And I'm bloody starving… What I need is something to eat.'

Flora flashed a helpless look at Ned, praying for him to come to her rescue.

'Here, Dad, have one of these to tide you over,' he said, pulling the biscuit tin from the side and handing it over. He turned back to Flora. 'We've had a really busy morning,' he added. 'Worse than usual. A line of fencing got broken somehow in the night and we've had to replace it. Dad's been hammering in the poles for the last hour.'

It was as much of an apology as Ned could get away with. Fraser wasn't normally this short, but it still didn't make Flora feel any better.

'I could make beans on toast,' she said, thinking on her feet. 'That wouldn't take long.' She bit her lip waiting for a response. 'And it's very good for you.' She didn't know what else to say. There was clearly no room for any alteration to the usual dining arrangements.

There was a scant nod and she got to work, hacking off two thick slices of bread from yesterday's loaf. She eyed the bowl that was resting on the shelf above the Aga. That was something else she had forgotten too. The dough she had managed to make earlier was still in the bowl where she had left it to rise. And it well and truly had. She looked away; she would have to fix it later.

Eventually, both Ned and Fraser had plates of food in front of them as well as a big mug of tea each. It was the best she could do under the circumstances but the kitchen was filled with a definite air of dissatisfaction and it lay heavy on her shoulders. It was ironic that, given the choice, Flora would much prefer to serve a breakfast like this than their usual fare. Cooking meat did not come at all naturally to her and the sight of bacon, sausages and black pudding swimming in fat every morning still turned her stomach.

Fraser ate fast and steadily as usual, quickly demolishing the lake of beans and helping himself to extra slices of toast. He made no further comment and it was left to Ned to cover the awkward gaps in conversation. She was sure he would have been genuinely interested in what she had been doing during the morning, but his embarrassment at his father's grumpy mood made his comments sound stilted, like polite small talk. It didn't take long for them both to fall silent.

'Would you like more tea, Fraser?' asked Flora, as he drained his mug. There was a pained expression on his face.

He belched, holding a hand against his mouth, before nodding.

'Aye, got something a bit stuck, I reckon.'

Flora dutifully poured another mugful which quickly went the same way as the first. She flicked a glance at Ned but he was busy finishing his own food.

He had hardly put his knife and fork together on the plate before Fraser got to his feet, motioning for Ned to do the same. 'Come on, lad,' he grumbled. 'We haven't the time to be sitting here.'

Ned pulled a face. 'I know, Dad, but at least let your food go down, eh?'

Fraser was rubbing the centre of his chest.

'Got bloody heartburn now,' he said. 'No offence, lass,' he added, 'but I don't get heartburn from sausages and bacon. I can't be doing with all this bread.'

Flora dipped her head. 'I'm sorry, it won't happen again.'

Fraser looked across at Ned. 'Now don't go thinking I'm being unkind by saying this, but I'm only doing so because I know that soft 'un over there won't. We have a way of doing things that suits us, Flora.

It's lovely having you here, don't get me wrong, and this 'un's got a spring in his step I haven't seen before. But don't go changing things that have worked perfectly well in the past. It will save an awful lot of heartache if you don't.'

And with that he lifted a hand in the kind of wave that signified the conversation was at an end and went through to the scullery where Flora could hear him pulling his boots back on.

There was an awkward pause while Flora waited for Ned to gather himself and decide what to say, but then she felt his arms go around her and his rough cheek rest against the top of her head.

'Oh, Flora,' he murmured. 'What have I done to you? Bringing you here where you don't know anyone and just expecting you to pick everything up and run with it.' He pulled away slightly to look at her. 'And believe it or not, in his own way my dad thinks he's being kind, which means he likes you. What he said wasn't meant with any ill feeling.'

There were so many conflicting emotions swirling through Flora, she didn't know which one to settle on, so she said nothing, but nodded glumly instead. It wasn't Ned's fault.

She managed a weak smile. 'Have a good rest of the morning,' she said. 'And I'll see you at lunch, okay?'

Ned kissed her, releasing her arms and giving them both a brisk rub. 'Listen, I've got to go, but I'll talk to Dad so don't you go worrying about things. And we can catch up later too, I promise.' He tipped his finger against the end of her nose and kissed her again. 'I love you,' he said.

'I love you too,' replied Flora, holding the smile on her face. 'See you later.'

The ticking of the clock above the Aga was suddenly loud in the room as the door closed behind Ned. She stared at it for a moment, trying to slow down the rush of emotions that were churning her stomach, and then her eyes settled on the bowl on the shelf underneath it where the dough was waiting for her. She took it down and brought it to the table, lifting the cloth that covered it and peering at the contents. Then she cleared the plates and mugs from the table in one fell swoop and stacked them by the sink. The bread wouldn't make itself and she might as well get on with it or she'd be in even more trouble. Then of course she could attend to the washing-up and begin the preparation of the soup for lunch.

She pursed her lips. Fraser was absolutely right, of course. He'd already done a hard morning's graft and expected to come in to the kind of breakfast he'd been provided with for umpteen years. There was no reason he could see why this should change and certainly not without any discussion or consultation. When she and Ned were married then things might be a little different, but for the moment she was effectively just a guest in their house and would do well to remember that.

She began to punch the dough, knocking back the rise as she had been shown and it wasn't until something dripped onto the back of her hand that she realised she was crying.

Chapter 6

And of course, it was at that moment that Hannah walked into the kitchen, tutting as she dropped her bag onto the table and pulled off her gloves and scarf before removing her coat. She sighed as she hung it over the back of one of the chairs.

'Honestly, I don't know why I bother going to these meetings…'

She stopped and looked up as Flora gave a sniff.

Flora had been on the verge of letting it all go. After all, she was on her own and was expecting to be for some time yet, so what would it have mattered? But now, Hannah's sudden appearance had caught her out and somehow that made it so much worse. Now she was embarrassed as well as upset and she could feel the dam holding back her emotions beginning to break. She looked anxiously towards the door, wondering whether she had time to fly, but Hannah's soft exhalation of breath let her know that her tears had been spotted.

'Flora, dear. Whatever is the matter?'

Hannah was around the table in seconds, quite rightly deducing that Flora was about to burst into noisy tears, but then she paused, looking awkward and unsure what to do next. Flora longed to have Hannah's arms go around her and be told that everything was all right, but instead she patted her arm and made vague shushing noises.

Flora gulped and held her breath, stifling her tears. Hannah's reaction felt like a wet blanket and she was clearly so uncomfortable it had an immediate effect on Flora. She drew herself up, nodding.

'I'm fine, honestly. Sorry, I'm not sure what came over me then… I just got a bit upset and… No, I'm fine now.' She mustered a weak smile as proof.

Hannah watched her warily as she slowly drew away a chair from the table and motioned for Flora to sit down.

'Even so, I've been thinking that maybe you and I need to have a little chat, so perhaps that time has come…' She laid a hand on Flora's arm. 'I'll make us a drink, dear, and then you can tell me all about it.' She got up and crossed to the chair where her coat was hanging, fumbling in the pocket before bringing something back to Flora. 'Here,' she said, passing her a tissue. 'It's clean. Give your nose a good blow.'

Flora took it gratefully, wondering how much of a state she must look. She'd always been an ugly crier – eyes that puffed up immediately, a nose that turned bright red and cheeks that blotched at the slightest hint of wet.

She shouldn't even be that upset. What had happened this morning had been entirely her own fault. She had known what needed to be done but she had allowed herself to get sidetracked, and Fraser had every right to say what he had; he'd even tried to be kind about it in his own bluff way. She wasn't normally so sensitive, but today the mix-up over breakfast had come at the end of a list of things that hadn't seemed quite right. And now Hannah had said that she'd been wanting to have a chat with her too. What else had she done wrong? She sat, scrubbing at her nose as she waited for Hannah to return to the table.

'You must feel dreadful, dear,' said Hannah, sitting down. 'And I know you're in love with Ned, but really a lot of this is his fault. I mean, if he had done us the courtesy of telling us what he was planning then we could have made better arrangements for your arrival, talked about the practicalities of you coming to live here so you wouldn't have been catapulted into the middle of all this. You would have known what was expected of you. I'm not surprised you hate it.'

Flora sniffed. 'I don't hate it... You've all been lovely, really, and in Ned's defence, I don't think he really knew what he was planning... In fact, it wasn't planned... it just happened. Him and me, I mean.' She hung her head. 'Oh, that sounds terrible, doesn't it? Makes it sound like it's not a proper relationship, and it is, honestly.' She looked up into Hannah's eyes. 'I'm not doing a very good job of this, am I?'

Hannah smiled, more gently. 'Explaining? Or being Ned's fiancée?' she asked. 'But you really don't need to worry about either of those things. It's simply a matter of adjustment and understanding how things are; you'll get used to it. Now, why don't you start at the beginning and tell me what prompted all these tears.' She pushed a mug of tea towards her.

Flora cradled her hands around it, grateful to have something to focus on while she caught her breath and tried to think of a way to start the conversation. Even though most of her wanted to slink away into her room and not think about anything at all...

'You and Ned haven't had a disagreement, have you?' suggested Hannah.

'No, nothing like that,' Flora replied, wondering what to say. 'But I messed up this morning, and I don't think Fraser's very happy with me...' She trailed off, not wanting to be critical. 'He wasn't unkind, it was my fault, after all – I got involved in something and forgot the time so breakfast wasn't ready when they got in. They had to make do with beans on toast which didn't go down terribly well and I can understand that... although I really didn't think it would matter for just one day. Sometimes it's good to do something a bit different, isn't it? Not to mention a little healthier.' She sighed. 'I just feel so out of place. Maybe I'm not cut out to be a farmer's wife.'

'Perhaps you're being rather hard on yourself, dear. You're not even married yet, and there's plenty of time to learn the ropes. After all, being a good wife isn't something that comes straight away, although you young folk don't always realise it. Being a farmer's wife comes with its own set of challenges, admittedly, but essentially it's much the same and you shouldn't try to run before you can walk. It takes years of practice, and I should know, I've had rather a lot.'

It wasn't exactly what Flora wanted to hear. What she wanted was more along the lines of 'she was doing fine and anyway who defined what the archetypal farmer's wife should be'. But Flora knew she wasn't going to get that response, because evidently there was such a thing, and it was she, Flora, who needed to change.

'Which is why I think it's rather unfair of Ned to simply expect you to slot right in here without even having the opportunity to talk about expectations... from both sides.' Hannah paused to lick her lips. 'Under the circumstances you've fitted in very well, and I'm very pleased to see your and Ned's obvious affection for one another, but...'

Here it comes, thought Flora.

'But... Oh dear, this is going to sound very harsh, and I don't mean it to at all, but this is still mine and Fraser's home and we've rather got used to doing things a certain way. I'm not sure either of us want that to change.'

Flora dropped her eyes. Because there it was, the crux of the matter. Whatever Flora wanted, whether she and Ned were married or not, this was never going to be her house, to do as she pleased...

'That said,' continued Hannah, 'it really is lovely having you here, so please don't think you're not welcome...' She broke off to pat Flora's hand. 'Ned is obviously very happy, and it's been a long time since there was anyone here who was quite so... colourful, and the flowers too... I can't remember the last time we had so many in the house. But although I know we're old stick in the muds, I'm afraid that rather suits us.'

Flora nodded, smiling. There wasn't much else she could do.

'And now I'm not being critical, because your artwork is lovely, but perhaps you need to think about whether it's something that you can continue to pursue? In the longer term... It could well take up rather a large amount of your time; time that you might be better served devoting to something else.'

Flora opened her mouth to speak, but Hannah held up a hand.

'Now I can see you'd like to argue your case, but I was brought up to believe that a wife's needs and desires were secondary to her husband's, which again is not a very popular opinion these days, and more's the pity.' She paused to take a sip of tea. 'The way I look at it is that I am living in my husband's house, and he's working hard to put food on the table and provide for me. The same will be true for you and Ned, and any little ones that come along. In my book that means that you do everything you can to support him.' She looked over the top of her glasses. 'For example, doing your bit to make sure that you don't fritter things away and be wasteful around the house.' She paused for a moment. 'I couldn't help noticing that you lit the fire in the dining room.'

Flora looked up, taken aback.

'There's nothing wrong with lighting the fire as such,' continued Hannah. 'But what happens when Ned wants to sit in the front room and have a warm-up after a hard day's work… and all the wood is gone? Are you seriously going to chop the logs?'

'Well yes, I would. I'd try anyway. I wouldn't expect Ned to do it.'

'Ah, but would *he* be happy with you doing it?'

Flora frowned. She hadn't thought of it like that. But Ned wouldn't mind, surely…

'After all, you wouldn't expect him to bake the cake for supper, would you?'

'I wouldn't expect him to, no, but I wouldn't mind if he did. I don't see that it's any more my job than it is his… It's about sharing the workload.'

'Which is fine if Ned worked in an office, but he doesn't. He works from early morning to late at night and it's hard, physical work which, however much you might want to, you couldn't possibly share. Believe me, there's nothing equal about the workload on a farm and these modern ideas are all very well, but they just don't seem to fit in with life here. You could spend an awful long time and a lot of heartache trying to find that out for yourself, or… you could just accept it.'

Hannah gave her a sympathetic smile. 'I do understand how you feel,' she said. 'And it's commendable that you want to do your bit to help on the farm, but if you want to feel useful then it's better if you realise that it's your job to support Ned in doing his, rather than to try and change things. You can still have your little hobbies and so on, and goodness, no one is saying that you have to do things exactly as I do…'

But they are, thought Flora, that's exactly what's being suggested.

'…You'll find your own way of doing things, put your own stamp on the household… which brings me rather neatly to the other thing I wanted to talk to you about.' She leant forward in her chair. 'Fraser and I have been talking, and I realise that there's a huge amount that needs to be discussed with regard to the wedding, but we'd very much like you to consider having it here. What do you think?'

Flora thought that this was a conversation she would rather be having with Ned at her side, but she couldn't possibly say so.

'Your offer is lovely, Hannah, thank you. I'll make sure I talk to Ned about it soon so we can decide, and please thank Fraser for me, it's a very generous gesture.'

'And it could be the most enormous fun, don't you think?' Hannah drank the last of her tea. 'A big upheaval of course, but I think we could manage it, and I've also been thinking…' She leaned in again. 'Now don't quote me on this, because it's not for definite yet, but I have made a suggestion to Fraser about our domestic arrangements, and I think he might be prepared to consider it.'

'Go on…' said Flora, sounding more cautious than she had intended.

'Some years ago when Ned was… well, when he was in a different relationship, Fraser and I decided that it might be the right moment to give Ned a little more space for… entertaining and the like.' Hannah broke off to clear her throat, slightly embarrassed at the mention of Ned's past. 'And the sheds at the far end of the yard are very well built so it didn't take much to start converting them into a cottage for us. It has always been our intention that, once Fraser and I retire, the farm would pass into Ned's name along with the farmhouse. The cottage would provide the perfect place for us to downsize, leaving Ned and this… person to take up the reins, raise a family and so on. However, when things didn't work out with the girl in question, it didn't seem sensible to waste all that time and money and so the work on the cottage stopped. But now that you're here it changes things again. Of course there are plenty of years left in Fraser yet, and so we're not about to retire immediately…' She broke off to give a rather forced laugh. 'But everything at the cottage is still in place so it wouldn't take much to restart the alterations. I wondered if it might provide a solution to any… difficulties we might have, all living under the one roof.' She sat back, clearly pleased with her suggestion.

'I'm sorry, Hannah. I'm not sure I'm following you.'

'Well, like I said, nothing is definite, but seeing as you and Ned are going to be married soon, I thought it might be rather nice for you to have a little more space of your own. It wouldn't be straight away of course, there's still a bit of work to do in finishing off the conversion for us, but I do think that Fraser might consider it. It wouldn't change anything as far as the running of the farm goes though,' she clarified, just in case Flora thought otherwise. 'At least, not at the moment. But if we moved out at some point you might feel that the house becomes more your domain than at present. Which in turn might also help you to settle in.' Hannah plucked at an imaginary piece of fluff on her sleeve. 'It's all about feeling in control, isn't it?' She smiled. 'Think of it as a wedding present, if you like.' She sat back, beaming.

But Flora didn't feel like it was a wedding present. She felt like she had pushed Hannah and Fraser out of their home. Was she really that difficult to live with?

Hannah inhaled a cleansing breath. 'I'm so pleased we've had the opportunity to have this little chat,' she said. 'Rather overdue, I suspect, and I am sorry you got so upset. But I hope that things are a little clearer now?'

Flora nodded dutifully.

'And you must always come and ask me if you need help with anything. Us women have to stick together, don't we?' Hannah glanced at her watch. 'Now, shall I finish off the bread and make a start on the soup? We don't want the men missing two meals, do we?' Her eyebrows were raised.

Flora got to her feet. 'Thank you,' she said. 'I might just go and tidy myself up a bit, if that's okay? Wash my face, that sort of thing.'

'Of course,' replied Hannah. 'It wouldn't do to have Ned see you looking like that.' She frowned slightly. 'Not that you don't still look lovely, I didn't mean it like that. But men don't really understand, do they? Ned will take one look at you, see that you've been crying and want to know why… and that's when it all gets rather complicated. Best not to let them see in the first place, dear.'

Flora was rather banking on Ned understanding, but she simply nodded instead. 'I won't be long,' she said, and slipped from the room.

But she didn't go upstairs. Instead she crept back into the dining room where her things were all still laid out on the table. The room was still warm, or warmer than the rest of the house at least, but the fire had died down and was now just a bed of glowing ashes. Flora picked up a poker from the set on the hearth and gave it a vicious prod. She could feel tears threatening again but, by inhaling deeply and clamping her back teeth together, she managed to keep them at bay. This was so much harder than she had thought. Ordinarily she would have spoken her mind, pointed out that Hannah's rigid ideals were entrenched in a past that had no bearing on how Flora lived her life. But how could she speak up when this was Ned's mother, and she had no idea how he really felt on the subject? She stared sadly at the table. Perhaps that was part of the problem. She didn't really know how Ned felt about anything much.

With a sigh, she began to clear away the debris of lino waste that littered the table. She had so nearly finished her print and had been pleased with how it had progressed, but she had no stomach to complete it now. The sketches she had made were almost finished too, and at least one of them was of sufficient quality that with a little extra work she could offer it for sale. But it would be going back in the box along with the rest of her things. Flora didn't really know when they would be unpacked again. And that meant no pictures for Grace to sell, and no money either.

Chapter 7

Lunch was fine. Normal service had been resumed and although Fraser was very quiet, he didn't appear to be harbouring any ill feeling. Flora could see that Hannah was relieved to have got things off her chest as well; it was just Flora who wasn't at all sure how she felt.

It was heading towards late afternoon by the time Flora was finally free to visit Ned. And she still wasn't sure which way to think. She veered between bouts of anger at the sense of injustice she felt, and guilt that she could dare to feel such a thing. She was the newcomer here. She had no right to expect things to change simply because of her arrival, and who was she to think that her way of doing things was any better than anyone else's? Hannah was obviously happy with her lot, as was Fraser, and even though their old-fashioned attitudes made her want to scream, it was just a different way of life. It didn't make them bad people.

And so, hens fed, she set off for the milking parlour in determined fashion. It seemed ridiculous that Flora hadn't yet ventured this far into the farm. Hannah had shown her where things were a little closer to the farmhouse and waved in vague fashion at the rest, but she'd had no need to go exploring on her own, or the inclination as it happened; it would have felt like trespassing. Ned had offered to take her but every time he was free it was already dark.

Reaching the milking parlour entailed walking right to the other end of the farm buildings, past the row of brick sheds, which Flora now realised were destined to be Hannah and Fraser's new cottage, and the assorted barns and other buildings that she guessed were used for storage.

As the troughs of flowers dwindled away and the level of mud increased, she realised she'd reached the 'business' end of the farm. It was different from the lush area surrounding the farmhouse, but still beautiful in its own right. The buildings around her were made from warm red brick and had an air of tradition and permanence about them. She crossed over the roadway which led into the bottom end of the farm and approached the low long shed she could see running along the other side.

The smell and the noise reached her before everything else. It was a warm sweet smell, but sour too, the type that invaded your nostrils and stayed there. And the noise was loud and clamorous, a rhythmic clanking to it, interspersed with the odd shout. It took Flora quite a few moments to take in what was going on and to even spot Ned among the machinery. And when she did, she saw he was not alone.

Caroline was leaning up against a metal railing that ran the entire length of the building, separating a raised walkway from the bright blue concrete floor of the parlour. The walkway was filled with cows, and everywhere Flora looked were legs and tails and bulging udders. Coils of pipework hung from machinery suspended on the ceiling, on the ends of which were four yellow tubes, and it was in among these that Flora had spotted Ned.

Caroline, in jodhpurs and a bright pink quilted jacket, had one arm draped casually over the railing, her hand lifting up and down as she talked, the other hand repeatedly running itself through her hair.

Despite her glamorous appearance, which was in direct contrast to the functional atmosphere in the shed, she looked very much at ease.

Ned, unusually, looked rather agitated. He had his back to Caroline as he worked, but every now and then he turned slightly towards her as she spoke. He looked as he always did whenever Flora had seen him in his work clothes, his wellies a dirty green, with a thick brown apron covering his navy blue overalls. But rather than the normal tiredness she was used to seeing, today, he looked harassed.

She had half a mind to turn and leave before she was spotted, but just at that moment, Ned looked up and saw her. And scowled.

Seeing the expression on his face change, Caroline spun around, her face breaking into a smile.

'Flora!' she exclaimed, coming forward. 'Goodness, I didn't think we'd ever get you in here.'

'Well, you know...' Flora muttered, looking past her to where Ned was standing, relieved to finally see a smile on his face.

'Is everything okay?' asked Ned.

'Fine,' replied Flora airily. 'I just thought it was high time I showed my face in here. I've just fed the hens and thought while I was out I should come on down and say hello.' She turned back to Caroline. 'I'm sorry, I didn't realise you were here,' she said. 'Or I'd have offered you a cup of tea.'

'Actually I'm just leaving, so don't worry.' Caroline turned back to Ned. 'I can see that things are a bit busy just now, but have a chat with Flora and let me know if that's okay. There's no rush.' She was having to raise her voice over the noise of the machinery and it was evident that she didn't like shouting.

Flora wanted to ask Ned if she could have a quiet word, but she wasn't about to do so in Caroline's hearing, and so she smiled and nodded. She wasn't about to ask what Caroline was referring to either, and she stood to one side to let her pass. As she did so she noticed another figure at the far end of the shed. Clad in red overalls, Fraser was standing, one hand on the rail, staring up at a point on the far wall a little bit higher than his head. She raised her hand in greeting, but perhaps he didn't see her. Or perhaps she wasn't quite out of his bad books just yet.

'What are you supposed to be talking to me about?' she asked Ned as soon as Caroline was out of earshot.

Ned looked blank.

'Caroline?' she prompted. 'You were supposed to be talking to me about something and getting back to her.'

'Oh that,' muttered Ned. 'Some bloody engagement party her mother wants to throw for us.'

'Engagement party?' Flora frowned. 'That's very generous, but a bit too formal for us… isn't it?'

'Yeah, like I really have the time to be poncing about at parties…'

'And I would have thought that if there was going to be an engagement party it would be something *we* would throw, seeing as it would be *our* friends who were invited…' She searched his face. 'Why on earth would Caroline's parents want to throw us a party? I mean, at the very least *your* mum and dad should organise it. It's a bit rude actually; I can't see Hannah and Fraser being very happy about it, that's for sure.'

Ned stared at her. 'You're right,' he said, and then shook his head. 'Sorry, Flora, I don't know how Caroline gets this stuff in her head at times.' He bent to kiss her cheek. 'Well, this is a rather lovely surprise,' he added, changing the subject.

She frowned again but then decided to let it go. 'Is it?' she replied. 'Only I seem to remember you didn't want me to come here this morning.' She gave him a cheeky smile instead. 'And I can see why. God it stinks in here!'

He grinned at her. 'It's an acquired taste, there's no doubt about that. But you don't really notice it after a while. Just as well, I suppose.' He looked behind him. 'Hang on a minute…'

She watched as he uncoupled the machinery from one of the cows, moving it along to the next, and then repeating the exercise several times. The ceaseless clanking seemed to increase in volume as she tuned back into it. As he walked back towards her she could see that his face had resumed its agitated expression.

'I'm sorry,' she said. 'I can see you're busy – I should let you get on. I guess I just wanted to come and say hello. I'll see you later, okay?'

She was about to go, when he reached out to touch her arm.

'Is everything okay?' He held her look for a moment. 'I asked you before, but with Caroline here, well… but now it's just us. So let me ask you again, and answer me truthfully this time?'

Her shoulders sagged a little as she sighed. 'I didn't intend to burden you with this now,' she replied. 'It can wait.'

She saw the tussle on his face; his desire to reach out to her against the pull of his work.

'Honestly, it can wait. You're busy and it's not fair.' She smiled. 'I'm okay though, in fact it's probably better if I wait until later to talk to you. I got a bit wound up and should calm down first.'

Ned cocked his head to one side. 'I don't know… if it's not one thing, it's my mother… Am I right?'

Flora blushed. 'That makes it sound awful, and it wasn't, not really. Your mum was lovely in fact.' She paused to chew at the side of her lip. 'I got upset after that stupid mistake over breakfast and Hannah came in just as I'd decided to start blubbing. It's okay, it was my fault after all, but after I'd cried all over her we had a little chat…' She broke off at the look on Ned's face. 'Which was fine… except that she mentioned the wedding, and one or two other things and… I'm really not sure how I feel about it all. I'm probably just being stupid. Hormonal or something, I don't know.' She threw her hands up in frustration.

'I doubt that,' replied Ned. 'Hormonal possibly, but how you feel is how you feel, you shouldn't try to ignore it, or pretend it's something else.' He touched the side of her face. 'Listen, I know Mum is stuck in the Dark Ages, and she's been a martyr to the "women's place is in the kitchen" cause for so long she doesn't know how to be anything else, but we're getting married, Flora, and that changes things whether she likes it or not. The important thing is that *you* don't get caught in the middle. We'll have a chat about it, I promise, all of us together.'

Flora nodded, smiling gratefully. 'Could we? I know now isn't a good time,' she said. 'But with her and Fraser potentially moving out of the farmhouse, it seems like a good opportunity to get a few things straight. I do understand her position… I'm just not sure I can be who she wants me to be, and that could cause problems, for us too, and that's the last thing I want to happen.'

'Oh, Flora,' sighed Ned. 'I do love you. How do you manage to be so sensible and yet so bonkers at the same time?' He scooped the hair back from her face and leant forward to kiss her, but then a sudden frown crossed his face. 'Hang on a minute, who said anything about them moving out?'

'Well, Hannah did, when we were talking. It's not definite or anything, she said she wanted to talk to Fraser first. I gather it's something they planned to do a few years back; she explained about the cottage and what they had planned for their retirement. Even though that's years away yet, it was a nice gesture, Ned, and it would give us a bit more privacy. I don't know how much work needs doing on the cottage, but—'

'Quite a bit. And we've neither the time nor the money for it at the moment.' His voice was harsh as he turned to look in his father's direction. 'Dad knows that. So does Mum for that matter.'

'Well I think it was more of a suggestion really rather than anything concrete…' Flora trailed off, wondering why there had been such an abrupt change of mood. She took a step backwards, peering around Ned's shoulder. Fraser had his back to them, one hand holding onto the lower rung of the rail, just as Caroline had earlier.

Ned turned back to her. 'Listen, I'd better get on.' His voice was softer now, more like the Ned she knew. 'But I'll try and have a chat with Dad in a bit, see what Mum's been saying. He's not in a talkative mood today though, so I dunno.'

Flora nodded, still staring down the length of the shed. She was about to shout goodbye to Fraser when she realised that there was something a little off about the way he was standing, leaning all his weight on his supporting arm, holding his body at an uncomfortable angle. As she watched, he suddenly bent forward and a spew of liquid splattered onto the floor.

'Fraser!'

She touched Ned's arm, alerting him to what had happened, and hurried down the shed, reaching Fraser just as he was gripped by a fresh wave of vomit. At her shout he had half turned towards her and she jumped backward, grimacing as the remains of his undigested lunch splashed onto her boots. She reached out a tentative arm.

'Fraser,' she said again. 'Are you okay?'

His eyes tried to focus on hers as he registered her presence, but they were staring wildly, full of alarm. His forehead was slick with sweat and, as he straightened slightly, his breath came in short pants. She reached out towards him, mindful that he might well be sick again, but still seeking to reassure him.

'I'm fine,' he said, gruffly, pulling his arm away from her reach. 'Just give me a minute. I've had bloody heartburn all morning; must have eaten something that's disagreed with me.'

A flicker of fear shot through Flora as Ned moved past her. 'Come on, Dad, let's get you out into the fresh air. Maybe you'll feel better then.' He took hold of Fraser's arm firmly and, avoiding the puddle on the floor, stepped backwards, trying to pull his dad with him. Flora tried to bring up the rear, making encouraging noises, but Fraser wasn't in any hurry to go anywhere.

'Shall I go and fetch Hannah?' she asked Ned, thinking she probably would anyway.

But Fraser's refusal was instantaneous. 'No!' He stopped dead. 'She'll only fuss… and will you stop manhandling me, I'll be fine.' He straightened up, but then his face creased into a grimace and he stooped again, clutching at his stomach, a low moan slipping from his lips.

Flora caught the look in Ned's eye as he nodded his assent, and she took off out of the shed and back to the house as fast as she could.

She returned within five minutes, an anxious Hannah in tow, and was glad to see that Ned had managed to get his father outside. You couldn't hear yourself think inside the shed, and what with that and the smell, it was enough to make anyone feel ill. Fraser was now leaning up against Ned, gulping in lungfuls of air. His face looked grey and sweaty.

Hannah clicked her tongue. 'Oh, would you look at you,' she said. 'Whatever is the matter?'

Fraser rolled his eyes in a 'told you so' manner. 'I'm fine. Just eaten something funny. Stop fussing, I'll be right as rain again in a minute.'

'You've said that several times now, Dad, and you're not getting any better, so what do you want to do?'

Hannah motioned for Ned to step away and moved forward to take his place. 'Come on, let's get you home,' she said. 'You need to get to bed.'

Flora hovered, unsure what to do, but she caught Ned's attention as he looked helplessly at his dad. 'Do you think we should even move him?' she whispered. 'Perhaps we should call an ambulance?'

Ned's eyes widened. 'An ambulance?' He turned back for another look. 'Why? Do you really think that's necessary?'

Flora didn't know what she thought. She didn't want to be alarmist but she had to say something. 'I don't know. It just… It just seems as if this came on a bit quick, and it's obvious your dad's not letting on, but I think he's in a lot of pain.' She thought back to their conversation of a few minutes ago. 'You said he hadn't been particularly talkative this morning…'

'Yes, I know, but nothing like this, Flora, just a bit quiet, that's all. But my dad's often a bit quiet.' She could see him trying to remember if there had been anything else unusual. 'What do you think it could be?'

Flora wasn't a doctor but she knew that there were several things it could be – some more serious, some less so – and she prayed that she was wrong; he could just as easily have a stomach bug. But from what? He hadn't eaten anything different from the rest of them, it didn't make any sense. She smiled reassuringly.

'Possibly just a bug, I don't know, but if he's in that much pain…'

At that moment Fraser stood up slightly, a tentative expression on his face. He looked around him, almost as if he were listening for something. 'There, see,' he said triumphantly. 'It's eased off now.' He shrugged off Hannah's arm, standing straighter. 'See, I'm fine now.'

Ned exchanged a look with his mum. 'Well, let's give it a few minutes,' he said. 'Just to make sure. Maybe you should go back to the house and have a sit-down?'

'Or I could just get on with milking the cows,' replied Fraser, pointedly.

'Yeah all right, Dad,' muttered Ned. 'I'll get back in there in a minute. I just want to make sure you're okay, that's all.'

'Well I am, so stop making such a fuss, all of you.' He all but glared at Ned, but just as he turned his gaze away, Flora caught a flicker in his cheek, a quickly covered flash of pain.

'Maybe you should have a break for a few minutes, Fraser,' she said. 'It wouldn't hurt, surely? Ned, can you finish the milking by yourself?'

He nodded. 'Course. Go on, Dad, she's right. We've been at it since early morning, it wouldn't hurt you to take a break.'

Flora thought he was going to argue again but, with a nudge from Hannah, he relented and began to move towards the house. As she watched, she wondered if she was the only one who could see how gingerly he was treading.

She loitered for a moment with Ned, giving Hannah and Fraser a little space, before she nodded back over her shoulder towards the milking shed.

'How much longer do you think you'll be?' she asked.

'We're on the second batch of cows,' replied Ned. 'So, another half hour perhaps. But I've got to clean down the parlour and the holding area afterwards.' He gave her a worried look. 'I'll be as quick as I can. Do you honestly think he's okay?' he asked.

'I'm sure he's fine,' she said, trying to keep her anxiety from showing. 'It's probably just like he said and he's eaten something that didn't agree with him.'

'Yes, but what? We've all had the same things today, and we feel fine.'

'I don't know. Perhaps it was the infamous beans on toast that did it.' It was meant to be a light-hearted comment but, as soon as she said it, she realised that Fraser hadn't felt right after eating them, he'd complained of heartburn then too. Which meant that he'd been suffering from it all day...

'I'll get back to the house,' she said. 'And I'll let you know if he gets any worse. Just come back when you can.' She stood on her tiptoes to kiss him. 'I'll see you soon.' She waited until he had disappeared back inside the shed again, and then she pulled her mobile from her pocket and peered at the screen, checking for signal. She opened her Internet browser and typed quickly, fingers held against her lips as she waited for the page to load. Then she absorbed the contents and hurried back to the house. It didn't tell her anything she didn't already know.

By the time she got there the kitchen was already deserted, and she could hear Hannah's voice from the hallway, speaking in a steady, soothing tone as she led Fraser up the stairs. Flora dithered about, crossing to put the kettle on to boil before changing her mind and taking it off again. She fetched a glass from the cupboard and filled it with water. She might not gain access to their bedroom, but she could at least give it to Hannah.

She caught up with them on the landing, waiting until they had turned the corner before following so that Hannah at least would catch sight of her. Fraser was still walking steadily, but he looked like he was holding his breath, as if the slightest jerky movement might trigger another episode of sickness.

'Come on now, let's get you into bed,' said Hannah. 'Best place for you, and you can sleep off whatever has got hold of you. And don't look at me like that, Ned will be just fine – he can certainly manage without you for a few hours.'

Flora was torn. She could see the sense in resting so maybe it was a good idea, but if she was right about what she believed to be going on, then Fraser shouldn't be lying down at all. The trouble was, how could she convey that without alarming either one of them? She looked down at the glass in her hand – it wasn't the perfect solution but the best one she could come up with at short notice. She hung back, letting Hannah guide Fraser into their room.

She heard the sound of boots being pulled off and a discussion over how best to get him out of his overalls, but after a few moments more, Flora decided it was time to interrupt before any further clothes were removed.

'I thought you might like a glass of water, Fraser,' she said, entering the room.

He was perched, somewhat hunched, on one side of the bed, while on the other, Hannah was trying to turn down the heavy eiderdown that covered it. It was the first time Flora had been in their bedroom and she was not particularly surprised to find that it was an almost exact replica of the room she shared with Ned. The same heavy furniture, similar wallpaper decorated with small flowery sprigs, and an old-fashioned brass bedstead. She had never asked, but the eiderdown was so similar to their own that she had a sudden vivid mental image of Hannah sewing them in front of the fire on long winter evenings. And fortunately, in one corner of the room, was a small pink Dralon-covered armchair.

'I'm not sure that's wise,' answered Hannah. 'He'll just be sick again.' She looked up, a set expression on her face. 'Food poisoning… that's what this is. Probably best if there's nothing in his stomach until it passes.'

Flora ignored her.

'You could just sip it, slowly, and it might take the nasty taste out of your mouth.'

Fraser nodded gratefully, a sheen of sweat still showing on his upper lip.

'Come over to the chair,' she added. 'You might be a bit more comfortable, and you can take your time then.'

She was almost certain that Hannah was shooting daggers at her, but she couldn't bring herself to meet her eyes and, instead, put out her free hand to Fraser's arm. To her relief he let her take it, and allowed himself to be supported into an upright position.

'Aye, I might be better sitting.' He stood taller, pulling in a deep breath as he tried to push his shoulders back. He winced slightly but nodded as if to confirm he was okay, and slowly made his way across the room, where he sank into the chair with an audible sigh.

Flora handed him the glass of water which he cradled in his lap for a moment before taking a sip. He smiled a thank you.

'I might just go and put the kettle on,' she said, desperate to remove herself from out under Hannah's disapproving gaze. 'I don't know about you, but I could do with a cup of tea.' At least in the kitchen she could pace without an audience as she anxiously awaited Ned's return.

It was a full forty-three more minutes before Ned finally arrived.

'Oh thank God, you're back,' she said the minute he entered the kitchen. She hadn't meant for it to come out quite as bluntly as it had, but then again, perhaps she did.

Ned's concern was instant. 'Is he—'

'There's no change,' interrupted Flora. 'But, honestly, trying to get through to your mother…' She took hold of his arm and led him to the far side of the kitchen, as far from the hallway door as she could.

'I'm sorry, Ned, I'm probably just being alarmist, but I can't get your mum to listen to me. She's convinced it's food poisoning, but I'm really not sure it is and, try as I might, she just brushes off my concern and says that he simply needs time to sleep it off.'

Ned looked towards the door. 'Is he asleep now? I'll go up and see him.'

'I'm not sure. He was dozing in the chair, and Hannah's with him now but, Ned, I really think we should call an ambulance, or a doctor at the very least.'

He stared at her, his mouth working but no sound coming out. His eyes narrowed. 'You mentioned calling an ambulance before… you're really worried, aren't you?'

Flora nodded quickly. 'I'm sorry, Ned, but yes, I really am.'

She saw the question form in his eyes, but she answered it before he could speak. 'I am really worried,' she said. 'Because I think your father's had a heart attack.'

Chapter 8

Ned stared at her for what felt like an eternity as he grappled with the impact of her words. She knew he was thinking about the farm, his mother, Fraser, of what to do, who to call, and all of it wrapped up in the sudden shock of realisation that his father could die. Flora didn't know Ned's past well enough yet to know whether he had ever been faced with such a crisis before, but she guessed from his reaction that he hadn't.

She was on the verge of gently repeating herself when he gave a sudden start, looking deep into her own eyes.

'Yes, of course,' he said suddenly, as if coming to. 'I'll ring them now.'

She watched as he hovered on the threshold between the kitchen and the doorway to the hall where the telephone stood on a small table.

'So, you're sure?' he asked, turning. 'It couldn't be something else?'

'It could be any number of things, Ned. But I think we need to find out. Let someone who can be certain make the judgement, that's all I'm saying.'

He nodded. 'Right... I'll go call them then.'

'I hope it's nothing,' she replied, but there was no point hiding her fear; it was a shared thing now, a thread tethering them to each other.

She waited while he phoned, and only then, as he came back into the room, did she take him in her arms, wordlessly laying her cheek against his. 'Go and see him,' she said and pulled away slightly as she felt his answering nod.

'What do I say?' he asked. 'And then there's Mum.' His eyes widened. 'Oh God, what do I say to her?'

'I could come up with you?' she volunteered. She had no idea what to say either, but she knew Ned needed her.

'Would you?' he asked.

But what if she was wrong about Fraser? In *her* head, the prolonged heartburn, nausea, dizziness and cold sweats could only mean one thing, but she might be making a huge fuss and drama over nothing and they would never forget it. She hesitated, but she had said it now and there was no taking it back. Besides… she had seen it in Fraser's eyes when she handed him the water, she knew she had; a silent cry for help, a pleading. His nod of thanks hadn't simply been for the drink he had received, he had been thanking her for what she'd been *about* to do…

She nodded, swallowing. 'Come on then,' she said, taking his hand.

They had almost got to the bedroom door before Flora pulled back slightly, causing Ned to look at her in alarm.

'I'm just thinking,' she whispered. 'I don't want to upset your mum, but I wondered if it might be an idea to get her to pack a bag for your dad, just in case the paramedics want to admit him. It would give her something to do?'

Ned nodded grimly. 'Whatever you think,' he answered, followed by a loud exhalation of breath. 'I haven't got a bloody clue.'

It would give Flora something to do as well.

Fraser was still sitting in the armchair. He'd been dozing when Flora last checked on him, but now he was looking much more alert, a little more like his usual self in fact. She saw Ned pause as he caught sight of him, obviously expecting to see him in a far worse state.

'Hiya, Dad,' he said cheerily. 'Glad to see you taking it easy while I do all the work. I should have known you were just after a crafty kip.'

Hannah looked up sharply, but Fraser just smiled.

'Cheeky bugger,' he replied. 'You'll be wanting the chair next.'

'That's not such a bad idea. A slice of cake and a cup of tea wouldn't go amiss either.'

Flora smiled. 'Dream on,' she said, catching Ned's eye as he looked at her, an unspoken question in his eyes. She nodded. *Yes, it's time to tell him.*

'Hannah,' she said, as brightly as she could. 'Can I have a word for a minute? I just wanted to ask you something.' From the corner of her eye she could see Ned kneel on the floor beside Fraser's chair, and she moved forward to intercept Hannah, leading her away to the other side of the room to where a large chest of drawers stood. And then, standing so that their backs were to the chair, she swiftly and calmly explained the situation.

'Oh, don't be so ridiculous. Fraser's a fit man. There's not many who could work all day the way he does. And he eats like a horse, there's nothing wrong with him.'

'But there is, Hannah,' she said gently. 'And I'm not saying that this is what *has* happened, all I'm saying is that it's a possibility given the pain in his back and tummy together with his other symptoms. He hasn't been well all day, in fact I don't think Fraser's felt right for a day or two, he just hasn't let on to anyone. He's short of breath too but he's trying hard not to show it. And if that's the case, it's because he's scared. So, if nothing else, let the paramedics come and put his mind at rest.' *Then you can all blame me,* she thought, but didn't say.

Hannah turned back to look at her husband. 'He's only sixty-four,' she said.

'Then he has age on his side,' replied Flora. 'Let's just wait and see, shall we?' She tried to smile, hating herself for resorting to platitudes, but that was what people did, didn't they? When they didn't know what to say.

A bark of laughter came from the other side of the room.

'Well, honestly. That's not going to help at all, Ned should—'

'No, that's a good thing,' she interrupted before Hannah could intervene. 'Fraser's obviously feeling better, and that's what we want. For him to be as relaxed as possible. Being stressed will do him no good at all.'

Hannah frowned, but even she could see the validity of Flora's words.

'So I thought we might pack a bag, just in case the paramedics want to admit him. Be prepared and all that.' She gave an encouraging smile.

'But you said yourself he's obviously better, what point is there in being melodramatic?'

'I said he's *feeling* better, Hannah. That's not quite the same thing. It doesn't get past the fact that he's just had quite a nasty turn and should the paramedics think he needs to go to hospital, they won't want to wait while you rush around.' She eyed Hannah's expression. There was only one thing for it. 'And I thought putting a few things together for Fraser might make you feel a little better – if you're organised, I mean.'

It did the trick. The threat that the paramedics might possibly think Hannah disorganised had her out of the room in a flash, returning a moment later with an ancient holdall which she laid on the bed. Flora used the opportunity to go and stand beside Ned.

'How are you feeling, Fraser?' she asked. Five simple words that hovered in the air between them for a moment. There was a knowing in these words, a myriad of silent questions and statements which sat between her words and which at this moment only Fraser would understand. *Are you in pain? Are you scared? You don't have to even tell me, I'll know. Don't worry about Hannah, or Ned, I'll look after them.* And of course the most important of all: *Don't worry, I'll keep your thoughts safe, I'll tell no one unless you want me to.*

And his reply, 'Aye, not so bad,' as his look held hers, which told her all she needed to know. *I don't know what's wrong, I'm terrified, I don't want to admit this is even happening.*

'That's good then,' she replied, as brightly as she could. She rested her hand on Ned's shoulder, gave it a quick squeeze and moved away. 'I'll just pop back downstairs for a minute.'

She didn't want to admit what was happening either, because upstairs there were people who had far more reason to be anxious than she did, but she couldn't ignore her thoughts, and she was thinking of herself when she shouldn't be. She should be thinking about Ned and how he was feeling, thinking of Hannah and Fraser, offering support, yet the insistent whisper at the back of her mind was clamouring to be heard. Because whatever was happening to Fraser would affect them all, including her… It could change their lives forever.

She looked round the kitchen. How long would it be before the ambulance arrived? Maybe she could peel some potatoes for tea or make a start on the apple crumble, but almost as soon as the thought popped into her head she flung it away again. Ridiculous. The garden was now dark beyond the window and she slipped into the scullery and out the back door to await the flash of headlights across the yard. The wind whipped around the corner of the house, slicing into her, but she didn't care. It was just punishment for her selfish thoughts.

*

It was the waiting that was the worst.

'Can I get anyone a drink?' offered Flora. 'I noticed there's a vending machine out in the foyer.' They were standing in an awkward huddle around Fraser's hospital bed.

Hannah seemed to look right past her, eyes focused on some distant object, but slowly she homed in on Flora and she shook her head. 'No thank you.' They were the first words she had spoken in quite some time. Up until then her gaze had remained glued to the monitor above Fraser's head which beat out the rhythm of his life, as if by doing so she was ensuring it continued. 'But perhaps Fraser might like some water?'

Fraser looked peculiarly affronted to find himself in hospital at all, particularly when, as he told anyone who would listen, he felt fine, and he turned to her now, tutting. 'Never mind the water, you can get me a cup of tea, lass,' he said. 'I don't know how much longer we're expected to wait, but a man could die of thirst in here.' He seemed completely oblivious to what he had just said, adding, 'And a Mars bar or something, it's nearly seven o'clock and I'm bloody starving.' He looked at Hannah. 'I don't feel sick any more,' he added.

'I'm not sure that's such a good idea, Dad,' said Ned, throwing Flora a nervous look. 'You know, just in case…'

'Just in case what?'

'You know… in case they have to operate or something, do tests… I don't know.'

'Oh, don't talk such rubbish,' replied Fraser. 'What are they going to do, cut me open right here? There's nothing wrong with me now.'

Hannah winced. And then she patted his arm. 'Fraser would like a glass of water, please, Flora,' she said. 'And nothing else until we've seen the doctor. Then when he's got over this bug he can have whatever he wants.' She fiddled in her handbag which had stayed resolutely thrust under her arm the whole time. 'I have some money here…'

Flora waved away her offer. 'No, it's fine. Ned? Would you like anything?'

He glanced at his mother's set expression. 'I'll come with you,' he said. 'And see what they have. You're sure you don't want anything, Mum?'

'I'm sure, thank you.' And the conversation was ended.

'Jeez…' said Ned, as they walked down the corridor towards the main waiting area in A&E. 'Mum's gone into full-on martyr mode and Dad's modelling grumpy old git. What are they like?'

'As bad as each other,' replied Flora. 'But you can't really blame them, they're both obviously scared, and I don't know, but I'm guessing they haven't been up against anything like this before.'

'Dad's never even been in hospital, and I can't remember the last time he went to see a doctor. Mum, too, for that matter. They just get on with stuff.'

'Maybe that's part of the problem,' said Flora, wondering just how long Fraser had been feeling unwell. 'But are *you* all right?'

Ned blew out air from between his teeth. 'I will be once someone tells us what's going on. It's the not knowing, isn't it? I can't keep hold of everything I'm thinking, there's just too much of it.'

Flora squeezed his hand. 'Then one thing at a time,' she said. 'That's all we can do.'

They had reached the vending machine.

'Christ, I could really murder a Mars bar now,' said Ned. 'I didn't think I was hungry, but now that Dad mentioned it, my stomach's gurgling.'

'Then have one,' replied Flora, sensing his hesitation.

He studied the machine. 'Nah, best not…' He straightened. 'Do you think that's what's caused this?' he asked. 'What we eat? I never really thought about it before, but what with you being a vegetarian and everything, and now Dad… He's only young, Flora, he shouldn't have had a heart attack…'

'We still don't know that he has,' she said gently. 'So let's not go there just now. There will be plenty of time to think about things like that once we know. And trying to lay blame isn't going to help.'

He studied her face. 'That's a non-answer, Flora, if ever I heard one, and not like you at all.'

She smiled. 'No, it's not, but for now, that's all you're going to get.' She handed him a couple of pound coins for the machine. 'Have what you want,' she added, changing the subject. 'We could be here for some time.'

'I'll just have a Coke,' he said. 'What about you?'

'Well I'm going to have the bloody Mars bar, I'm starving too.'

Ned didn't need much persuading to have one as well, but rather than take them back and eat the contraband in front of Fraser, they slipped outside for a minute. There, leaning up against the wall of A&E, they both shovelled the chocolate into their mouths as fast as they could. Flora held out her hand for Ned's wrapper.

'I'll go and find a bin,' she said. 'Get rid of the evidence.'

'What do you suppose they'll do, if it is a heart attack?' Ned's face was suddenly serious.

She swallowed, pushing away the images from long ago in her mind. She couldn't even begin to answer his question. 'I'm sure someone will tell us,' she said instead.

He was staring up at the sky. The clouds had lifted and the dark sky was shining with stars. 'It's like someone's stopped the world, isn't it?' His eyes dropped to hers and he shivered. 'Come on, it's freezing out here.'

He led the way back inside, waiting while she darted across the room to a bin she spied there. A woman was perched in the seat next to it and she looked up and smiled as Flora dropped in the chocolate wrappers. She was sitting next to a man who was hunched over in his seat, elbows resting on his knees as he cradled his head in his hands. The woman didn't say a word and yet her smile spoke volumes. They were all the same, these people here, waiting endlessly for their lives to restart again. Not all of them would, Flora knew that, and others would be changed irrevocably. Only time would tell which of these was waiting for them.

She hurried back to Ned and together they made their way along the length of corridor that was divided off into bays by regulation blue curtains. Flora glanced at the numbers above as they walked, momentarily lost, but then she realised that it was because the curtains to Fraser's bay had been open when they had left. Now they were closed and there were voices coming from within.

Flora held back to allow Ned to step through and, despite only moving the curtain a fraction, the angle meant that she had a clear line of sight past his bulk to the bed within. It wasn't clear whether Hannah was holding Fraser's hand or the other way around, but they were locked together, a look of stunned incredulity mirrored on each other's faces.

As the curtain opened wider, she could see a tall man, who though not overweight, seemed to occupy a huge proportion of the room. He was holding a sheet of paper and Flora reckoned his hands were twice as large as hers. But very neat looking, still slender. Artist's hands.

'So until we establish the degree of damage, it's very difficult to say, but I'll organise those tests straight away for you. In the meantime, we'll send you up to the ward once a bed becomes available, so for now just try to get some rest.'

It was Hannah who recovered herself first.

'Thank you, Doctor,' she said. 'So it's nothing to do with his stomach then, not a sickness bug?'

'No, I'm afraid not. The nausea is a common symptom, as is the stomach pain. Not all heart attack victims suffer from the classic chest pain one normally associates with them, so you did the right thing by getting it checked out.'

He turned and glanced at Ned, giving a tight smile. And then he was gone.

'Dad?'

Ned crossed to the side of the bed where Fraser looked up at him and then straight to Flora, who was still hovering by the curtain.

'Your beans weren't to blame after all, lass,' he said. 'Reckon I owe you an apology.'

Chapter 9

There was scarcely a word said as they filed through the scullery door back at the farm. It was gone eleven o'clock and Hannah would have stayed at the hospital the whole night if they'd let her. One of the few things Flora knew about Ned's past was that he had been born at home, so not even childbirth had separated his parents. Tonight would be the first night in over thirty years that they had ever been apart.

The kitchen was still, the house in darkness as they entered, the steady thump of Brodie's tail against the floor the only greeting. Ned crossed to flick on the light and the room was suddenly filled with harsh reality. Nobody knew what should happen next and they smiled weakly at one another, looking for clues. It was Flora who went to slide the kettle over to boil. If nothing else, it would bridge the awkward gap between coming into the house and going to bed, an act which would finally bring an end to the day. Right now none of them knew whether this closure was a good thing or a bad thing.

Flora poured the tea and then she cut three slices from the honey cake she had made earlier that afternoon because she'd needed to keep busy. It felt like a lifetime ago. She laid a plate in front of Hannah, hoping that the chance to comment on her culinary skills might at least break the silence she had settled into. But although its arrival elicited a momentary glance, Hannah said nothing.

Ned pounced on his. Apart from the Mars bar he had eaten at the hospital, he'd had nothing to eat since lunchtime. The ingredients for the vegetable stew that they should have had for their evening meal were still in the fridge. What would have happened if Flora had not gone to the milking parlour? Would Fraser have carried on working, hiding how he had been feeling from Ned, just like he had all day? Getting steadily worse and worse until possibly… she shuddered. Might his heart have stopped altogether? She ran through the events of the afternoon, wondering if there was anything they could have done differently, but then her hand flew to her mouth as she thought of something else.

'Oh, my God, the chickens! Hannah, I've left the hens out… I'm so sorry… I'll go now, I'll—' She stumbled over her feet in her haste to get to the door.

'Leave them!'

Hannah's voice was harsh in the quiet room.

'But I can—'

'I said, leave them! It's far too late to go out now.' Her voice had a sharp edge to it that Flora hadn't heard before. And even though they were talking about the chickens, her tone still managed to convey all her upset, all her anger, all her fear, just as easily as if they had been talking about Fraser.

Flora threw a hasty glance at Ned but he gave an imperceptible shake of his head.

Hannah got to her feet. 'I'm going to bed,' she announced, picking up her handbag from the table.

Flora's eyes darted around the room. She couldn't let Hannah leave like this. Not by herself. Her eyes sought out Ned's once more, imploring him to help her find a way to reach his mother.

'Look, I'll… come up with you, shall I? In case you need anything. Maybe you might like the little heater on in your room? It's bitter out there tonight and it won't take a minute to set it up for you. I always think you feel the cold more when you're tired…' She trailed off. Or when your husband isn't there beside you in the bed, she thought.

Ned stood up, taking his mother's arm. 'Good idea, Flora. Come on, we'll all go up together.'

It seemed to take an age for Hannah to digest what had just been said to her, but eventually she nodded her head. 'Thank you,' she said, and that was all.

Flora needed no further encouragement and fled upstairs, trying not to look at the armchair in the corner of Hannah and Fraser's room. The air felt frigid and she turned down the covers on the bed before moving back out onto the landing and dragging in the oil-filled radiator that lurked unused at the end of the corridor. She switched it on. It might smell for a little while, but Hannah needed to be warm.

Half an hour later she finally sat down on the side of their bed as Ned wearily began to remove his clothes. Neither of them had said a word about his mother's outburst and, since then, Hannah had continued to speak in a monotone. Questions had been met with polite responses and reassurances met with a slight smile. It was a relief when she had succumbed to their ministrations and climbed into bed, bidding them both a goodnight.

Flora undressed and was about to get into bed herself when she realised that there was no way she could, not yet. There was still one thing more she had to do. Telling Ned that she wouldn't be long, she pulled on her pyjamas and crept back downstairs, grabbing a torch and oilskin from the scullery and whistling for Brodie to join her. They slipped out into the night together, making their way across the yard.

She would never forgive herself if she didn't check and, as she picked her way through the dark, her heart began to beat faster and faster. She had no idea what massacred chickens would look like, but she didn't imagine it would look pretty. There would be blood and guts, gore and body parts and she had no idea how she would clear them all away in the dark, but she would, however long it took. Whatever happened, come morning, there was to be no trace of the death and destruction that had taken place.

An owl hooted, making her jump, but other than that, the night was still and she was grateful for the absence of rustling noises as she reached the coop. She swung the beam of the torch in front of her, lighting up the ground as she scanned for the inevitable. But there was nothing. Just the muddy uneven scrub of the chicken run and the wire mesh of the enclosure, glinting in the torchlight. The wooden door was hanging open just as she had left it, but of the hens there were no sign. Nor was there sign of anything else.

She let out a slow breath. She knew that the hens put themselves to bed automatically so it wasn't a question of searching for them in the undergrowth, but perhaps instead they had been ambushed, attacked while they slept. Did hens even sleep? She didn't know. She moved closer, circling the coop until she was back to where she started. Nothing.

Satisfied that she wasn't about to come face to face with a wild animal intent on its dinner, she moved purposefully to the hutch and lifted the lid at one end. Taking a deep breath, she shone the light inside, and there, perched on the struts, presumably asleep, but very much alive and unmauled, were seven chickens. She breathed a huge sigh of relief.

It was at that point she realised how cold she was. And that the fine drizzle she had hardly noticed as she left the house had nonetheless managed to soak through the thin cotton of her pyjamas. She pulled the oilskin tighter around her and turned her face to the sky. What on earth was she doing here, in the middle of the night, in a dark, cold, muddy chicken coop? The few stars not covered by cloud winked back, but they had no answers for her and after a few more seconds she carefully secured the door to the coop and walked slowly back to the yard.

She paused for a moment and turned off the torch so she was standing in complete and utter darkness. It was hardly any more disorientating than the rest of the day had been. How had her world turned so completely upside down in such a short space of time? The morning had started off with promise as she had sat immersed in her artwork enjoying the glimmer of hope that her life at the farm was beginning to settle; there was routine and familiarity, she was with people she cared for, doing things she loved. But from there the day had rapidly disintegrated into chaos and she felt caught in a tide of things far beyond her control. And now, here she was, standing in the dark in the middle of the night, far from anything she could call home. How ironic that she had come to live at the house at Hope Corner when all hers seemed to have been well and truly dashed. She glanced back up to the sky, hoping for a glimpse of the moon, but that too was hidden from view. She could certainly do with some hope right now...

And then she thought of Ned, alone in their room, and she had a sudden overwhelming need to be back beside him. To feel his warm body against hers banishing the cold and doubt. As if reading her thoughts, Brodie shoved his wet nose against her hand, and together they hurried back to the house. She stripped off her wet things and left them beside the washing machine, padding naked through the still house until eventually she was able to crawl into the warm space that Ned had created, snuggling up against him.

'Are you asleep?' she whispered.

There was a soft sigh. 'No… not yet.' He turned over, pulling her into his arms. 'Where have you been, you're freezing?' he murmured into her hair, not flinching at her cold limbs but instead enfolding his skin around hers.

'I went to check on the hens,' she said. 'I thought they'd all been killed…'

'Oh, Flora,' was all he said, holding her tighter, and then the pair of them lay soundlessly waiting out the remaining few hours of the night.

*

Hannah apologised for her outburst in the morning. It was the first thing she said as she entered the kitchen.

'I don't know what came over me,' she said. 'I'm so embarrassed. What was I thinking?'

Flora crossed the room to stand in front of her, unsure whether to hug her or not. Although very caring, Hannah wasn't a particularly demonstrative person, not like Flora's family, who all threw their arms around each other at the drop of a hat. British reserve, that's what it was, but she looked so small this morning, so much less of herself than normal. Flora put out a hand tentatively, but ended up stroking Hannah's arm a little awkwardly when she made no move in response.

'I don't think any of us were thinking straight last night,' said Flora. 'It's been a massive shock for everyone.' She motioned to the table. 'Come and sit down and I'll get you a drink.'

'But the hens…?' Hannah's eyes darted towards the door.

'Are fine,' replied Flora, smiling in a reassuring way. 'I checked on them last night after you'd gone to bed,' she explained. 'Scared myself silly out there in the dark, but everything was okay. I had convinced myself I'd find them all ripped apart…' She trailed off, realising that

Hannah probably wouldn't appreciate her graphic flights of imagination. 'Anyway, they weren't.'

Hannah sat down. 'You went out last night?' she asked. 'On your own?' Clearly it was not something she would have contemplated.

'Well, I took Brodie…' Flora nodded. 'Ned was already in bed.'

She turned back to the Aga, lifting the kettle as it came to the boil. 'I'll go and feed them in a bit, make sure they're none the worse for their nocturnal visitor, even if it was only me.' She smiled, but Hannah still looked rather uncomfortable.

'I don't know what to say…' she said. 'Except thank you, that was a very thoughtful thing to do.'

Her words were a little stilted and Flora moved swiftly on, recognising the embarrassment that Hannah must be feeling. 'Now, one cup of tea coming up and how about some breakfast? A bit of toast, or something a bit more substantial?'

Hannah stared at her in horror and then looked around her as if only just realising where she was. 'Where's Ned?'

Flora looked at her watch. 'Milking,' she replied. 'He went out a little earlier this morning,' she said gently. It was seven o'clock and Ned had already been gone for several hours.

'But what are we going to do?' Hannah's voice was beginning to rise a little. Flora had been thinking much the same thing, and so had Ned. In fact, as they took their first cup of tea together a little after four this morning, the conversation had centred on little else. But they had come up with a plan…

She poured the boiling water into the teapot and brought it to the table where two mugs were already waiting. Then she sat down, opposite Hannah, and tried to relax, hoping that her posture might communicate itself across the space between them. Hannah looked crumpled. Her normally smooth hair was unbrushed and there was a large greasy smudge right in the centre of her glasses, which Flora thought must be incredibly annoying. She was wearing yesterday's clothes too.

'Ned and I have been chatting,' Flora began. 'And I've already rung the hospital so firstly, you needn't worry. Fraser had a good night and is quite comfortable.' She wasn't quite sure what Hannah's expectations were about the day, but Ned had suggested that it might be better to have certain things put into place. That way Hannah might be less inclined to fret… 'The nurse explained that he will have a couple more tests this morning and will then see the consultant around eleven who will be the one to decide what happens next. Apparently we won't get any more information until then.' She picked up a spoon and gave the tea a stir.

'I see,' said Hannah. 'That doesn't sound very good. Why doesn't anyone want to act with any urgency? It was the same last night.'

'I think perhaps that's a good thing…? He isn't considered an emergency, you see.'

'But he is an emergency. To me he is!'

Flora smiled. 'I know he is, Hannah, I know. And we can go and see him just as soon as you want to. There's open visiting on the ward he's on, but the nurse did say that there's really little point until later on this morning, after the consultant's been,' she repeated. 'I'm sure he's in safe hands.'

'Well, I'm not.' Hannah made a grab for the teapot and then held it in mid-air looking at it for several seconds. She returned it to the table.

'I meant, what are we going to do?' she repeated, more forcefully this time. 'About the farm? The work? It's hard enough with just the two of them, but we simply can't afford to pay anyone else and Ned can't do it all on his own. We'll get even further behind… And then there's the house, and jobs around the yard and the garden – I can't look after Fraser and be expected to do everything else as well. He's going to need round-the-clock nursing and—' She broke off abruptly, staring at Flora, who took a deep breath and then let it out slowly.

She nudged the mugs closer to the teapot and carefully poured out the tea, trying to give herself a little time to think. There were lots of things to think about, that much was true, but Flora could sense that Hannah could quite easily work herself up into a real lather given half the chance and, apart from the fact that Flora wasn't sure she could cope with that by herself, it wouldn't help the situation at all. Better to try and stay calm and rational.

'I think we need to wait and see how Fraser is first,' she replied. 'Before jumping to any conclusions. Ned and I soon realised that it was hard to decide what we should do because we haven't got a clue what's going to happen next. Until we do, there's little point in speculating, so…' Flora looked anxiously at Hannah to see if she had noticed how rehearsed how her words were, but Hannah's face was impassive so she carried on quickly before that changed. 'So… We thought that I could take you to the hospital today while Ned gets on with business as usual. Hopefully we'll hear some good news. They might even be able to give us an idea of when Fraser can come home.'

Hannah looked up. 'Do you really think so?'

'I think what we have to remember,' said Flora carefully, 'is that, to us, all this is scary and completely alien, but to the hospital it's just routine. I don't mean that it doesn't matter,' she added quickly, 'but that they deal with patients who've had heart attacks every day. They know what to expect and what the procedures are for every step of the way.'

'I know you're right…' Hannah got to her feet. 'I'm sorry, Flora. I just feel so…'

'Helpless?' suggested Flora.

'And completely frustrated too,' she added, nodding. 'I don't even know how I'm supposed to feel.' She paced around the table. 'One minute I think Fraser's going to die and…' She shuddered. 'And the next I think it will all be something or nothing and he'll be home in a day or two as if nothing has happened.' She stopped by her chair. 'I just want things to stay the same, for heaven's sake. Is that too much to ask?'

'No,' said Flora gently. 'But I think we have to understand that they probably can't…' There was no point trying to dress it up. 'Look, why don't we have a cup of tea, and a bit of something to eat, and then decide what to do next. There's still a few hours before we can go to the hospital, and we probably ought to do something to keep ourselves busy, otherwise we'll just go mad.' She gave a small smile. 'I am at your service, Hannah, and I'm even prepared to scrub the floors, or clean out cupboards. You name it, and I'll do it.'

For the first time that morning Hannah smiled. A proper smile that lit up her eyes, bringing out the creases that gathered there. 'I was going to make marmalade today,' she said. 'So we could do that if you like? It's Fraser's favourite and stocks are somewhat low at the moment.'

'Marmalade it is then,' said Flora, grinning. 'But first, let's have some breakfast. Toast or cereal?'

Chapter 10

'Oh my goodness, I came over as soon as I heard!'

The scullery door crashed open, and suddenly Caroline was in the kitchen, striding across the room and crushing Hannah in a fierce embrace.

Despite the abruptness of her arrival, there wasn't a hair out of place and Flora wondered what it would take to make her look even a tiny bit flustered.

Caroline pulled away from Hannah to look at her, still clutching both her arms. 'Oh, poor you. How dreadful. You must be feeling absolutely awful.' She stopped then as she suddenly realised what was going on around her. 'Whatever are you *doing*?'

'Making marmalade,' replied Flora. 'Morning, Caroline.'

'But I thought…' She trailed off, looking around her. 'I thought Fraser had had a heart attack?'

'Yes, dear.' Hannah's eyes narrowed. 'And which little bird told you, I wonder. Aren't you here a little early for breakfast?'

Caroline glanced at her watch. 'Oh, I just popped round to ask Ned something. I wasn't necessarily planning on having breakfast, but naturally he told me…'

'Was it the same question as yesterday?' asked Flora. 'Only we haven't had a chance to discuss that yet… obviously.' For some reason she felt intensely irritated by Caroline's presence.

'No, quite…' Caroline looked a little disconcerted for a moment. 'Oh, but that doesn't matter now anyway… What on earth has happened? Is Fraser all right?'

Hannah wiped her hands on a tea towel. She had just removed the softened oranges from the enormous preserving pan full of simmering water and they were sticky with juice. She looked at Flora. 'Did you put those plates to cool in the freezer, dear?' she asked.

Flora nodded.

'Thank you.' She nodded at the oranges lined up on a chopping board. 'Now we need to leave these to cool and then we'll halve them, scoop out all the flesh, pips and pith to leave just the peel, which we'll shred.' She smiled. 'Fraser likes it nice and fine.' Then she turned to Caroline. 'Fraser is as well as can be expected; I think that's the expression, isn't it? He has had a heart attack, but we don't know any more than that at the moment. I expect we'll find out more once we get to the hospital.'

It had been a good plan, putting Hannah in charge of something, particularly something where she had to show Flora the ropes. It had allowed her to recover her composure.

'Oh, but then I'll take you…'

Hannah shook her head briefly. 'No need, thank you, Caroline. Flora has already offered.'

'But I really don't mind,' she replied. 'You must have things you need to do, Flora.'

'I do indeed. And taking Hannah to the hospital is one of them. It's very kind of you to offer though.'

Their eyes locked and, for a moment, Flora thought she was about to argue again, but then Caroline smiled. 'Well then, at least let me help you finish the marmalade. I can't believe Hannah wants to be bothered with it at a time like this. I mean, I don't suppose any of you got much sleep last night and, while it's totally understandable under the circumstances, if you don't mind my saying, you do look a little peaky, Hannah. Why don't you go and put your feet up for a bit? I can look after things here.'

Hannah's eyebrows shot through her hairline. 'And why would I want to do that?' she asked. 'It's only being busy that's keeping me from fretting about Fraser,' she said. 'Flora very sensibly suggested it might be a good idea, and it has been as it happens. I might look peaky, Caroline, but I feel absolutely fine.'

Caroline paled slightly. 'Oh, of course… Gosh, we're all different, aren't we? You never know quite how you're going to react in a crisis until one is thrust upon you.'

'I don't think we're quite at crisis point yet, dear, but I'll be sure to alert you if that happens. We may have need of your help then.'

There really wasn't anywhere for the conversation to go after that and Caroline left soon after, promising to ring later in the day to see how things were. Flora would have liked to hug Hannah again but she didn't quite have the nerve.

'Now then, the marmalade,' asserted Hannah. 'I've quite lost my train of thought. Where did we get to?'

Flora reminded her and, once the oranges had cooled enough to handle, Hannah passed half of them across to Flora and showed her how to remove everything except for the peel, which was now nice and soft.

'Peaky indeed,' tutted Hannah. 'And what was the burning question she needed answered anyway?'

Flora smiled to herself. She clearly wasn't the only one that Caroline had managed to irritate.

'A conversation about an engagement party, I think,' replied Flora. 'Which under the circumstances can wait.'

Hannah nodded. 'Oh, is that all? I didn't realise you were even going to have an engagement party.'

'We're not, as far as I know…' she replied, anxious to change the subject. 'Am I doing this right?' she asked, pointing at the chopping board in front of her.

'Perfect,' replied Hannah. 'Just the way Fraser likes it.'

After chopping the peel between them, the orange 'innards' were scooped into a muslin cloth, tied at the top and then lowered back into the cooking water together with the thin shreds that gave the marmalade its distinctive flavour. A ton of sugar went in last and then the whole lot was set to boil.

'This next bit is supposed to be the tricky part,' remarked Hannah, 'although I've never yet had a problem getting my marmalade to set.'

'Is this one of those things, you know, like horses?' quipped Flora. 'Where you never show your fear?' If it was, Flora might have a rather sticky problem on her hands.

Hannah frowned. 'I'm not sure it works quite like that, but I think it's the same with most things in the kitchen. A little confidence goes a long way.' But she darted Flora a small smile. 'That, and buy decent oranges in the first place.'

They stood watching the boiling liquid for a while; periodically Hannah took a metal spoon and lifted the frothy scum from the top to discard it.

'If you don't take this off, the resulting marmalade won't be very clear or have that lovely glossy finish to it.'

Flora nodded, watching the fat bubbles rolling around the pan. It was almost mesmerising. Breadmaking still held a weird fascination for her, a very strange alchemy indeed, but this was right up there. A bit of fruit and sugar boiled up together, who would have thought it? She wondered idly who had come up with the idea in the first place – Mrs Beeton perhaps. No, probably way earlier than that. And then she caught herself grinning. *Flora Dunbar, what are you doing, thinking about stuff like this? For goodness' sake, this is the epitome of domesticity and you are not a domestic goddess, nor do you aspire to be. Stop it this instant.*

'What's the smile for?' asked Hannah, holding the spoon aloft.

'Oh, I was just thinking,' replied Flora. 'I've never made anything like this before, and I can see the attraction of it… But at the same time I can't help wondering if it's all worth it, when a jar of marmalade only costs a couple of pounds at most.'

'Does it…?' Hannah paused. 'Do you know, I've never really thought about it before; I've just always made my own.' She looked across at Flora, her brow furrowed. 'Well now… we'll have a dozen jars by the time we're finished and the cost of the oranges is about a fiver, the sugar a couple of pounds, so… seven pounds…' She wrinkled her nose. 'I can't work that out, but it's less than a pound a jar…'

Flora squinted. 'About sixty pence, I think…'

'So, much cheaper than you can buy…'

'And you're going to tell me much nicer as well…'

Hannah smiled. 'See, you young ones don't know everything…' She licked her lips, enjoying the moment, but there was no malice in her words. 'And even the really posh marmalade, which I think might cost about five pounds a jar, isn't as nice as this. Believe me, you can really taste the difference.'

Flora pulled a face. 'You might be able to. I'm not honestly sure I could, not being a marmalade connoisseur and all that.'

Hannah cleared the last of the scum from the top of the liquid. 'Well then, tomorrow you shall have marmalade on toast for breakfast, and we'll see… You might even surprise yourself. Now, let's have a plate out of the freezer and we'll test this to see if it's ready.'

Flora smiled inwardly at the reference to any normality over the coming days and did as she was asked, watching as Hannah spooned a little of the liquid onto the cold surface.

She waited a couple of seconds and then gently pushed her index finger into the mixture, giving a satisfied nod as she did so. 'There now, see that? How there's a skin formed already which wrinkles when you push it? That's how to test when it's done; it works the same with jam too. Of course it doesn't always happen first time, it which case you just leave it to boil for a wee bit longer and then test again.'

'It's still very runny though?'

'It will thicken as it cools,' replied Hannah. She pulled the pan from the heat. 'Would you like to spoon it into the jars for me? There's a ladle in that drawer there.'

Flora nodded as Hannah removed a tray of jam jars from the top of the Aga and carried them across to the table. They had been washed in incredibly hot water and left there to dry.

It didn't take long, and once they were done, Flora stared at the line of jars filled with the amber preserve. They glowed golden in the sunlight which slanted across the kitchen, but it was nothing compared to the unexpected glow of satisfaction that filled Flora up from the inside. She stood back, appraising the table.

'I'm rather proud of those,' she said.

'And so you should be.' Hannah wiped her hands on her apron. 'A new skill learnt and, now you know how, there'll be no stopping you. Look at your breadmaking – that's come on in leaps and bounds. All it took was a little help from Caroline in the first instance, and you have mastered it already.'

Flora smiled in agreement, but then her face fell as she re-ran Hannah's words through her head. 'You knew I didn't know how to make bread?' she asked, a spark of anger igniting within her.

Hannah patted her hand. 'Yes of course, dear, but it's nothing to be ashamed of. It's probably considered quite an old-fashioned skill these days, and…' She leant in closer to Flora. 'Don't tell anyone, but yours is almost as good as mine!'

It was a massive compliment but Flora was suddenly furious.

'Did Caroline tell you she'd helped me?' she asked, trying to keep her voice even.

Hannah stopped for a moment, frowning as she tried to recall the memory. 'Well, yes I suppose she must have done, or how else would I know?'

Hmm, thought Flora, how else indeed? She looked back at Hannah, who was surveying the table, not in the slightest bit perturbed. It was hardly the point, but at least Caroline revealing herself as Flora's aide hadn't made Hannah think any less of her. Nevertheless, Flora still couldn't help thinking that Caroline might have done it on purpose.

'There's enough marmalade there for a couple of months with any luck,' said Hannah. 'Fraser can get through a whole jar in a week no problem at all, and well…' Her eyes sought out Flora's. 'I guess we'll have to see, won't we? But anyway, they're done now. There for when he wants them.'

Hannah looked so pleased that Flora couldn't stay cross. 'Which I'm sure will be soon,' she said, pulling Hannah into a quick hug. 'He *will* be all right, Hannah,' she added. 'And you know he really is in the best possible place. They can do amazing things these days…' She looked back at the table and smiled. 'Why don't I sort the washing up and then we can have a cup of tea before we go to the hospital? There's still plenty of time.'

'And I'd like to make some sandwiches and pack up some cake and a few other bits and pieces,' Hannah replied. 'Whatever else he's doing, he won't be eating properly, that I do know. I would imagine that the hospital food is quite dreadful.'

Flora turned away so that Hannah couldn't see her smile. Some things never changed.

Chapter 11

The day they cut Fraser open and stopped his heart dawned like a bright beautiful spring morning. It was a Friday, in the very middle of February, and came after a day and a half of torrential rain. But then suddenly the skies had cleared and a fresh wind had blown in, chasing away the clouds. The temperature had risen and they had crawled wearily from their beds to feel the first tentative stirrings of the new season. It was also Valentine's Day.

Flora had been first up, and now she stood, eyes locked on the garden beyond the window, seeking a sign that everything would be okay. The day itself must be auspicious; surely the universe wouldn't take a husband and a father on Saint Valentine's Day, would it?

The echo of the consultant's words, delivered only two days ago, still rang in her head.

'Mrs Jamieson, I'm sorry to have to tell you, but our tests showed that two of your husband's major blood vessels which supply the heart with oxygen have become narrowed to such an extent that surgery will be required to bypass them.'

A heart bypass. Open heart surgery. That's what Fraser was facing. And almost as soon as the information had been imparted to them, they were handed over to a bubbly and alarmingly efficient nurse coordinator, named Mandy. She swiftly provided forms and leaflets and spoke about all the things that would be happening to Fraser in terms of percentages; the percentage of people who went on to lead relatively normal lives, the percentage of people who died or had a stroke during the operation itself.

The numbers were all designed to be reassuring, but Flora found them trite and offensive; that someone could even consider that Fraser's life be reduced to a set of statistics. These percentages were all people, for heaven's sake; somebody's husband, wife, son, or daughter… What Flora wanted to know was whether the surgeon would take good care of Fraser's heart. Would he cradle it gently in the palm of his hands? Love it and care for it like Hannah did? But no one could tell her that.

They had said goodbye to Fraser at 8.32 yesterday evening, although none of them had actually used the word goodbye. It was too painful, too final, so Hannah had told him that she loved him, Ned jokingly told him not to give the surgeon a hard time, and Flora told him she would see him tomorrow. And now that day was here and she prayed that her wish would come true.

Outside the kitchen window the daffodils' heads were waving gently in the breeze and, more than anything, Flora longed to throw open the door and run. Run as far and as fast as she could and feel the air rushing past her, feel her own blood pulsing in her veins, anything to make her feel alive instead of the stifling slow demise of responsibility and care that was settling upon her. She had sent off an email to Rowena late last night, longing to hear that she was finally beginning to put her life back together again. Anything to give Flora hope that, despite what had happened, loving Ned and moving to the farm had been the best decision she'd ever made. A cheerful response came pinging back, but even that wasn't enough to lift her spirits. Flora felt trapped and she hated herself for it.

Heavy footfalls sounded on the floor behind her and she turned around to see Ned standing there. He was wearing his usual overalls, his feet already encased in his work boots. He came to stand beside her.

'I'm sorry, Flora,' he said as he bent to kiss the top of her hair. It could have been an apology for many things. Sorry that it was Valentine's Day and he hadn't bought her a card, let alone a dozen red roses…? Sorry that this wasn't the life that he had promised her? But, more likely, it was an apology for not being able to wait out the agonising hours of Fraser's operation with her, and for leaving her alone with his mother instead. There was no point in blaming him, he hardly had any choice in the matter, but that didn't make it easier either and she still felt disappointed.

'I'll phone,' she said. 'As soon as we know anything. They said to ring at half twelve…'

'I know.'

'He'll be okay…'

Ned stared at her and swallowed. And then he left the room.

Hannah entered shortly after, her face pale and blotchy. She was wearing fresh clothes and had brushed her hair, but she had applied more make-up than Flora had ever seen her wearing and it looked all wrong, too harsh on her soft, natural face.

'I thought we could have omelettes this morning,' she said as she entered the room. 'We haven't been making cakes recently so we have far too many eggs, and I cannot abide waste.'

Flora turned from the window. She was about to gently refuse when she saw the look on Hannah's face and stopped. In fact, her expression was so defiant that Flora almost took a step backward.

Hannah continued. 'Now I don't know about you, but I always favour three eggs per omelette, so could you fetch me nine eggs? It seems scandalous to be using so many simply on breakfast, but I can't see the point in making cake today, can you?'

Flora didn't want to argue, but even she could do the basic maths required. 'Hannah, I don't think we'll need quite so many, Ned has already gone out.'

'Nonsense. Where on earth has he gone?'

She shrugged. 'He didn't actually say, but I assume it was to start work…'

'So then he'll still be needing a breakfast inside of him.'

Hannah all but glared at Flora, who cleared her throat. 'I got the impression that he wouldn't be back until lunchtime… I'm not sure he was terribly hungry.'

'Oh, for goodness' sake.' Hannah gave a loud tut. 'We could do without that silly behaviour.'

'Perhaps we should just eat ourselves, and then if Ned does come back we can whip him up something then, can't we?'

It seemed the most sensible suggestion, although the thought of working her way through a mountain of rapidly cooling egg made Flora feel sick. But on no account would she contradict Hannah, not today.

'Hmmm.' The dissatisfaction in Hannah's voice was clear. 'It doesn't seem as if I have a choice, does it?' She crossed to the pantry door. 'Right, just the two omelettes then.' She half turned. 'I'll put four eggs in yours,' she added. 'You could do with feeding up.'

Flora's groan was almost audible, but she clamped a hand over her mouth just in time.

'You know, if you're worried about there being too many spare eggs, I could always take some to the village for you?' offered Flora, willing Hannah to agree. It would be a great excuse to go and see Grace again. 'Didn't you say the shop is always happy to have them?'

'What, today?' Hannah's brow creased into a row of furrows. 'Well, I don't see how you could possibly go today…'

Flora weighed up her desire not to upset Hannah against her desire to do anything to get out of the house.

'I just thought it might be helpful,' she said. 'We can't go to the hospital today, can we? So even once we know that Fraser is okay, there would still be time.'

Hannah's look was long and cool. 'No, I don't think so. Not today.' And that was the end of that. Flora clenched her teeth together.

'Shall I give you a hand with breakfast then?' she asked.

Another look. 'I am perfectly capable of making omelettes, Flora. Goodness, I've probably been making them since before you were even born.'

Flora inhaled and let the breath slide out of her, long and slow. 'Okay,' she muttered under her breath. 'Looks like I'm on tea-making duty then. Again.'

From his space beside the Aga, Brodie raised his head, giving Flora a baleful look. *You and me both, Brodie, you and me both.* 'I'll take you out in a minute, boy,' she whispered. 'I promise.'

She watched as Hannah removed the special omelette-making pan from the cupboard, and then the special small bowl into which she would first break the eggs to check they were fresh, even though they could only be a day or two old at most, before finally slipping these into the special bowl she reserved for beating the eggs.

Collecting the teapot from the table, Flora saw, almost in slow motion, the moment when Hannah brought the first of the eggs down sharply on the side of the bowl to crack the shell. Perhaps she had slightly misjudged the angle or used a little too much force, but either way the side of the bowl dipped alarmingly, causing it to roll away at speed. Flora watched in horror as the bowl reached the edge of the work surface, teetered for a lengthy second and then fell straight down, hitting the quarry-tiled floor with a sharp crack that cleaved it straight in two. The egg Hannah had been holding at the time followed suit.

In her scramble to catch the bowl, Hannah's hand also knocked several of the remaining eggs that were lined up beside her and, before Flora could even react, they too were on the floor.

'No! Oh… no, no, no…'

Hannah sank to her knees, grabbing the broken pieces of the bowl before frantically trying to salvage the mess. Miraculously, one egg was still intact and she scooped it from the floor, gently cupping the yolk in her palm so that it nestled there as she sought desperately to keep the stringy egg-white from slipping through her fingers. Her gaze met Flora's and in that instant, through Hannah's eyes, it was Fraser's heart she saw, cradled in Hannah's hand, his life blood seeping away as she clutched frantically to save it.

The next second Flora was beside her, sunk to her knees in the devastation around them, clutching at Hannah, who was sobbing Fraser's name over and over again. The two of them rocked back and forth as Hannah finally released the pain and fear she had been holding tight to her for days.

'Don't leave me, Fraser,' she whispered. 'Oh, God, don't leave me.'

Flora's own face ran with tears and she offered up a silent prayer. She glanced at the clock on the wall. Fraser would be two hours in to his operation by now.

It took at least fifteen minutes before Flora even thought about moving from the floor. Her eyes had been shut tight as she clung onto Ned's mother, letting the storm of Hannah's tears slowly subside until she was spent. There was egg stuck to her tights, her hands, even in her hair. It was sticky and slippery both at the same time, and the sensation made Flora want to heave. She looked down to find she too was covered in it and suddenly, more than anything, she wanted to get it off her. Panic rose in her throat as she gagged, sucking in air as fast as she could to try to calm her breathing. She picked a spot on the wall and tried to focus on it. *Everything is going to be okay. Everything is going to be okay.*

She felt a tentative lick on her hand, and looked up to see Brodie's questioning look, his eyes warm and soft on hers. The old boy was worried too. She pulled him closer and his tail gave a soft thump as he wriggled against her, seeking his own reassurance. They must have looked quite a sight, huddled on the floor together. She kissed the dog's head, realising that he too had been out of sorts over the last few days.

'Come on, boy,' said Flora, as Brodie continue to lick at her hand, realising then that there were spoils to be had on the floor. It broke the spell and at last she and Hannah were able to get to their feet, where they looked at one another one more time before a final warm embrace marked the end of whatever had just happened.

Flora looked down at the floor. 'Perhaps we should have had cereal, after all?' she suggested, a flicker of a smile pulling on her lips as the absurdity of the situation suddenly hit her.

Hannah looked up, her hand flying to her mouth. 'I've just remembered… You don't even like eggs!' And then she burst out laughing.

The two women looked at one another for a moment, Hannah's laughter subsiding to a warm smile. 'Oh, Flora… How on earth are we going to get through the day?'

Flora squinted at the window. 'Well, I don't know about you, but I'm sorry, I don't think I can stay inside. I need to be where there are trees, plants, that kind of thing…' She broke off, wondering whether what she wanted to say next would sound stupid.

'Go on,' said Hannah, spotting her hesitation.

'It sounds a bit… kooky… but I always feel more *hopeful* when I'm out in the garden. More alive…'

Hannah nodded. 'So what do you suggest?' she asked. 'If it's okay with you, I think I'd like to be outside too. You're right, it does feel like what we should do.'

'Well, Brodie would like a walk… and there are still eggs to take to the village, but apart from that, well, I wondered – if it was all right with you – whether I could use the greenhouse, to plant some seeds?'

'Seeds?' She cocked her head at Flora. 'I don't mind in the slightest – as a matter of fact, it would be good to see the greenhouse being used again – but what kind of seeds?'

Flora hesitated. 'I brought them with me actually,' she admitted. 'Which sounds a bit presumptuous, I know, but they're flower seeds… Ned told me you had a big garden, you see, and back in Birmingham I only had a flat, so no garden of my own. I've always wanted to plant masses of flowers…'

'A florist wanting to plant flowers, I've never heard anything like it,' said Hannah with eyebrows raised in amusement. 'I think that's a lovely idea. We mainly have lots of shrubs, as I'm sure you've spotted, flowering ones granted, and the roses here are beautiful, but apart from the spring bulbs, very few flowers… I'm not entirely sure why.'

'Too much bother, I expect,' replied Flora. 'I mean, they're not really, but you do have to pander to them a bit to get the best out of them. I don't suppose you've ever really had the time. But your gardens are lovely, just the same.'

Hannah stared wistfully out of the window. 'You should see Grace's garden, full of flowers; now that *is* beautiful. Colour everywhere and in summer, the smell… oh, there's really nothing like it.'

'Grace?' queried Flora. 'Grace from the village shop?'

Hannah nodded. 'Yes, she lives next door.'

'Does she...? Well, I never knew that. But by next door I guess you mean about three miles away?'

Hannah smiled. 'Not quite...' She turned in the other direction and pointed towards the field beyond the garden. 'Just over the rise. Her house is on the hill, actually, but you can't quite see it from here. She has the most amazing views.'

'Strange. She never mentioned that we're neighbours even though she knows I live here.' She frowned.

'Grace is a very private person,' replied Hannah. She leant a little closer. 'Her husband is, well... rather well known, and she doesn't like everyone to know. They do know of course, but that's not the point.'

'What do you mean by rather well known?' asked Flora. 'Is he a notorious criminal or something?' she joked.

Hannah gave her a searching look. 'You're not far off the truth actually... Not a criminal, no, but what in our day we would have called a scoundrel.' She lowered her voice. 'Chases anything in a skirt,' she added. 'Catches most of them too...'

'Oh.' Flora's hand went to her mouth. 'Poor Grace... And everybody around here knows that, do they? That must be awful for her.'

'Which is why she rarely talks about herself, at least until you get to know her well. Of course what doesn't help is that her husband is Paul Maynard – you know, the one from the telly. Does all those quiz shows and documentaries.'

Flora wrinkled her nose. 'But he's a smarmy slime ball—' She stopped suddenly. 'And Grace is lovely. What on earth does she see in him? Apart from his money, of course... Sorry, that sounds rather uncharitable.'

'And there you have it,' replied Hannah. 'That's what most people think and one of the reasons she likes to keep her private life very much to herself. But Grace met Paul when he was just nineteen, and they've been together ever since… thirty-odd years all told.' Hannah ran a finger across her lips. 'Of course it's never discussed, and I would never say this to her face, but I would say that Grace herself is the reason that Paul has been so successful…'

'Ahhh,' intoned Flora. 'The "behind every successful man is a woman" theme… I've never been sure about that myself, but whatever the dynamics of their relationship it still doesn't seem right for her to be treated that way. No wonder she likes her private life to stay just that.' She paused to think. 'I really liked her when I met her though, I should try to get to know her a bit better.' She gave a nod as if to underline her thought process. 'Now, what were we doing? I can't even remember how we got talking about Grace.'

'Her garden?' prompted Hannah. 'The flowers?' She tutted gently. 'And I thought it was me whose brain was scattered to the four winds…'

Flora held a finger in the air. 'Ah yes…' She grinned. 'Right, I expect we had better clear up both ourselves and this mess, hadn't we? Although Brodie looks to have done most of the hard work for us. And then I'll go and get the seeds, shall I?' And with another quick glance at the clock she crossed to the sink and began to run the hot water.

*

Not long after, they were both standing inside the greenhouse surveying the debris around them. Despite the spring-like feel to the day it was still far from being warm, but inside at least the glass magnified the heat from the sun and it felt warmer.

'As you can see, it's been a long while since I've been in here,' said Hannah, pulling a face. 'And it's become something of a dumping ground.'

Flora looked around her. 'I know.' She gave a wry smile. 'I should probably own up to already having had a bit of a nosey,' she said. 'But it won't take much to tidy all this stuff. I'd have done it but I wasn't sure if these things were still needed. Some of it looks like rubbish to me.'

Hannah nodded. 'I'd say most of it is rubbish. It's certainly been in here far longer than it needed to be. Let's just clear off that work bench for starters and then we can put what we need on it for now and stack the rest under the benches on the other side. We can throw as we go.'

'I've already spied several bags of compost and loads of pots,' said Flora. 'Buried under that lot. Shall we try to pull those out first?'

Hannah was staring where Flora pointed but Flora could tell she wasn't really seeing it.

'Do you suppose he's doing okay, Flora?' she said, suddenly.

Flora looked up as if scenting the air. 'Yes,' she replied firmly. 'I think he's doing fine.' She checked her watch. All being well, Fraser would now be halfway through his operation. She lightly touched Hannah's arm. 'Come on, let's not stop now, eh?' They needed to keep busy.

With a visible effort Hannah pulled herself out of her reverie and met Flora's eyes. 'Won't it be lovely for Fraser – to see all these beautiful flowers come the summertime.'

There was a sudden lump in Flora's throat. 'Do you know what his favourite is?' she asked.

'Love in a Mist,' Hannah replied without thinking. 'And cornflowers, blue like my eyes…'

Flora turned and picked up a pile of old sacks from the floor behind her. She couldn't say another word.

With the two of them working systematically, it wasn't long before order was restored and soon they had cleared a work bench and laid out an assortment of pots and trays. Importantly, they had found two more big bags of compost languishing in the corner, more than enough for what they would need, and Flora dragged these over to the bench. Fifteen more minutes saw the pots and trays filled with soil and finally Flora was able to pull the packets of seeds from her pocket and spread them out.

'I'm a bit of a hoarder,' she admitted, grinning. In front of her were at least twenty different varieties of flower seeds. 'Once I'd started collecting them I found it hard to stop.'

'You don't say…'

Flora pulled a couple of packets forward. 'So these, obviously, for Fraser…' she said. 'And what else, Hannah, what are your favourites?'

Hannah immediately snatched up a packet. 'Oh, larkspur,' she said. 'Anything old-fashioned like these.' She touched another. 'Ranunculus, too.'

Flora smiled at the joy on her face. 'Right, then, we'll start with these.' She looked down at the bench. 'How about we do two of the big pots of each of these, and then see what we've got left over?' She handed two of the packets to Hannah, who smiled at them dreamily.

'I had ranunculus in my wedding bouquet,' she said. 'Goodness, that was a long time ago…'

'How long *have* you two been married?' asked Flora.

Hannah's head came up slightly. 'It will be thirty-five years this year. In May. We got married on May Day.'

'Well, then we need to make sure that this year is *extra* special, don't we? Fraser will be up and running about like a spring chicken by then, so it will be perfect…' She had expected to see Hannah's face light up, but was surprised to see it fall.

'I was rather hoping that perhaps you and Ned… but now I'm not at all sure that's going to be possible. I can't see how we could make all the arrangements in time, not now there's this…'

Getting married on May Day? Flora wasn't entirely sure how she felt about the idea. She knew there was no rush, but… She pursed her lips. What bothered her was the nagging doubt that if they didn't get married soon, they wouldn't get married at all. It would be quite some time before Fraser was able to take up his former role on the farm and they would continue to be as busy. It would be difficult, if not impossible, to take time away from the farm.

'Hannah, there's no rush. Ned and I can get married any time. What's important is that Fraser makes as full a recovery as possible, and then once things are more settled we can think about it then.'

She tore off the top of the packet of seeds she was holding, trying to judge how to pitch her next statement.

'And it might be that it will be easier to have the wedding somewhere else and let them take the strain, rather than having it here, with all the extra work that involves. I expect there are some lovely places around.'

Hannah considered this for all of a millisecond. 'No, I don't think so,' she said. 'I think we'd hate that.'

Flora gave a tight smile. 'Well, then… as I said, plenty of time to think about it.' Today was really not the day to have this conversation. She stared at the packet in her hand. Still, at least the seed of the idea had been sown. Oh, the irony…

She sprinkled a few seeds over the tray of compost. 'These are going to look so gorgeous,' she added, trying to lighten the mood. 'We'll have to have a look and see where the best place will be for them once they've grown on a bit and can be planted out. Where do you think they should go?'

'Well, as we'll have so many, I think I'd like to have some for the cottage garden as well. If we do ever get to move in there's only a patch of lawn at the back so a few flower beds would look very pretty. The rest I was thinking would look lovely on the big triangle between the two houses. It's where we have the table and chairs out in summer, under the shade of the big chestnut.'

Flora nodded. 'Imagine how great they'll smell too. Well, I think that's settled then. We'd better get a few more done.'

The hands of the clock were creeping round, and by the time they had finished and tidied up, watered their seeds and washed their hands, Flora reckoned it might be time for a cup of tea. And a phone call.

Chapter 12

Flora's heart was literally pounding in her chest, and she hoped to God that Fraser's still was too. She felt like she was choking; as if her stomach had somehow risen, leaving her lungs with no room to expand. One look at Hannah's face confirmed that she was feeling just the same. Flora shook her head. Of course she was. How ridiculous to think she could be anything other than terrified.

They were both sitting at the kitchen table, a mug of tea and a plate of biscuits in front of them. The biscuits lay untouched and, although Flora's mouth was dry as a bone, she couldn't bring herself to drink. She had completely underestimated the amount of time they would need to finish up in the greenhouse, and making a pot of tea had taken all of three minutes, not the twenty they had until it was time to make the call.

'Would you like me to ring for you?' Flora asked. She didn't want to at all, but she had to offer.

Hannah inhaled a deep breath. 'No, I should ring. That's kind of you, Flora, but…' She couldn't finish the sentence. She stared out across the room, her fingers wrapped tightly around her mug, drawing comfort from the warmth.

The hospital hadn't rung them; that had to be a good sign, thought Flora. If anything had happened during the operation they would have made contact. She swallowed and sneaked a glance at Hannah, reaching down to stroke the top of Brodie's head, which was pressed hard against her knee and had been since the moment they'd sat down.

'I think I'll ring now,' announced Hannah, getting to her feet. 'I can't stand this. Even if they tell me to ring back, that's okay. It'll be something.'

Flora nodded and watched as she left the room. Should she go with her, to stand by her side? Should she loiter by the kitchen door and try to hear what was being said? Or should she just give Hannah some space and wait for her to return? She leant forward and buried her face in Brodie's fur. 'What do I do, boy?' she whispered. 'What would Hannah want?'

But she knew what *she* would want, and so she slowly got to her feet and went out into the hallway.

Hannah's hands were shaking as she dialled the number, but as she waited for it to connect she smiled gratefully at Flora. It must have rung about twenty or thirty times before it was answered and, as Hannah made her request, Flora's stomach shifted, fizzing with anxiety.

There was a long pause and then Hannah closed her eyes, her lips murmuring, her breath leaving her in short pants. 'Oh, thank God…' She held out the receiver to Flora and melted back down the corridor.

Flora stared at it in surprise. 'Hello?' she said.

The voice at the other end sounded just as confused as she was.

'No, I'm sorry, this is… I'm Fraser's… daughter-in-law. Yes, I think his wife's just gone to sit down.' She listened for a moment. 'Okay, no, that's lovely, thank you. Oh… we're so relieved… Yes, I will. Thanks… Bye.' She hung up, a rushing noise in her ear, trying to keep the nurse's words in her head so that she could repeat them.

Hannah had returned to sit at the table, her back to Flora as she entered the room and, as Flora moved back to her original seat, she could see slow silent tears making their way down Hannah's cheeks.

'I thought I'd lost him,' she said, as soon as Flora sat down.

She reached over to take her hand. 'I know,' she said. 'But it's over, Hannah.' She beamed. It wasn't over, not by a long chalk, it was only just beginning, but Flora wasn't about to divulge any of her memories or the things she'd uncovered during her Internet research. 'The nurse said the operation went well and, although he's not awake yet, he's in recovery. You can see him tomorrow.'

Hannah gave a series of rapid nods, and clutched briefly at Flora's hand before her grip went slack again.

'Shall I make us some more tea?' Flora asked, but there was a swift shake of the head. 'Are you sure, because I'm going to have another?' Flora's tongue was now welded to the roof of her mouth. She got up to re-boil the kettle. 'We must let Ned know too,' she added, turning back around, but Hannah was still staring into space. 'Hannah?'

The vacant eyes slowly refocused on her.

'Would you like to give Ned a ring?'

It seemed an age before Hannah answered. 'No, dear... you can speak to him. If you don't mind I think I might go and have a lie-down. I'm suddenly feeling incredibly tired.'

She looked exhausted. As if the strain of keeping everything under control had suddenly collapsed and she could no longer even control the way her face looked. Flora smiled warmly.

'No, you go, it will do you the power of good.'

Suddenly the long afternoon stretched ahead of her. She paused for a moment, wondering how best to phrase what she wanted to say next.

'Before you go though, Hannah, when we were talking before, about the wedding, it made me wonder about other arrangements as well… Have you thought about what you're going to do when Fraser comes home?'

There was a sideways glance. 'What do you mean?'

'Well, practical stuff, I guess. Where you'll sleep, for one.'

Hannah was concentrating on the table in front of her. There was a pause and then she looked up, a surprised expression on her face.

'Do I need to think about that? I haven't really…' She trailed off.

'Hannah,' said Flora gently. 'Did you read any of the leaflets that the hospital gave you?'

There was a slight shake of the head. 'No, I couldn't. I don't want to know. I just want him home.'

Flora feared as much. 'Okay,' she said lightly. 'Well, we can talk about it as and when we need to, it's no big deal. Fraser won't be out of hospital for a week or so anyway, so we have a little time, but the one thing I think we do need to sort out is sleeping arrangements. I don't think he'll be able to manage the stairs for a few days, and he may well need help with certain… personal things…' She stopped when she realised that Hannah clearly hadn't thought about any of this. She gave a small smile. 'Fraser's a big man and you might not be able to manage on your own…' She cleared her throat. 'Ned and I were talking about it last night and we wondered if it might be better if we made up a bedroom for Fraser downstairs?'

There was silence for a few moments as Hannah stared at her hands.

'We just thought that might be easier for you,' added Flora. 'And we could make the room really nice.' She smiled again. 'Anyway, we don't need to think about that now this minute, but if you like I can make a start this afternoon. The dining room is never used. It's a huge room, quite airy when the curtains are open, and… it has a fire. I expect Fraser will feel pretty fragile and the last thing he'll need is to feel cold…'

Hannah got slowly to her feet. 'I'm really not sure that's necessary,' she said. 'And I certainly can't think about it now, dear.' She gave a weak smile and, crossing to trail a hand across Brodie's head, left the room.

Flora stared at the doorway, and the sudden huge empty space of the kitchen. Now what was she going to do? She needed to contact Ned first of course, but after that… The prospect of a free afternoon held little appeal – there were far too many things to think about and nothing she wanted to dwell on. She stared at the kettle. She must be practical and keep busy. There were any number of things to attend to, and the dining room would need a lot of sorting if it was to become what she had in mind. She walked out of the kitchen, Brodie trailing behind her.

It only took a few moments standing in the quiet space to realise that this was the last place she wanted to be. She had a desperate need to get out of the house again and, as she looked down at Brodie's upturned face beside her, she knew what she would do. Brodie was sure to want a walk, the surplus eggs needed a new home but, more importantly, she needed a friendly face and she knew just where to find one of those.

It took several goes before Ned finally answered his phone. That wasn't unusual – he often didn't hear it or wasn't in a position to answer straight away – but when he did answer Flora could tell she'd called at a bad time. He was clearly talking to someone else as he connected the call, his voice loud and strident, but then he paused for moment and she had a sudden mental image of him checking the caller display before he softened his voice to greet her.

'I'm sorry, Flora, I'm with the vet.'

'Oh… problems?'

There was an audible sigh. 'Always. Listen, never mind, have you heard?'

'Ned, he's okay. I've spoken with the hospital and the operation went well. We can't see him until tomorrow, but he's in recovery at the moment and then he'll be moved to intensive care. The nurse said they'd take good care of him… Ned?' She had lost him for a moment.

When his voice came back on the line it was choked with emotion. 'Sorry, Flora… that's good, isn't it?'

'It's all we can hope for at the moment. But there's no reason to think that things won't go well from here. Your dad's a strong man.'

'Aye…'

She hated hearing him so upset and would have given anything to be able to wrap her arms around him. 'Listen, isn't there any way you can come to the house, just for a little bit?'

There was a long pause. 'Oh, Flora, you don't know what you're saying. I wish I could, but it just isn't possible.'

She could hear him pulling himself together, and that made her feel even worse. She wished that he didn't have to, that he could just let all his emotion go.

'Is Mum okay?'

Flora smiled down the phone. 'Relieved. A bit stunned actually. She's gone to have a lie-down.'

'Okay… listen, Flora, I'm sorry, I have to go. I'll see you later, yeah?'

'You will… Things *will* be okay you know, Ned.'

There was a long pause. 'I'll see you later… Love you.'

'I love you too…' But Ned had already gone.

Right, that's it. It was time to leave the house. She marched back into the kitchen and opened the pantry door, taking several trays of eggs and placing them into the wicker basket that Hannah used to transport them.

'Come on, Brodie,' she called. 'Get your coat, we're going out.'

She scarcely even thought about what she looked like, jamming a purple hat onto her mass of curls and pulling on her boots. It was definitely milder today, but she'd still need her warm coat and the fact that it clashed horribly with her skirt and leggings was of no concern. She was ready to go before Brodie had even made it to the door.

It was only after a couple of minutes, when she realised that Brodie was lagging way behind her, that she slowed her pace and waited for the elderly dog to catch her up.

'I'm sorry, boy,' she said. 'I've got a bit of a route march going on. And you don't know what's in my head, do you? So if it looks like I'm trying to run away, well…' She trailed off as the dog reached her. Then she took a deep breath, ruffled the fur on top of his head and started off again, much slower this time.

The air was still a little fresh, but it felt like the first time for days that Flora was actually breathing it in. She pushed back her shoulders and consciously tried to let them drop, relaxing into the rhythm of walking rather than hunching herself over.

Under normal circumstances a day like today would have filled Flora with joy. She would have revelled in the beauty of the natural world around her and the sheer wonderment of all it had to offer. And she could feel this same sensation today, but it felt as if it was behind glass and she couldn't quite reach it. She knew there was a huge amount to feel grateful for, but this only made her sense of detachment from the outside world worse. She cared for Fraser and Hannah, and it broke her up to see the family so upset and in total disarray, Ned especially. But in a very short space of time her life had also changed beyond measure and, right now, she had no idea where it was headed. Everything was in total freefall, and yet she felt trapped at the same time.

She stopped and looked around her. There was nothing she could do about it, nothing any of them could do about it. One day at a time was all she could cope with. Get through it and on to the next, and trust that somehow, in some way, the path would become clear once more.

After checking that Brodie was happy to wait outside, Flora pushed open the door to the shop with its tinkly bell and walked inside, amazed again at just how much was crammed in here, and how much it looked like her parents' front room when she had been growing up.

'Afternoon!' Grace's sunny greeting was like a breath of fresh air. She was about to say something else but instead she stopped and came around the counter, taking Flora's arms gently and easing her to one side.

'I heard about Fraser,' she said in a low voice. 'You must be out of your minds with worry.'

'Well…' Flora was hesitant. The fact that Fraser's heart attack was seemingly common knowledge ought not to surprise her, given how small a community it was, but she still didn't want to say too much.

'More importantly,' continued Grace, 'is there anything I can do to help?' She looked around her at the shop, which was empty of customers. 'I could put the kettle on?'

Perhaps there was something in Flora's face that had given away how she was feeling; the suggestion was perfect.

'Do you know, that would be wonderful.' She gave a grateful smile.

Grace slipped back behind the counter, reappearing a few moments later with a packet of chocolate Hobnobs. 'Get one of these in you first,' she said. 'The tea won't be long.' She patted a stool next to hers behind the counter and Flora needed no second invitation.

'I just came in to drop off some more eggs actually.' She held out the basket for inspection. 'Are you sure it's okay?'

'What, the eggs? Of course it's okay. I think Hannah has a pretty firm arrangement with Bill. He takes whatever she can provide.'

Flora smiled. 'I didn't actually mean the eggs… I meant the tea and sympathy…'

Grace took her own seat and fixed her with a stern expression. 'Friendship, Flora. I'm not the vicar's wife, I don't do tea and sympathy.' The corners of her mouth twitched and Flora's smile widened into a grin.

'That's me told then,' she said.

'Yep… and if you don't mind me saying, you look like you could use a friend right now. You look as if your brain's going in twenty different directions at once.'

Flora groaned. 'It feels like it. There's been rather a lot to take in.'

Grace nodded in understanding. 'Now, first things first. How is Fraser?'

'Double bypass,' she said, swallowing. 'He had it this morning. We've just found out it went okay, but he's in recovery now and we can't really see him until tomorrow. So, Hannah's gone to have a lie-down and I've—'

'Escaped?'

'You'll think I'm awful…'

Grace narrowed her eyes. 'On the contrary, I think you're behaving entirely normally.' She shook her head. 'I had no idea it was so serious though, Caroline didn't mention anything about an operation.'

'Caroline?'

There was a long pause. 'You didn't realise? How else do you think we all know what's going on?'

Flora sighed.

'Take no notice of her, Flora. Caroline is a shameless gossip. I think she sees it as her duty to the community in some way, keeping us all informed. Mind you, they do own most of the land around here, and quite a few of the people as well—' She clapped a hand over her lips. 'Hush my mouth, what am I *saying*?' She winked. 'I just mean that when you're in that position it's only natural to want to keep tabs on what's happening locally, and Caroline does a very good job of fulfilling her obligations in that regard. She's very well *networked*… if you catch my drift…'

'Oh, I can imagine.' Flora rolled her eyes.

A shrill whistling sound came from the little kitchen. Grace hopped off her stool. 'Back in a sec,' she said.

Flora pulled the packet of biscuits towards her and took out two of the intensely sweet treats. She stuffed the first one into her mouth practically whole.

'So, backtracking a little,' said Grace, putting down a mug of tea a few moments later. 'A double bypass sounds harrowing stuff. I imagine that must be pretty hard for all of you to get your heads around. How is Hannah taking it?'

Flora weighed up the question. 'At the moment? I'm honestly not sure. She's very upset obviously, and she's gone through every emotion possible in the last few days. It's going to mean a massive adjustment for everyone at the farm, and I'm not sure she's fully realised quite what that's going to mean.' She paused. 'I'm not being critical, I don't know how I'd react in her situation and everything has happened so fast. I'm not actually sure how you're supposed to deal with it. Time, I guess.'

'A great healer, so folks reckon,' replied Grace. 'Not sure that's always true. Sometimes the longer something goes on the more unbearable it becomes…' She stopped and took a sip of her tea, staring out across the room. 'But even then, I suppose what does happen is that you learn to develop coping mechanisms… But in this case I'm sure things will improve day by day. Fraser's a tough old boot. I can't see him giving up without a fight.'

Flora blew across the surface of her mug to cool her tea. She wasn't entirely sure Grace had been talking about Hannah for a moment, but she nodded.

'And I've known Hannah for years,' added Grace. 'She's got a heart of gold, even if she has always been a bit of a stick in the mud...'

'Yes, you live next door,' said Flora, looking up. 'Sorry, I didn't know.'

Grace pulled a face. 'I should have said when we first met. Force of habit, I'm afraid. I don't always mention where I live... a lot of people around here know the house and jump to conclusions, usually the wrong ones.' She tutted. 'But that's my story, for another day. So, Fraser is probably going to be okay, and Hannah as well as can be expected. What about Ned? And you of course, who seems to have been dumped in the middle of all of this from a great height.'

Flora stared at her.

'What? Well you have, haven't you?'

Flora wasn't about to disagree; she just hadn't banked on such a shrewd assessment from someone she barely knew. She gave a rueful smile.

'It has been a bit of a shock,' she admitted. 'But there's not a lot I can do to change anything. It's Ned I'm worried about though. There's too much work for just one person, and he's pretty stressed already. Worried about his dad of course, but now with all the added responsibility he's going to have to take on, I can see him making *himself* ill if he's not careful.'

'And in one fell swoop, Flora has gone from beautiful siren, yet thoroughly respectable prospective daughter-in-law, to carer for the whole lot of them.'

Flora blushed. 'It's not that bad,' she protested, but then she leant closer. 'I've never been called a siren before,' she whispered. 'Goodness…'

Grace grinned. 'Jet-black hair, huge green eyes, an obvious artistic temperament and possessing a way of wearing clothes I could only dream of… Who are you kidding? No wonder you have Ned well and truly under your spell.'

'I think you must be a little bit witchy yourself,' said Flora, sitting back.

Grace tapped her nose. 'I talk to my bees,' she said. 'They tell me *everything…*' She stretched out the last word for several seconds, and then burst out laughing.

'Of course!' Flora slapped her forehead. 'The honey we buy… It's yours, isn't it?'

Grace simply smiled. 'You must come over and see my hives sometime,' she replied. 'You were a florist in a previous life and bees like flowers.' She put down her mug. 'In fact, if you could see your way to planting a few more up at the farm that would be perfect. It's not a good time for bees just now.'

'No, I've heard.' Flora's face brightened. 'But you know, when Hannah and I were trying to keep busy this morning, we planted up a load of seeds as it happens. Come the summer we'll be overflowing with flowers.'

'Well then, you must definitely come and see them. And my garden is my absolute pride and joy; you might enjoy seeing that too.'

Flora blushed again. 'I'd like that, thank you. I've been wondering a little what there might be that can get me out of the house. That sounds awful, doesn't it, but… I have a feeling I might have need of it.'

Grace smiled. 'I'm certain of it,' she said. 'I'm only here two days a week –Wednesdays and Fridays – and apart from that I'm usually at home, so come and visit whenever you like, there doesn't need to be a reason. And don't forget I still want to see your prints, so perhaps you can bring them with you next time?'

Flora's face fell. 'I'd have liked to have completed a few more by now, but it's difficult at the moment as you can imagine. There isn't much time for airy-fairy stuff.'

'Oh…? That doesn't sound like you.'

Flora chose her words carefully. 'It's been pointed out that my role on the farm is to support Ned's work, not indulge my hobbies.'

'Ah. Now that sounds like Hannah talking.' She smiled. 'We've been friends for nearly thirty years and there are many things I greatly admire her for, but her artistic ability is not one of them. She's just not made that way, Flora. But it's only her opinion, don't forget; it doesn't mean you have to put that side of you to bed. Granted, things are harder at the moment with Fraser being so poorly, but they will improve.' She broke off, thinking. 'In fact, if it helps, you're very welcome to visit just so that you can have a quiet space in which to draw. I've got plenty of room.'

'Could I?' asked Flora, astonished. 'Would you really do that for me?'

Grace smiled. 'Of course! You're welcome to visit whenever you like, and for whatever reason.' She pushed the packet of biscuits back towards Flora. 'Don't underestimate the strain Fraser's illness is going to put on you, Flora. You're a strong independent young woman, anyone can see that, but you're going to have to wear several hats over the coming months, and I'm not just talking about the fetching number you have on today. That's not going to be easy, but when the going gets tough, surround yourself with the things you love and remind yourself that there will be a reason why you're here, why all this has happened, and when you discover what that is, everything else will fall into place…'

Flora's eyes widened and her hand hovered somewhere near her heart. 'You really believe that, don't you?'

'Of course I believe it,' she said, throwing her head back and laughing out loud. 'Because it's true.' She lowered her voice again. 'The bees told me, and didn't I tell you, they're *never* wrong...'

Chapter 13

'Oh, my God, Ned, it was dreadful. It didn't even look like him. Fraser was in there somewhere, but on the surface you couldn't see him at all.' And then she stopped. 'Oh shit… sorry, that came out so badly…' The images that had played on a loop through her head the entire time she had been driving home from the hospital were slowly beginning to lose their sharpness, but they would stay with her for quite some time to come.

'It's just that your dad's such a big bloke, and he looked so small surrounded by all those wires and tubes and monitors.' She took a deep breath and squeezed Ned's hand. 'But… the main thing is that he's okay, and the nurses say he's right where he should be at this point. In fact, he might even be able to move out of intensive care and back up to the normal ward tomorrow, all being well, and then home just before next weekend. I mean, how is that even possible? How can someone have such major surgery and be home in a week? I don't know whether to think it's irresponsible or just plain miraculous.'

She was aware that she was jabbering, trying to fill the silence that Ned was making no attempt to fill himself. It was lunchtime and he was steadily making his way through a plateful of sandwiches that Flora had made in a daze.

Ned swallowed and nodded. 'Where's Mum?'

'She's popped out to get a few things for Fraser.' She paused. 'I think she wanted a little time on her own… this morning came as a bit of a shock. But it's early days, you know. And he'll be better tomorrow, and the next day…'

Ned took another bite of his sandwich and Flora watched him, tucking her hair behind her ears. She wasn't sure he had properly looked at her yet. She reached out a hand.

'Ned?'

He looked up.

'Your dad was asking about you. He'd love to see you, you know.'

He gave her a sheepish smile. 'I feel a bit pathetic actually. It's not that I don't want to see Dad, I do, but he'll ask me about the farm and I really don't know what to say to him. How can I tell him that we need him here and that it's killing me doing everything by myself? Even if I don't tell him, he'll know anyway. He'll take one look at me and tell me it's as plain as the nose on my face, you know what he's like. I can't do that to him, think how he'll feel.'

She knew there had been some reason for his reluctance. 'Oh, Ned,' she said gently. 'Do you not think he'll feel like that anyway? He's not daft, he knows the score, and yes, he probably does feel guilty as hell, but he'd still like to see you.'

She could see the indecision on Ned's face. It was understandable, and she was still convinced it was tinged with a fear of what he might find when he got to the hospital, but nonetheless it worried her. She hadn't thought Ned was the type to keep secrets and yet she was beginning to wonder if things were worse than he was letting on, even to her.

'I know,' he said finally. 'We'll go tonight.'

He leaned forward across the table and she did the same until their noses were just touching. 'I'm sorry, I'm such a pain in the arse,' he murmured. 'But I do love you, Flora, and I promise when things have calmed down a bit I'll make it up to you.'

Her stomach rumbled as she walked Ned to the door to say goodbye. Neither she nor Hannah had been able to stomach anything to eat after returning from the hospital and she knew she wouldn't stop to eat now. Ned wouldn't be back until teatime and she had the whole afternoon ahead of her. She wasn't sure what time Hannah would appear, if at all, but no mind, she knew exactly what she was going to do with the intervening hours. She snatched up her mug from the table and marched through into the sitting room, looking around her with an appraising eye. And then she set to work.

There were three reception rooms on the ground floor of the house, but although the smaller of the two sitting rooms was perhaps the nicest room, sadly it had no fireplace so wasn't suitable for what Flora had in mind. The dining room, however, was never used and would be large enough to accommodate a bed, two if Hannah wished to sleep in the same room as Fraser, a couple of chairs, and at least one chest of drawers. To make the arrangement work would mean moving most of the dining room furniture out and into the other rooms, but with a bit of shuffling, Flora was convinced it would all fit.

An hour later she had squeezed the table and chairs from the dining room into the second sitting room, and ferried the remaining pieces of furniture into new homes elsewhere. All that was left was a huge oak dresser and matching sideboard which were far too heavy to move, but once tidied or possibly emptied would provide Fraser with some storage space for any clothes, underwear and other personal things he might want around him.

She crossed over to the sideboard and pulled open a drawer; the topmost one from a set of four in the centre between two cupboards. It was full of cutlery. Drawers two and three seemed to be full of cloths, napkins, and old placemats, while the bottom one housed an assortment of candles, napkin rings, old playing cards and what looked like the novelties from long-ago Christmas crackers. She was certain that none of it would be needed for now.

During her earlier assessment of the rooms she had spotted a large oak blanket box in the main sitting room which, partially covered with an embroidered cloth, was doing service as a coffee table. She quickly went to check and was pleased to find it empty apart from some very old magazines which had probably been shoved in there a long time ago and promptly forgotten. There was more than enough room to stash the contents of the drawers in there for now.

She got to her feet and was about to make a start when she heard the back door bang.

'Halloooee!'

Caroline's voice was unmistakeable.

Flora rolled her eyes but put on a smile and went to greet her.

'Oh, goodness, Flora, you poor thing. However are you all coping?' She came forward to give Flora a hug. 'Why don't I make a nice cup of tea for us both. I've just seen Hannah down in the village, so I know you're all on your own. I expect you could do with the company.'

Flora, who didn't want company at all, gave a weak nod. 'That's very kind, Caroline, but I'm actually sick of the sight of tea, I've drunk that many cups of it over the last day or two. You go ahead though, I don't mind if you'd like to stay and have one. I was just in the middle or rearranging some furniture for when Fraser gets home.' The last thing she needed was a heart-to-heart with Caroline.

She received a sympathetic look. 'It seems impossible that Fraser could even be in hospital, he's always seemed so strong, but for them to send him home again after only a week when he's had such a major operation—' She stopped suddenly and cleared her throat, a slight look of alarm crossing her face for an instant. 'Oh, I, er, met Ned coming through the yard, he filled me in on how things are...'

'So I see...' Flora couldn't help herself.

'I was on my way over, obviously, just to see how Fraser was doing, how you're all doing. Ned mentioned how amazing you've been, looking after everyone.'

Flora ignored the last comment. 'No, well, it's early days, but he's through the worst now. Moving forward is what's important, for everyone. Things aren't going to improve overnight, but every day will be better than the last and soon Fraser will be back to normal.' Even if she wasn't sure this was the case, Flora made damn sure her face said so.

Caroline's brow wrinkled a little. 'Oh, I hope so, after all this it would be desperate if Fraser had to sell the farm.'

'What on earth makes you think he'd have to sell the farm?' The comment had caught Flora completely off guard and her voice rose as she replied. 'I don't think that's even been considered, nor should it be.'

A hand fluttered to Caroline's chest. 'Oh, no... I didn't mean. Oh goodness, this has got all of us in quite a tizz, hasn't it?' She reached out a hand. 'I'm so sorry, Flora, I didn't think what I was saying. Of course that won't be necessary, I was just thinking silly thoughts, but Fraser will be fine, I'm sure of it. I guess it was seeing Ned so stressed just now, you can't help but wonder what's going to happen. Under the circumstances that's hardly a surprise.'

'No, he's having to work harder than ever at the moment, but that won't be for long. Besides, I'm going to be helping him out once Fraser is settled back home.' She held Caroline's look, at a complete loss to know where her last statement had come from. She hadn't even considered the possibility before. Perhaps she should have… 'And then as far as we're all concerned Fraser will just pick up where he left off once he's able to. A few things will have to change in the short term, but…'

Caroline was nodding heartily. 'Yes, yes, of course. Well, that is good news, I'm so relieved. And you mentioned you're getting things ready here for when Fraser comes home. I expect that will be a huge help to Hannah, but let me know if there's anything I can do, won't you?'

Flora was on the verge of refusing when it suddenly occurred to her there was something which Caroline could help with after all. She smiled to herself. A rather wicked smile.

'Actually… You could give me a hand with something if you wouldn't mind?' She motioned for Caroline to follow and led her into the dining room. 'I hope you're feeling strong?'

Caroline stared at the virtually empty space, a hand at her throat. 'Goodness, I don't think I've ever seen this room changed in all the years I've been coming to the house.'

'No, well, Fraser's never had a heart attack before either, but he's going to need somewhere on the ground floor for a few days once he's home. There are far too many stairs up to his and Hannah's bedroom and it's right the other end of the hallway from the bathroom. This will make a perfect bed-sitting room though. It's right opposite the downstairs cloakroom too, and of course next to the kitchen. Plus, it's the only room in the house apart from the kitchen that we stand any chance of keeping warm.'

She gritted her teeth. *For goodness' sake, Flora, shut up, you don't need to justify yourself.*

'But for what I had in mind, it would be better if the sideboard were shifted along a bit so it's closer to the dresser.' She pointed. 'But it's too heavy to move by myself so it's lucky you came along just when you did.'

Caroline gave her a wary smile. 'Oh, I see… well I…'

'So if you could just grab that end there, it won't take a moment.'

She watched with an amused expression while Caroline deliberated the possibility of either not being able to manage the task requested of her, or looking like a complete fool while she was doing it.

'I've already emptied the cupboards so it shouldn't be too heavy.' It would be, it was a dead weight, Flora knew that. She did pause to wonder quite why she was being so wicked when all Caroline had done was pay a friendly visit, but whenever they met there was just something that Flora couldn't quite put her finger on and today she wasn't in the mood to pretend otherwise. She moved to take up her own position.

'Thanks so much, I don't know what I'd do without you.'

There was a slight lip on the top of the sideboard which made it a tad easier to find something to hold onto, but it was still only a finger-width wide.

'We might just have to shuffle it over bit by bit, let's see how we go. Ready?'

Caroline nodded, still fidgeting with her grip.

'And lift!'

It took an absolute age as they walked the sideboard along the wall inch by painful inch, which was all Caroline could manage before she had to put it down again, and, by the time they had it more or less in situ, Flora was glowing slightly. Caroline, though, looked positively scarlet and a small strand of the low bun she favoured when she was riding had come loose and, for some reason, seemed to be annoying her inordinately. She tucked it crossly behind her ear once more, standing straighter and blowing out her cheeks.

'I really think we should have taken the drawers out or something,' she huffed. 'It would have been an awful lot easier.'

Flora clapped a hand to her head. 'Oh, God, you're right!' she said, turning away to hide her grin. She stood back to survey the positioning of the piece. 'Never mind, it's done now. Ah, that looks so much better.' She motioned to the empty space. 'Everything needs a bit of a clean, but we can put the beds there, coming this way, the table in between and an armchair in the corner.'

'Yes, I suppose,' answered Caroline. 'Although it does seem weird seeing the room like this. In fact, I can't remember when it was last used. Almost certainly at Christmas, but it would have been years ago; Ned and I were considerably younger, that I do know… And I seem to remember that Ned did suggest once upon a time that this be used as a more cosy sitting room, because of the fire, but of course Hannah wouldn't hear of it. I'm not sure why this room is sacrosanct but I'm glad that Hannah has come to her senses; this would seem a much better use of the space under the circumstances.'

'Sacrosanct…' faltered Flora. 'I didn't know that…'

'I think it's something to do with the dining table. Her mother's maybe? I can't quite remember. But I guess it doesn't matter much where the furniture is at the end of the day, just that it's still around.'

Flora could feel her heart sinking. The dining table. The one she had dragged unceremoniously down the hallway and hidden behind a door in the other room. But there was absolutely no way she was going to let on to Caroline that she hadn't even asked Hannah about moving the room round. They had sort of discussed it the other day, and even if Hannah hadn't actually agreed to it, it would still be a nice surprise, wouldn't it?

She nodded and rubbed her hands together as if they were dusty. 'Right then, did you want a cup of tea, Caroline?'

But Caroline shook her head, scowling as she inspected a manicured fingernail which hadn't taken too kindly to manhandling furniture. 'No thanks, I'd better get going actually, but I'll try and visit Fraser tonight. I expect he could do with seeing some friendly faces.'

'No—' The word was out of Flora's mouth before she could stop it. Caroline looked up sharply.

Flora winced. 'Sorry, what I meant was it would be better if you didn't go this evening... or possibly for a couple of days actually. Ned hasn't seen his dad yet, but apart from that, Fraser's not really up to visitors at the moment. He's still in intensive care for one, but I also think you might be better to wait until he's a bit more...' Flora still couldn't get the image of Fraser from this morning out of her head. '...He looked awful, Caroline,' she said bluntly. 'You'd hardly recognise him.'

She wondered whether Caroline might take offence at being contradicted but to her relief she looked more grateful than anything.

'No, well then, I'll wait. Maybe even until he's home. I don't... well I don't really *do* illness, I...' She broke off and shuddered. 'I'll get going then and let you get on. Give my love to everyone, won't you?' She edged towards the door. 'And I'll see myself out, don't worry.' She was almost out the door when she suddenly paused and turned. 'You know, you really should come riding with me tomorrow.'

Flora looked up, horrified. 'Oh, I don't think...'

'No, you should, honestly. A few hours out in the fresh air, instead of being cooped up in the house, worrying about things.' She looked Flora up and down. 'You're looking peaky actually. I think it would do you the world of good.'

'It's not really a good time, Caroline, and I don't ride, I think I mentioned that before, and—'

'Then it's the perfect opportunity to learn. I can see how stressed you are and with everything that's going on you need to look after yourself too, Flora – have a little bit of "me" time.' She patted the side of her hair. 'I'll pick you up at eight tomorrow which will give us plenty of time.'

'Yes, but the hospital…'

'Oh, we'll be back well in time for visiting, don't worry.' She backed out of the door. 'I'll see you then!'

And then she was gone, leaving Flora standing in the middle of the room, her heart sinking rapidly. She had no desire to go riding, not now, and certainly not with Caroline. She heaved a sigh and stared around the half-empty space. As if she didn't have enough on her plate. What on earth was she going to do with the room?

She had honestly thought she was helping by trying to create somewhere more suitable for Fraser, but now she was seriously questioning her motives. She knew how much Ned's mother hated change, particularly when it included any alteration to the domestic arrangements, so why hadn't Flora included her in her decision making and chosen to do it on an afternoon when Hannah was around? Was it to do with the fact that she didn't want to spend the afternoon alone with her own thoughts? Or because she wanted to be the one who was holding everything together in a time of crisis? Was she trying to carve a role for herself as the perfect prospective daughter-in-law and would-be wife as an alternative to the life she wanted, the one that was slipping away from her? But if not that, then what? Where would she go, if not here? No money, no home. She shook her head angrily. No, she mustn't think like that. This change was for Fraser; it was the right thing to do.

She crossed to the sideboard and yanked open the top drawer, pulling out the wooden box that held the cutlery. She had started now so she might as well finish, and if Hannah hated what she'd done, then she'd just blooming well put the room back to how it was before, and

Hannah could come up with something. Flora carried the box through into the sitting room and, removing the cloth from the blanket box, opened it up to lay the cutlery inside. Then she doubled back and collected the bottom drawer to repeat the exercise so that all that was left to do was move the tablecloths and other linens and Fraser would have several drawers at his disposal.

She reached inside the drawer and lifted a handful of the cloths, pulling them out towards her. They were heavier than she'd anticipated and she felt something slip from within. Trying to stop it from sliding with her knee, she realised it was a file of some sort, which must have been wrapped inside. But with her hands full she was hampered and she watched helplessly as it crashed to the floor. It landed edge on, bounced slightly, and out slipped a sheaf of papers which fluttered in all directions.

Damn.

Dropping to her knees, Flora set down the linen and picked up the blank cardboard file. Darting a look to the door, she began to pick up the loose papers, anxious to retrieve them as quickly as she could. Whatever they were, they'd obviously been hidden from someone, and she didn't want to be the one caught with them. As she gathered them together, she couldn't help but notice that they looked a lot like bills, and she quickly averted her eyes before she could be accused of snooping.

Carefully stowing them back in the file, she made sure all the pages were face down, and arranged them neatly so it wouldn't look like they had been rifled through. Then she wrapped them back up again inside the bundle of cloths and carried them through into the living room.

Another half hour or so later and she had manoeuvred an upright armchair into the corner of the room and even found a small side table which could sit beside it. A lamp completed the trio and she gave an affirmatory nod. She didn't even know if Fraser liked reading, but he would need something to occupy him over the coming weeks, and now at least he had somewhere to sit which would either have good light from the window during the day or be a cosy spot of an evening.

All that was needed now was to move the beds in here and Ned could help her with that later. She gave the room one last look. It was the best she could do for the moment. Later on, when Fraser was home, she'd put some flowers in here of course, and Hannah could bring some of his personal things if he wanted them, even some cushions and a throw for the chair. It would be warm and comfortable, but more importantly, close to them. She tried to regain some of the feeling she'd had earlier when she first started; a positivity. But it was gone. Since Caroline's visit she'd started questioning her motives, and now there was no denying she had meddled, plain and simple. And in doing so she had seen things she wasn't supposed to see, and given Hannah twenty different reasons to be annoyed with her.

She closed the door quietly behind her as she left.

*

'What have you done with my table?'

They had already been eating dinner for ten minutes or so and the question came out of nowhere. Flora almost choked, looking across at Ned, but he hadn't seemed to notice anything untoward.

Flora had heard the front door close just as she was checking on the pie for tea some half an hour earlier and she'd braced herself for the inevitable questions. But it wasn't until she was spearing a carrot to check if it was cooked that she'd heard a creak on the stairs and realised that Hannah had gone straight up to her room. Had she not even seen the alterations in the dining room? Or, thought Flora ominously, has she seen them and chosen not to comment?

The time in between had been agony for Flora as she waited on tenterhooks, but when Hannah finally appeared she had greeted Flora normally and bustled about the kitchen helping with the last-minute dinner preparations.

But now this.

Flora looked up and smiled, determined not to let her own misgivings about the room show. 'Oh, I popped it in the other room,' she said lightly. 'I can show you what I've done after tea if you like.'

Hannah's knife clattered onto her plate, making Ned jump. 'I rather thought I might put it back again,' she replied sharply. 'It's the dining room, Flora.' She placed her fork down rather more quietly. 'And that table was my mother's.'

'Yes, Caroline took great delight in pointing that out, don't worry.' She had told herself over and over not be defensive about what she'd done to the room and that if Hannah didn't like it, it wouldn't matter, but now faced with her scorn she could feel her indignation rising. 'So the table is quite safe. It's in the small sitting room, tucked out of the way so that it doesn't come to any harm… not that it's going to, seeing as no one ever goes in there anyway.'

Ned had sat up, his own knife and fork now resting on his plate. 'Caroline…? And what table?' He frowned, looking at his mother's angry face. 'What's going on?'

Hannah picked up her cutlery and started to eat again.

'Flora has taken it upon herself to move all the furniture out of the dining room which, although we had discussed very briefly, I certainly hadn't agreed to.'

'Oh… is that all? For goodness' sake, I thought she'd painted the room black with orange stripes the way you're going on, Mum. I take it this is to make some space so that Dad can move in there when he comes home?'

Flora nodded. She couldn't trust herself to do any more.

'Excellent idea.' He slid his hand down Flora's knee and grinned at her. 'You can show me what you've done when we've finished eating. I bet it looks great.' His eyes stayed on hers the whole time he was speaking.

'It isn't finished,' murmured Flora. 'Because obviously I can't move the beds by myself, and I haven't moved any of Fraser's personal things either.'

'No, obviously,' replied Ned, his eyes still on her. 'Mum can do that, can't you, Mum? Make it really cosy for Dad, with everything he'll need on hand. He'll feel so much better for knowing he hasn't got to worry how on earth he's going to get up the stairs.'

Flora was very glad for his response, and squeezed his fingers in reply, but he had also put her firmly in the middle.

'I honestly thought it would help,' she said.

'And it does. Mum's very grateful for all your hard work, aren't you, Mum? It's such a generous thing for you to do, thinking about Dad like this. I don't think it would have even occurred to me.' He was staring at his mum, eyebrows raised.

Hannah fidgeted with the edge of her placemat. 'Hmmm,' she said. 'I would still have liked to have been consulted.'

Ned loaded his fork with mashed potato. 'What did you get up to this afternoon then, Mum? Did you get the things you wanted?'

'Yes, thank you. A couple of books from the library, his *Farmers Weekly* and some new pyjamas. I don't like seeing your dad in those old ones, they're fine here, but not at the hospital.'

'Brilliant,' Ned replied. 'It sounds like Dad's going to get spoilt rotten, he'll enjoy that, despite what he says. We'll go and see him in a bit,' he added. 'And then we're one day closer to having him home again.' He smiled. 'It won't be long now, Mum.'

It was a valiant effort and Hannah did show a flicker of a smile, but the rest of the meal was finished in virtual silence. Despite Ned's attempts to make her feel better, Flora felt every second keenly.

Chapter 14

'… And then she said you'll have to sell the farm.'

Ned had just taken a huge bite of toast and suddenly paused mid-chew, eyes wide. He waggled his fingers and Flora waited until he was able to speak. 'Caroline said *what*?'

'That you're going to have to sell the farm,' she repeated.

Ned stared at her.

'I know. She said it without thinking and I wouldn't have mentioned it except for the fact that, well, I could be wrong, but I've heard that Caroline likes a bit of gossip… Imagine how Fraser will feel if he hears that kind of thing going round. It's bad enough now,' she added. 'Even if it is a rather old-fashioned view. In Fraser's eyes he's the head of the household and I know you don't mind holding the fort while he's ill, but it's obvious he feels terrible about saddling you with everything. And then you get people like Caroline making stupid assumptions, which isn't going to help anybody. I just hope Fraser never gets wind of it, that's the last thing he needs.'

'I'll speak to her.' Ned's mouth had set in a hard line.

Flora nodded. 'I think that's a good idea. She apologised as soon as she'd said it, but it's the kind of knee-jerk conclusion people jump to without thinking. It will take time, but there's no reason why Fraser won't be able to get back to work eventually.'

'Well, Caroline should know better. And yes, things like that do have a habit of gaining ground.' He swallowed the rest of his toast. 'So, when exactly did she say this?'

'Yesterday.' Flora rolled her eyes. 'When she also told me that moving the dining table was the biggest mistake I'd ever made and that Hannah would hate what I'd done to the room. Which she did, of course.'

'I'm sure Caroline didn't say it quite like that…'

Flora looked up. 'I think "sacrosanct" was the word she used,' she replied, not quite ready to let the matter drop just yet.

'Ahhh…' Ned pulled a face. 'I'm sorry, Flora. Mum will get used to the idea, you'll see. She's just not used to anyone showing any initiative around here; that's what comes of living with two clod-hopping farmers. But she'll soon see what a brilliant idea it was, and Dad will be chuffed to bits.'

'Hmmm, we'll see.'

And as it happened Ned was right. Less than ten minutes after he had left, Hannah came into the kitchen, or rather she hurtled in and stood there staring at Flora.

'Oh, thank goodness you're here!'

Flora wasn't entirely sure where else she would be.

'I wanted to apologise,' she said. 'For yesterday. I really don't know what came over me. You worked so hard, taking me to the hospital, doing all the cooking and taking Brodie out. You did all the washing-up too, and caught up with the ironing. Don't think I didn't notice that! And then, of course, you made the dining room so perfect for Fraser, and I think I just…' She stopped, realising she was rambling. 'Well, I'm sorry. For what I said. And the way I said it.'

Flora took off the washing-up gloves and placed them carefully beside the sink. She wasn't sure whether to hug Hannah or not, but in the end she didn't; something about the way she was holding herself so stiffly made her think it would just be something else that was too awkward for words. She smiled instead.

'It's okay, Hannah, really. I understand. It was the shock of everything catching up with you, I think, but I should have asked you about the room first. I guess I was trying to keep busy too, and I thought I could just get on with it while I had the time.'

'Even so, my reaction was uncalled for. You did it with the best of intentions, and what did I do? Spent most of yesterday trying to ignore everything, instead of doing what you did which was to try and think about things in a practical way, something which I usually pride myself on. So, I gave myself a very stern talking-to last night, and I'm pleased to say that I feel much better this morning.' She was wringing her hands, still standing in the same spot. 'Now, what time are we visiting Fraser today, the same time as yesterday?'

Flora glanced at her watch; it was a little after half past seven.

'Actually, Caroline has invited me out to go riding with her this morning.' She pulled a face. 'But I'm not all that keen on going so I'd be quite happy to give it a miss and go to the hospital instead.'

'Nonsense, you'll have a wonderful time, and it will be lovely for you to have some fun with a friend for a change. In fact, if we visit Fraser after lunch, that will give me plenty of time to give the room a thorough clean before we go and then I can start to move more of his things downstairs.'

'I did give it a clean yesterday.'

'I know, dear, but everything must be wiped down and disinfected. There mustn't be any trace of germs anywhere in the house. Fraser will be very susceptible, and we must all be very careful.'

She drew in a long breath, which Flora didn't like the sound of.

'Then, once the dining room is done, we can work through the other rooms in turn, finishing with the kitchen. If we aim to do one room a day, by the time Fraser comes home everything will be shipshape. Now, where did I put my notepad, I must make a list.' She looked around the kitchen and then back at Flora. 'Go on then, off you go and get changed.'

'Right,' said Flora faintly, looking down at her bright red tights. Why did she always feel like it was one step forward and two steps back?

*

'What?' Flora sighed as Caroline's eyes travelled up the length of her body, taking in the skirt and leggings she'd changed into before heading down to the yard. 'It was the best I could do. I don't own any jodhpurs and the one pair of jeans I do have are too tight to be comfortable on a horse. These are elasticated, plus they're old, and I don't mind if they get a bit muddy.'

Caroline arched her eyebrows. 'I can't take you out looking like that…' she drawled in a not quite fake posh accent. 'Not that you don't look lovely,' she added hastily. 'Just that, well, you'll see when we get there… Fortunately I have some spare riding clothes that I'm pretty sure will fit. You can change once we get to my house.'

Flora wasn't sure she liked the sound of that, but she followed Caroline meekly to her car and got in. Their farm might be next door, but in the countryside that meant at least two miles away by road or a really good walk across some fields. However, it also meant that, as Caroline was driving, Flora could drink in the views from the passenger seat. It felt like she had hardly been away from the farm since she had arrived and yet she had meant to get out and explore every day. So far that had been impossible; Shropshire might be home, but it still only amounted to a farmhouse, a few buildings and the odd field or two. And the hospital of course.

The high hedge they were passing ended and suddenly the horizon expanded in front of them. Flora drew in a quiet breath. It was stunning and she reminded herself that she had resolved to enjoy herself. Today was an opportunity and she mustn't spoil it by being negative.

'So this is *chez moi*,' said Caroline as they turned in through a pair of large stone gates. 'Otherwise known as Micklethwaite Stud and, as we go up the hill here, you can actually see Hope Corner across the fields to your left.' She smiled. 'Where no doubt Hannah is hard at it whipping everything that dared step out of line back into shape.'

Flora pursed her lips a little. Hannah wasn't that bad.

'So have you lived here all your life then?' she asked Caroline, changing the subject.

'I have, all thirty-two years. And my dad grew up here too, we're third generation.'

'Blimey…' Flora couldn't even conceive of such a thing. Her own family was scattered to the far corners of the country and had been for years. A brother in Norfolk, where he ran a guesthouse with his wife, and her younger sister in Cornwall where she managed a gallery for a very rich businessman who she was currently trying to entice into her bed, without much success as it happened. Her mum had retired a couple of years earlier, where she was now living an idyllic life with her stepdad in a small village on the Dorset coast. And then there was Rowena, of course. She felt the familiar weight of guilt that settled on her every time she thought of her elder sibling. Maybe one day they would be able to resume the same easy relationship they had once shared. Flora frowned, thrusting the thought aside; she had no space in her head for it today.

They were driving up a long straight track with open fields on either side but, as they approached a stand of trees, Flora could see another set of gates protecting a large red brick house, much like Hope Corner, although at least four times bigger. As they swept through the gateway the courtyard opened up in front of them, a large expanse of gravel providing a turning circle in front of the house before disappearing in between two rows of long low buildings to the left. Several other vehicles were already parked in an area to the right and it was towards these that Caroline headed, lurching to a stop with a spray of chippings.

'Come on,' she said. 'Let's go and get you sorted out, the girls are already here.'

Flora threw her a confused look, but Caroline was already climbing out of the car and she had no choice but to follow.

There was scarcely time to marvel at the grandeur of the double-height hallway before Flora was drawn up an oak staircase with a huge balustrade that led to a galleried landing on both sides. Her feet sank into deep carpet as she reached the top, hurrying towards to a door to the right that Caroline was holding open for her.

Caroline's bedroom was vast and incredibly untidy. With its tall ceilings and double aspect it was a beautifully airy space, decorated in pale lemon and blue with soft furnishings to match. But the enormous double bed was unmade and heaped with clothes, as were an old blanket box at the end of the bed and an armchair in one corner. Even then, there were still clothes on the floor, and a large number of cosmetics and hair products had spread from the dressing table to the window sills and a mantelpiece over a cast-iron fireplace. Flora shuddered to think what Hannah would make of it. At least she and Caroline had something in common then.

Flinging open the doors to a large walk-in wardrobe, Caroline rooted around for a moment before pulling out a pale pair of jodhpurs and a striped blue shirt, which she then thrust at Flora.

'There you go, I'm sure these will fit.' She crossed to the window which overlooked the courtyard and peered down. 'Oh look, Georgia has just arrived as well.'

Flora stared at her. Who the hell was Georgia?

It was clear that Flora wasn't to be offered any privacy to get changed and, judging by the speed at which Caroline was moving, time was of the essence. With a grimace Flora pulled off her boots and began to peel off her leggings.

'You mentioned the girls just now, Caroline,' she said, as she danced about the floor trying to get her feet into the jodhpurs. 'And now someone called Georgia… Am I right in thinking it's not just you and I that are going to be riding?'

Caroline turned back, a puzzled expression on her face. 'Oh, didn't I mention it? The girls always come hacking with me in the morning… Chloe, Emilie and Georgia, so there's just the four of us, well, five now you're here. But I know you'll love them. Gosh, we've been friends for… well years, since we were little.'

Flora gave a wan smile and heaved at the jodhpurs, which had glued themselves to her legs. 'So you're all experienced riders then…?' She let the question dangle as she pulled her skirt down and, by some miracle, managed to get the jodhpurs done up. Stepping out of her skirt, she carefully laid it on a clear area of the bed. 'Won't that be a problem?'

'Won't what be a problem?' Caroline came forward and picked up the shirt, handing it to Flora, who was pulling her old top over her head.

Flora waited until her head was free from her jumper before replying. 'The fact that I don't ride… Won't that be a problem, seeing as how you're all so experienced? Won't I hold you up?'

Caroline waved an airy hand. 'Oh, I don't expect so. It's not like we're going to be performing dressage or anything, it's just a gentle hack. I'm sure you can manage that.' She grinned. 'Oh, that looks much better, but do tuck the shirt in. It's not the done thing to have everything all flapping about.'

'I don't think I can,' muttered Flora. 'There's not really much spare room in here, Caroline,' she added, tugging at the fastener at her waist.

'Nonsense,' replied Caroline. 'You have a lovely figure, Flora. You might as well show your curves off.' She eyed her closely. 'Lie down on the bed if you can't get the jodhpurs done up again. They're meant to be skin-tight, and if you lie down and breathe in, it helps.'

Flora did as she was told. This really was not going to end well. She struggled back to her feet.

'See, look,' said Caroline. 'That's perfect!' And she turned on her heels again. 'Come on, let's go and meet everyone.'

They were all blonde, all a size ten and Flora found it hard to distinguish between them. Chloe was slightly taller, while Emilie was the shortest, and Georgia had brown eyes not blue but, apart from that, they all had the same big, white-toothed smiles, peaches and cream complexions and laughed far too much at things that simply were not funny. And the worst thing was that Flora found herself doing it too. Within minutes her cheeks were aching from maintaining such a wide smile, and giggling in a high-pitched way she had *never* done before.

The laughter stopped the minute she tried to get on the horse. She had already suffered the indignity of Caroline trying to find her a hat which would actually fit. Then a young lad whom Flora wasn't even introduced to brought forward the biggest horse that Flora had ever seen. It was white, with big brown eyes that stared right into the very centre of Flora's soul. Samson, she was informed, was a really gentle old boy, but that didn't do much to allay her fears. Nemesis would have been a better name.

The simple matter of swinging her leg up and into the stirrup seemed an impossibility but, after several goes, she at least managed to get her foot through it, although the rest of her was going nowhere. By this time the others had all mounted their horses and, after several more attempts and an embarrassing exchange with the young lad, who didn't know where to put his hands, Flora was still very firmly on the ground. No one was laughing, but then it was implied in the silence that dragged on longer and longer…

Eventually, Caroline got off her horse and led Samson over to a stone trough at the far end of the stable block which, with some help, Flora managed to stand on without falling in. From there, it was a short step up into the stirrup and a gentle swing of her leg over Samson's back.

'Easy-peasy,' said Caroline.

To give him his due, Samson didn't move a muscle throughout the whole shameful debacle, but Flora soon realised that this presented her with another huge problem. She had no idea how to make the horse go and, unaccustomed as she was to being not only so high up, but also seated on the back of a massive animal, she would have been perfectly happy if they had not moved at all.

Re-mounted on her own horse, Caroline doubled back to her and came alongside, scooping up the reins and making a clicking sound through her teeth that caused Samson to shift forward as she handed the reins to Flora.

'You are a bit rusty, aren't you?' she said.

Flora stared at her. 'Nope,' she said. 'Not rusty. Completely and utterly clueless…'

Caroline gave a slight glance back over her shoulder and leaned in a little closer. 'But I thought you were *kidding* when you said you hadn't ridden before,' she said, her voice barely above a whisper.

'Caroline, why would I even make that up?' Flora replied, trying to keep the edge out of her voice. 'I honestly have never been on a horse before in my life.'

For a moment Flora thought that Caroline was just going to abandon the whole thing as a ridiculous idea, but then she gave Flora a warm smile. 'But the girls have come over especially. I really wanted you to meet them, they're such fun and well… otherwise, who are you going to make friends with?'

She had a point. Flora could already see that life on the farm wasn't going to give rise to many opportunities for social outings. Ned worked too long hours and unless she wanted to go out by herself, which she didn't, where would Flora meet anyone her own age? And besides, she was the stranger here, the townie without a clue, and Caroline was doing her best to help her fit in. She pulled the smile back onto her face. How hard could this be?

'You're right,' she said, 'I'm just a bit nervous… well, a lot nervous actually. But we've all got to start somewhere, haven't we? And I'm sure I'll get the hang of it if you just show me the ropes… or rather the reins…' She lifted the leather straps and grinned. 'I don't even know how to hold these.'

Caroline showed her. 'And as long as you don't pull on them too hard, you'll be fine. Samson will just trot along behind us and—'

'Trot?' squeaked Flora.

'Sorry, a figure of speech… What I meant is that he'll just follow us. We normally ride two abreast but I'll ask the girls to ride together so that I can keep an eye on you. Just sit so you have a straight line through your ear, shoulder, hip and heels – don't let your legs fly forwards or lean back; then just relax and let your body move with the horse. You'll be fine.'

Flora tried to do as she was told but she felt anything but relaxed, and they weren't even moving yet. She nodded at Caroline. 'Okay,' she said. 'Let's do this.'

The first hour was the worst… *who was she kidding?* At this rate she wouldn't make it past the first ten minutes. Flora was hanging on for grim life and, despite a constant stream of chatter from Caroline and the others, she could scarcely take in what they were saying.

She concentrated on trying to go with the flow, letting her body move in time with Samson's, but just when she thought she'd got the rhythm right, she would miss a beat and bump uncomfortably in the saddle.

'Sorry, Caroline,' she said. 'I missed that. What did you say?'

They had just passed through a gateway into a field and the five of them were able to spread out a little.

'I was just asking what your wedding plans were?' she replied. 'I asked Hannah, but I got the feeling she didn't want to tell me, or she didn't know…'

Flora risked a glance across at her. 'No, well, Ned and I all happened so fast that we didn't really have time to discuss anything before I came to the farm and now, what with Fraser, well… but we were thinking of sometime in the autumn, when things are a bit quieter, hopefully.'

Chloe was riding to her right. 'Yes, that's awful isn't it, about poor Fraser. Oh, but it's still exciting though. We haven't had a wedding around here in ages. Not a proper one anyway. Mind you, you'll need to get a move on. Won't everywhere worth having be booked up? The Castle has a waiting list as long as your arm, but then I suppose if you're not in any hurry, you could always make it next year, that way you'd get where you wanted.' She gave Flora a searching look. 'You're not in any hurry, are you? You know…' She patted her stomach suggestively.

'God, no,' spluttered Flora, blushing bright red. 'Is that what everyone thinks?'

Chloe exchanged a look with the others. 'No, I'm sure Caroline was just teasing when she said that, weren't you? Although…'

'Oh, take no notice, Flora,' said Caroline. 'Of course I was. Chloe's just jealous because her fluttering eyelashes didn't attract Ned's attention. I think it's very romantic having such a whirlwind romance.'

Flora returned her smile but wasn't altogether sure how to take the girls' comments. While it was true she and Ned hadn't been together very long, they were both in their thirties and pretty sure of who they were and what they wanted from life. To her it didn't feel whirlwind, it just felt right. Except that the conversation felt miles away from her life at the moment. She'd almost forgotten that she and Ned were meant to be getting married at all.

'What's this castle place you mentioned though, Chloe? It's not an actual castle, is it? That sounds a bit grand for what we'd have in mind.'

'Oh, it's terribly grand, but that's why you have to have it there of course. Anyone who's anyone around here does. Its real name is Ravenswick Hall, and it's a hotel, but it has a turreted tower at each end of the building so everyone calls it The Castle. My cousin had her wedding there last June, and oh my God…'

Flora shifted her weight cautiously, trying to find a more comfortable position. She wasn't sure she wanted to be 'anyone' – she just wanted to be her.

'Well, that's one to bear in mind then. Thanks for the tip, Chloe. Obviously I'll have to see what Ned would like, and Hannah and Fraser too. I rather get the feeling that Hannah might like to have the reception at home…'

'No question about it,' said Caroline, from her other side. 'Which is all the more reason why you need to have somewhere in mind. Otherwise, if you don't have an alternative ready when it comes time to decide, you'll get stuck at the farm without you even realising it's happened.' She clicked her heels slightly against her horse's side. 'Come on, Flora,' she said. 'It's too nice a day to dawdle and we'll never get back in time for coffee at this rate.'

Flora felt Samson pick up his pace as Caroline pulled ahead of her, and she jostled uncomfortably in the saddle, trying to keep her balance.

'Don't go too fast,' she cautioned, 'or we'll never get back at all.'

'Oh, but you're doing brilliantly!' cried Emilie, moving from behind at a trot before slowing right down to walk alongside her. 'You're obviously a natural. We'll have you cantering in no time, just you see.'

Flora gave her a nervous smile.

The conversation continued in fits and starts as the group made their way out of the field and onto a track which wound its way through a small wooded area before beginning to climb. Flora managed to join in with some of it, but she didn't watch the television programmes they were discussing, or know the hairdresser's in town which had just *absolutely butchered Lucinda's hair*, and now that Samson was going uphill, she was pretty busy trying to master a slightly different technique for hanging on.

Fifteen minutes later however, she no longer cared as they crested the hill and the countryside opened up in front of her. It made every moment of the uncomfortable ride up there worthwhile. The land was still seasonally bare, but even in winter it couldn't hide its majestic beauty; swathes of bright yellow gorse followed the line of one slope, while on another, a purple haze from the heather that grew there. More than anything she wished she could climb from her horse and immerse herself in it, but she knew it was a futile desire. No one around her even seemed to notice the glory that surrounded them, and so she consoled herself with the knowledge that she could always come back another day, on foot.

Even with the wind whistling around them, Flora would have liked to stay up on the ridge for longer, but within moments the party was on the move again, turning directly back down the hillside as they followed a path through the gorse. By necessity, the horses fell into line, each following the other and, for a moment, conversation became next to impossible. Suddenly there was a burst of movement from the head of the line and a peal of laughter rang out. Flora sensed what was going to happen but, before she had time to even think, she felt Samson's muscles tense for a split second before they took off at speed, following the other horses. Catapulted forward, she just managed to cling onto the horse's neck as they shot down the slope, her thighs slapping horribly against the leather of the saddle. And bit by bit, the peak of her hat began to slip down over her eyes, lower and lower, until she could no longer see.

She clung on for grim death, blinded, and with the sound of her blood rushing in her ears, until by some miracle they finally came to a stop. How on earth had she managed to stay on? She pushed the hat up from her eyes and a wave of embarrassment swept over her. The others looked so composed and relaxed and she suddenly realised that, despite what it had felt like, they had hardly been going at speed at all. A canter possibly, but more likely just a trot. She felt her cheeks begin to burn.

Caroline turned and rode back towards her. 'Well, look at you! Well done! Sorry… Georgia's horse took off. It's what we normally do here and the others just followed her lead before I could stop them, but you did ever so well. Did you enjoy that?'

Flora's heart lifted a little; perhaps it hadn't been as bad as she had feared. But then it sank again even more rapidly. Caroline was simply trying to be kind, that was all.

She gave as bright a smile as she could muster and nodded, even though her heart was still racing and her shoulders beginning to ache.

From then on she gritted her teeth the whole way home and, just over an hour later, they arrived back beside the stable block. The girls slipped from their horses with practised ease, leaving Flora grappling with the tricky problem of how to dismount. In the end, the stable boy came to her rescue yet again.

Relieved to be back on solid ground at last, she looked around to see where the others had got to. They were huddled together a little distance away but, as Flora caught Georgia's eye, the haughty smile on her face faded as she realised Flora was looking at her. She could tell from Caroline's posture that whatever Georgia had said was hugely funny and, as Flora thanked the young stable boy for his help and walked towards them, she was struck by a sudden flash of insight. They were laughing at *her*.

Today wasn't about helping her to acclimatise, or giving her the opportunity to learn to ride, and neither was it about making friends. Everything about today had been orchestrated; from making such a fuss about her clothes to the carefully engineered conversations designed to make her feel left out. The speedy descent of the hill was no accident either. Caroline knew she couldn't ride and had shown her off to be the laughing stock she was. And worse, she had fallen for it. Taking their kindness and encouraging comments as genuine when in fact, as her chance catching of Georgia's eye had revealed, they were nothing of the sort.

A wave of angry hurt washed over her, but without her own car she was at Caroline's mercy for transport home, so it was another hour before she was finally able to reclaim her clothes, sit through the silence of the car ride back and slink through the door of the farmhouse. She would have collapsed in a chair and cried had her backside not been so sore.

Chapter 15

Flora leaned back in her chair and looked around the room. She didn't think she had ever been anywhere quite so soothing before. From the elegant colour palette of soft greens, powder blues and delicate pinks to the clean lines of the simple, unfussy furniture, everything was beautifully put together.

From the outside, Grace's home appeared to be a rambling series of white-washed buildings glued together at different angles and heights, but once inside, some very clever artistic touches had made the most of the building's originality and quirkiness and Flora had spent the first few minutes there staring around her in open-mouthed awe. It was worlds apart from the farm's dark colours and heavy oak furniture, and there was something about it that spoke to Flora's soul like an old friend.

Here, at last, was somewhere she didn't feel out of place with her bright clothes and wild hair, and Grace's warm welcome had already done much to dispel the memories of the morning's intense cleaning. She could still smell bleach, despite the beautiful vase of heavily scented lilies that sat on the table in front of her. She closed her eyes and breathed in deeply, feeling more relaxed than she had in days.

'Here we go,' said Grace, entering the room with a laden tray and heading for the table. 'I found us some biscuits too. And you, if you don't mind me saying so, look like you could do with some sugar.'

Flora pulled a face. 'Is it that obvious?' she said.

'Only a little,' replied Grace generously. 'And don't worry, I only know because I recognise the signs. Tough morning?'

'You could say that. And I must apologise for the smell… It's Eau de Dettol!'

Grace gave Flora an appraising glance. 'First things first,' she said. 'How's Fraser?'

'A lot better than yesterday,' answered Flora truthfully. 'Which was absolutely awful. I think it scared us all, seeing Fraser so frail. Today, things seemed a little better.'

'But?'

Flora smiled. 'Again, is it that obvious?'

Grace didn't reply but began to pour the tea before picking up a plate and offering Flora a biscuit. 'Take two,' she said. 'Otherwise I shall be forced to eat them all myself.'

It was a moment or two more before Grace finished pouring and handed Flora a cup. She took one for herself and settled in a nearby armchair with her own mug.

'So, let me guess, Hannah has now sterilised everything within a ten-mile radius of the farm and woe betide anyone who touches anything.'

'How did you know? Did your bees pick up the scent of disinfectant on the wind?'

Grace laughed out loud. 'No, don't forget I know Hannah of old and it's always been her reaction to a crisis. Clean everything to within an inch of its life. I can imagine how all this has sent her into overdrive.'

'And some. We all have different ways of coping, I know that. And at least today Hannah is feeling more positive instead of taking to her bed, even if she has driven me absolutely mad. But if I thought my muscles were sore from riding, it's nothing to what Hannah has put me through.'

'So, you've been riding as well? Blimey, you poor thing. You have had a rough few days.'

Flora grimaced. 'Yes, well I don't think I'll be going again, so that's a relief. Not only was I spectacularly bad but… how can I put this…'

'You don't need to explain, Flora,' interrupted Grace. 'I can't see how you and Caroline would ever really hit it off. Her friends are a rather particular kind of person and I'm pleased to say that you are not like them. Don't forget that I've known her for years and she's always been the same. Nice, pleasant enough, but… well, I don't think I'm her kind of person either.'

'Oh, thank the lord,' said Flora. 'I thought it was just me. Everyone else seems to think the sun shines out her…' She rolled her eyes.

'Now then,' said Grace. 'No more talk about Caroline, riding, Fraser, Hannah or Dettol – plenty of time for all that another day. I'm dying to see all these lovely prints you've brought with you, so come on, let's have a look.' She shuffled forward in her chair as Flora reached into the bag at her side.

'I haven't had a chance to finish the new ones I've been working on, but these will give you an idea.'

Flora handed over a folder stuffed full of her designs which had been put together over the last few years. She took a bite of her biscuit while she waited for Grace to flick through them. And then another as the minutes stretched out.

Grace didn't say a word the entire time, but finally she reached the last piece and slowly closed the folder. Her expression was inscrutable.

'How much do you charge for these?' she asked, blinking.

'Well, it depends. The original paintings usually around forty pounds and the prints fifteen. Greetings cards, postcards and the like, a lot less obviously.'

'It's not enough,' said Grace bluntly. She pulled out an original illustration that Flora had subsequently made into a print. It was of a hare sitting in front of a hedge, grass and dandelion clocks at its feet and three fat blackberries on a stem above its head. 'I would like this for myself,' she said. 'But I won't pay you any less than one hundred and twenty pounds.'

Flora nearly choked on a biscuit crumb. 'Grace, I can't accept that!'

'Why ever not?' she replied levelly. 'It's worth easily that much.'

'Because… because…' Flora threw up her hand.

'If you're going to say, because I'm a friend, don't you dare do yourself such a disservice.'

Flora shut her mouth, which had hung open, but there was no evading Grace's admonishing stare.

'Okay, okay!' She laughed. 'Blimey, remind me never to get on your wrong side.'

Grace held up the picture and beamed. 'Then you've made me very happy,' she said. 'I'm also honoured that you consider me a friend,' she added. 'And getting down off my high horse for a minute, I really do think that you should start taking yourself a little more seriously as an artist. That's not a criticism by the way, but modesty is far easier to adopt when you're not very talented, and you, my dear, have it by the bucket load. Bugger modesty.'

'Me?' Flora protested. 'What about you? I couldn't help noticing the wall-hanging you have in the hallway. And the fact that it's made with horse chestnut leaves. I bet you made it, didn't you? Only I've never seen anything quite like it before. It's absolutely stunning.'

Grace beamed. 'Do you know, it had been on the wall for nearly a week before my husband even noticed it,' she said. 'He doesn't *do* creativity, and if he had his way, the house would just be painted beige! It's one of my favourite pieces though and, as such, I can't imagine how anyone could fail to even notice it, let alone marvel at how wonderful it is. God, I'm so brilliant!' She laughed with abandon, throwing her head back so that her earrings swung wildly. It was the first time Flora had noticed them, a pair of crescent moons. 'You can tell I don't get out much, can't you?' she added, and then smiled a little shyly. 'In all seriousness, I'm glad you like it, that means a lot.'

The hanging was simply two layers of sheer fabric spun from the finest golden threads which had been sewn in sections so a series of pockets were formed, a bit like a sheet of ravioli. Each section was home to an individual leaf, in glorious autumnal shades of pale yellow, through to a deep blazing bronze.

'I love it, Grace, but you're going to have to tell me how you did it. They look like real leaves but I don't understand how you got them to stay fresh and not shrivel and die.'

Grace tapped the side of her nose. 'It's a neat trick, isn't it?' she replied. 'And so simple. You just take a small branch with several leaves on it, stand it in a glycerine solution for a few days and, as the plant drinks, the glycerine preserves the leaves so that they stay soft and retain their colour. I use them in decorations all the time.'

Flora's creative imagination went into overdrive imagining all the wonderful things she could do with this new trick. Oh, how she had missed talking about these things with someone. Ned understood. It was one of the things that had first attracted him to her, how he could marvel and wonder at the smallest of things – the sublime colour of a petal, the texture of a leaf. But here at the farm, there was no time for any of that and, given the current situation, no likelihood of returning to it.

'I should apologise now,' said Flora. 'Only I can see I'm going to be spending rather a lot of time here.'

Even as she said it, she knew that Grace wouldn't mind and that, moreover, the suggestion had been just inches from her own lips. Her smile curved around the rim of her cup as she drank the last of her tea.

'Then I'm glad you've come round,' said Grace, smiling warmly. 'Perhaps when we've finished our tea I can take you out to meet the hive, and see the garden too? If you're anything like me, all it takes is a bit of time outside and I find the inspiration just starts flowing.'

Flora nodded vigorously. 'Actually, one thing I'd really love is to paint your bees. Do you think they'd mind?'

'I should think they'd be honoured,' replied Grace, draining her cup. 'Let's go and ask them, shall we?'

She rose and beckoned Flora to follow her through the house, stopping by the front door so that Flora could collect her boots. From there, she led her down another wide hallway until they arrived in the enormous kitchen.

'How close to the bees do you want to get?' asked Grace. 'I have a spare hat if you want to get really personal, but sadly I can't show you inside the hive just yet, it really isn't warm enough, and they've only just started properly foraging again.' She raised her eyebrows. 'Although if you're nervous we can just watch them from further up the garden.'

Flora could feel her mouth drop open and made a conscious effort to close it. She hadn't imagined she'd be doing this today. 'I'm not frightened of them; wasps and hornets, yes, but not bees…'

'Up close it is then.'

Grace's garden was just as beautiful as she'd described, and nestled in among a huddle of trees towards the far end were her hives, three of them, a few feet apart. The low winter sun would soon be gone but, for now, its golden rays were slanting across the tops of the hives, filtered by the branches of the trees. From there the garden sloped away allowing an uninterrupted view across the fields, fields which, Flora knew, lay just behind the farmhouse.

'Come and stand on this side,' said Grace. 'That way you'll get a better view of the bees on the wing and you won't be directly in their flight path. They're only just beginning to gather food again, but the last few days of warmer weather have really helped.'

'Can I go closer?'

Grace nodded. 'As close as you're comfortable with. If any bees land on you just wait quietly until they fly off again. They'll soon work out that you're not bearing gifts of nectar.'

Flora took her phone from her pocket and crouched in the grass. Turning on the camera, she increased the zoom until she was focused right on the entrance to the hive. She took several shots straight off.

'They're beautiful,' she said. 'I love the way their wings catch the light, like tiny slivers of gold.' In her mind she was already beginning to see how she might transform the photos into art.

She took a couple more pictures and straightened again. 'One of my favourite designs is a print of a thistle head with a fat bumblebee feasting on it. And it's all the more extraordinary because the thistles were in a big bunch in a bucket outside my shop in the middle of a busy street. The bee just flew along and helped himself. I prayed no customers would come along for a few minutes so I could quickly sketch the scene, and that night I cut the lino block to make the print in record time. It was the most perfect composition, and I loved how the whole thing came together so effortlessly.'

Grace looked delighted. Flora could see she understood perfectly how that felt and she needed to say no more.

'Well, I hope that next time you come you'll have more wonderful work to show me,' said Grace. 'I'd love to see it. In fact, bring anything. I'm going to take what you've already brought to the shop if you don't mind, and put up a display. I'm certain we would sell them, but I'm only going to do it on one condition.' She looked at Flora expectantly.

'Which is…?'

'That you let me decide what price to put on them.'

Flora didn't reply and Grace took her silence for discomfort. 'I'm sorry,' she said quickly. 'I've embarrassed you.'

'No, it's not that.' Could she confide in Grace? Flora wondered. Everything she knew about this woman told her she could be trusted, but it was a big thing for Flora to take her into her confidence. She screwed up her courage; there were bigger things at stake here. 'I'm incredibly flattered that you like my art so much, and if you really think they'd attract a higher price then… well, that's incredible!' She couldn't help a glimmer of excitement slipping out. 'But, well, it's a bit of a difficult subject.'

'Talking about money always is. But spit it out, Flora, it's the only way.' She smiled in encouragement.

Flora took a deep breath. 'It's not a secret as such, what I do. In fact, Ned has wonderfully supportive but… well, since coming to the farm I don't have any means of making any money of my own and I don't like to ask Ned for it. He doesn't mind at all, but I'm trying to save a bit, you know, for the wedding and—'

She didn't need to finish. 'Don't worry,' Grace said. 'When they sell, because I'm sure they will, I'll make sure that just you and I know about it, how's that? I've spent years being a kept woman because my husband liked it that way, while *I* hated every minute. You don't need to say any more.'

Flora heaved a sigh of relief. It wasn't quite the whole truth, but it was close enough.

'Thank you, Grace. I really appreciate it.'

'Not another word,' she replied, smiling. She paused and a more sombre expression crossed her face. 'I know that things are a little difficult for you at the moment because of Fraser,' she said. 'And they have every chance of being difficult for some while to come, but your art is important to you, Flora, it makes you who you are. It brings you peace, and solace too when you need it, but it also fires you up and gives you the energy you need to go on. The joy that radiates outward from you at that moment is good for other people too. Hold onto it, Flora, don't ever let it go.'

Flora nodded, seeing the wisdom and sincerity in Grace's brown eyes. She had a feeling that something rather important had just happened and she stood for a few moments, drinking in the quiet and serenity. Whether that came from the view, the garden, the bees, or Grace herself, Flora wasn't sure, but it was profound.

'Penny for them?'

Grace had moved to stand beside her, with her face turned towards the sun.

The question surprised her. Flora hadn't realised she'd been thinking about anything much, but then she realised that she had. There was a vision in her head that was so clear it could have been real. And the smile that had curved around her lips had come completely in response to it as she looked out across the field that was no longer a grassy meadow. Instead, it had become a riot of colour from the rows and rows of flowers planted there, heads waving in the softest of breezes, just enough to release the most wonderful scent of summer…

She shook her head, laughing, suddenly a little embarrassed at her flight of fancy. 'You wouldn't believe it if I told you,' she said. 'I've always had the most overactive imagination…'

Grace regarded her quietly. 'No,' she said. 'I think I'd believe you. I've often stood here and imagined the future. Maybe that's what you've seen.'

A tingle ran up Flora's spine. That's exactly what it had felt like…

Chapter 16

Flora scarcely had time to think over the next few days. Her mornings started early, rising with Ned so that at least they could share a few minutes together before he left for the day. As he was working by himself, he no longer came in for a proper breakfast, but instead Flora would make up a parcel of sandwiches and fruit and take it over to the main barn, from where Ned would collect it at some point. It wasn't ideal. On the one hand, she was pleased that he wasn't eating a fat-laden breakfast every day, but on the other it meant that Ned didn't stop for a break either; with lunch consumed the same way, he was effectively working twelve-hour days.

Given Hannah's deep mistrust of hospital food, early mornings also included making lunch for Fraser which they would take with them when they visited later in the morning. Then, after lunch, they made yet more food ready for when Flora visited again after dinner, with Ned this time. Flora suspected that Fraser gave most of it away, but she didn't dare say anything.

In the scarce moments Flora wasn't helping to prepare food, she was systematically cleaning the house from top to bottom according to Hannah's instructions. Curtains were taken down and washed, carpets were cleaned, window sills and skirting boards were scrubbed. It left Flora exhausted and with little time to think about Grace's words, but they stayed with her, at the back of her mind, biding their time.

Now, one week and two days after his operation, Fraser was finally coming home, and Hannah was as nervous as a kitten. By now, she'd read all the information that the hospital had given her so many times she'd practically committed it to memory and would repeat it verbatim to anyone who dared suggest what Fraser would, or wouldn't, be able to do when he came home.

Despite her initial misgivings over the use of the dining room, Hannah had now taken the furnishing of the room very seriously and had seemingly brought most of Fraser's possessions down from their bedroom. The room was consequently stuffed to the gills with things that he might need, and just looking at it all made Flora feel claustrophobic.

'Come on, let's go and bring him home,' said Flora, as she watched Hannah plump the cushions on his bed for the zillionth time. 'He's waited long enough, let's not keep him any longer.'

'Yes, yes, of course.' Hannah looked flustered, and Flora took her arm.

'It will be okay you know,' she said. 'I know the thought of having him home is scary for all sorts of reasons, but we'll all be here to help, and the hospital wouldn't let him go if they didn't think he was ready.'

Hannah smiled gratefully. 'You're right, I know, but…' She trailed off, looking around the room again, and Flora began to wonder if she'd ever get in the car. Flora took a deep breath; Hannah wasn't the only one who was nervous.

*

After the last few days of milder weather, the temperature had been getting steadily colder as if reminding them that winter wasn't quite over yet. The evening was bitter and, as early as teatime, a frost was already beginning to form outside. But Flora didn't mind; being outside was far preferable to being inside, and Brodie, bless him, was a willing accomplice.

Fraser had been home now for exactly one hour and forty minutes and Flora already felt like screaming. In fact, if she heard Hannah ask him how he was feeling one more time, she probably would have. To give him his due, Fraser, despite catching her eye with a wry smile on one or two occasions, didn't seem to mind. He was just pleased to be home, delighted with his new room, and obviously exhausted from the journey.

She hadn't intended to walk as far as she had, but the clear sky was lit by an almost full moon and the garden was enticingly silvery and mysterious. It drew her onward until she realised that she was standing by the fence at the bottom. In front of her lay the sweep of fields she had walked through her first morning at the farm.

She hadn't a clue what had prompted her vision a few days ago, but it had been as clear to her as her surroundings were now and, as she stared around her, the echo of Grace's appeal to never let go of her art made the hairs stand up on the back of her neck.

Before speaking to Grace, Flora had almost come to terms with having to give up her creativity; at least she thought she had. She'd packed away her art materials and decided to throw everything she had at life on the farm. Except that now she realised that she just couldn't do that. The call of nature and art was stronger than ever, and it just might be the only thing that could save her sanity. She felt her heart lift slightly as her decision settled in her head. Fraser was home, and things would surely improve. Somehow she would just have to find the time she needed.

Turning around, she scoured the garden for Brodie and spotted him by the back door. Now used to her bouts of introspection, he was waiting patiently for her to finish so he could return to his place by the Aga. She hurried over and threw her arms around the old dog.

'You understand, don't you, boy,' she said. 'Otherwise I think I might go completely mad. I mean, I know I'm mad already, but mad in a bad way...'

Brodie's dark eyes glinted in the moonlight as he licked her hand. He was a very wise dog indeed.

'Come on then,' she said. 'Let's get back inside. Best foot forward and all that.'

But her heart sank again the moment she opened the back door to the sound of Caroline's trilling laughter coming from the kitchen. Resisting the urge to turn on her heels and run, she pasted on a smile and went to join the others.

Ned was sitting at the table but barely looked up when she came in; he was clearly exhausted. Hannah was standing in the middle of the room looking flustered and Caroline was just taking possession of a small tray filled with two mugs of tea and a plate of biscuits.

'Hannah, please go and sit down and take a breather for a bit. I can entertain Fraser for a few minutes, and I promise I will call if there's anything wrong.'

Hannah looked from Caroline to Ned and back again but, met with no reaction from Ned, reluctantly drew back a chair from the table and made to sit down.

'Well then, see if you can get him to eat something,' said Hannah. 'He's had virtually nothing all day.'

'Mum, we've only just had tea. He isn't going to want anything else,' said Ned, without looking up from the table.

'Yes, and he barely ate a thing. A couple of biscuits won't hurt.'

'Leave him to me,' said Caroline, smiling. 'I'll see if I can entice him.' The way she said it left Flora in no doubt that Caroline had every faith in her ability. 'Hi, Flora,' she added.

Flora nodded. 'Hi,' she replied. 'Blimey, it's freezing outside. It's very brave of you to venture out tonight.'

There was a tight smile. 'No, well, when I heard that Fraser was coming home today, I just had to pop over and welcome him back to the fold. I feel bad that I didn't get to see him in hospital, so it's the least I can do.'

'Just don't expect too much,' said Hannah. 'He's still very poorly.'

'Don't worry. I won't be too long.' She smiled directly at Flora, who went to take a seat opposite Ned.

'We might have to go and rescue him,' she whispered once Caroline had left the room. 'It's really kind of her to visit, but I would imagine that Fraser is worn out from the emotion of being home as much as anything. He probably just wants to be left alone.'

'Caroline's a very old friend though,' said Hannah.

'And Fraser might be pleased to see her,' added Ned.

Flora bit her tongue. 'Yes, of course,' she said instead. 'Sorry, I'm just concerned that Fraser will overdo things, that's all. We all are, I know.' She trailed off. There wasn't much else left to say.

'I might have that cup of tea now after all,' she added. 'Would anybody else like one?'

Ned groaned. 'Not for me, thanks, I'm sick of the sight of the stuff.'

'No, thank you, dear,' added Hannah.

Flora didn't really want one either – what she wanted to do was draw. With her new-found resolution still fresh in her head, she wanted to lose herself for several hours with just her pencils and a pad of paper for company. She looked around the kitchen but there wasn't a single other thing she could think of doing, and she really couldn't bring herself to sit at the table for hours and stare at the other two while making what felt uncomfortably like small talk.

On an impulse, she pulled her phone from her pocket to look properly at the photos she had taken the other day in Grace's garden and, although she had taken several of the flowers and foliage, it was the bees she was particularly keen to see. She clicked on the first of the pictures, a shot from a little distance away, and scrolled through them until she came to the ones she had taken close up. They were perfect. She was still smiling as she left the room.

When she returned a few minutes later, art materials in hand, Hannah had gone. Ned had also moved from the table and was now slumped on the sofa against the wall, the evening paper in his hands, but Flora could tell from the angle of his head and the steady rise and fall of his chest that he would be asleep in moments. She sat down and opened her sketchbook.

Totally engrossed in her drawing, it wasn't until a shadow fell over her that Flora realised Caroline had come back into the room, and was now standing right in front of her, peering at what she was doing.

She reached down and picked up Flora's phone, squinting at the image on the screen.

'The weird woman next door keeps bees,' she said idly.

Flora felt her shoulders hunch.

'Oh, do you mean my friend Grace?' she said. 'Yes, these are hers.' She carried on drawing, adding in another line of detail. 'They are truly amazing creatures,' she added, 'so I'm not surprised to find they've made a home with her. I only hope I can paint them well enough to do them justice.'

Caroline peered closer. 'Well, I can see you've a way to go yet, but that looks okay. Rather you than me though, I can't stand bugs...'

'Well, I rather love my flowers, so I'm happy to have the bugs as well,' she answered. 'It seems a small price to pay.'

She was aware of Ned putting the paper down. 'Thanks for coming over, Caroline,' he said. 'I'll see you to the door.'

Flora was grateful for Ned's interruption, but if Caroline was put out by his tone she didn't show it. 'I'll just go and give Hannah a hug,' she said. 'I'm sure she could use one after the day she must have had. What *are* you going to do?'

'About what, Caroline?' Ned challenged.

Flora didn't dare look at Ned, but stilled her pencil.

'Well, Fraser of course,' Caroline whispered back. She glanced towards the door in case Ned's raised voice had summoned anyone. 'Goodness, Ned, I know you warned me that seeing Fraser might be a little scary, but seeing him like that... ugh, it's awful. The poor man.' She paused for a moment. 'I'm worried about you, Ned, darling. How on earth are you going to manage? I can't see Fraser ever being able to get back to doing what he was.'

'We'll manage,' he said through gritted teeth.

For a moment his words hung in the air between them and then Caroline gave a soft sigh. 'Of course you will,' she replied in a soothing tone. '*Of course* you will. It was a figure of speech. I didn't mean that you wouldn't be able to manage, *of course* not, but I can see that Fraser is going to need a lot more than just a couple of weeks off.'

Flora placed her pencil down gently before she broke the nib.

'Caroline, the man has just had his chest carved open, of course he's going to need more than a couple of weeks off, nobody here thought otherwise. But we'll all muck in and we'll get through it. Together.'

'Yes, yes, of course. Well, I'll just get off now, don't worry about coming to the door, Ned, I can see myself out.'

It gave Flora little satisfaction to hear Caroline flustered, but her own heart was beating fast with indignation. She might be an old friend of the family, but who the hell did she think she was?

She turned back to her drawing as Caroline left the kitchen, trying to pick up from where she left off, but if her head had been full of worries before, now it was overflowing. She just hoped to goodness that Fraser hadn't heard any of their exchange.

When she had waited long enough for Caroline to be out of earshot, Flora looked back up to speak to Ned but was surprised to find that he had silently left the room. A trickle of unease pooled in her stomach. Had he gone to see his dad? She quickly rose from the table and went through to Fraser's room to check.

Ned was not there, however, and nor was Hannah. There was just Fraser, hunched in his chair, his face lowered towards his lap. At first she thought he was sleeping, but then she realised that his eyes were open.

'Fraser?'

He didn't even move.

'Fraser… are you okay?' There was a sudden flutter in her own chest.

She stood there, almost not wanting to move, until she saw a tiny nod of his head. She let out the breath she'd been holding, and moved forward to sit on the edge of the bed. The room was softly lit and, as she approached, he looked up slightly and the glow from the fire lit up his cheek and an expression full of sorrow.

'Oh, Fraser…' She took his hand, and knelt beside him on the floor. 'I'm so sorry…'

His shoulders heaved.

'They stopped my heart, Flora. Ripped me open like a chicken caught by a fox...' His words caught in his throat. 'And I'm thinking maybe they should have left me dead.'

He looked up then, and she could see his eyes, dark with pain. Her own eyes began to fill with tears.

'I'm so sorry, Flora,' he mumbled. 'So sorry...' He pulled his hand from Flora's grasp.

'What are you talking about, Fraser? You've got nothing to be sorry for, nothing at all...'

But Fraser shook his head, refusing to be comforted. 'I've ruined everything... And now this.'

'Listen to me, Fraser,' she said softly. 'You haven't ruined anything at all. You've been really poorly, that's all, but now you've come back to us.'

'Aye and no use to anyone.'

'Nonsense, try telling that to Hannah, or to Ned...' She ran her thumb over the back of his hand. 'And don't you dare believe anyone who tries to tell you otherwise. We both know that in many ways what comes next is going to be the hardest part. There may well be bloody awful days up ahead, but we'll tackle them one at a time until a day arrives that might not be quite so awful... then we might have a few which settle for being merely mediocre, and then before you know it, there might be a tiny glimmer of good, and I sincerely hope after that, completely and utterly wonderful. We will get through it, Fraser. I promise you.'

He squeezed her hand. 'That's a nice thought,' he said.

'That's life, Fraser. Whatever it throws at you, throw it back if you don't like it and wait for the good stuff. It will come, *if* you plant the seeds... and now you get to choose which ones to plant, just like the flowers in the garden... You might decide that some bits of your life need a good old prune, and other bits need more nurturing, but one thing is for sure, you're going to have plenty of time to figure out which. And that's okay, it really is.' She leaned forward to kiss his cheek. 'You take all the time you need. Just concentrate on getting better, and don't worry about anything else. Just know that every day brings you a step closer to where you want to be.'

'You're a good lass,' he replied, his voice gruff. 'I don't normally talk much about my feelings, but… I am grateful to you, for all you've been doing for us. And I'm pleased to see Ned so happy.'

She looked at him for a moment. His face was lined and drawn, but it was the face of a good man nonetheless and he didn't deserve to be made to feel like this. She could bloody murder Caroline. Old friend of the family or not, she should know better.

'You get some sleep,' she said after a moment. 'You've got a lot of catching up to do.'

She gently withdrew her hand. 'Is there anything else you need?' she asked, checking that the fire was still burning brightly.

'No, I reckon I'm all set.' His gaze drifted to the table beside him, which was laden with drinks and tempting treats, newspapers, books… She caught the ghost of his smile.

'You're a lucky man having Hannah to look after you,' she said.

'Aye, that I am, lass, that I am.'

She dropped a kiss on his forehead. 'Then I'll say goodnight, Fraser.' She rose and walked to door. 'Sweet dreams,' she added, but Fraser's head was already bent.

It wasn't until Flora was halfway down the hallway on her way back to the kitchen that Fraser's words suddenly came back to her. *I've ruined everything,* he had said. *And now this.* Two sentences. Two separate admissions.

Oh, Fraser, she thought. Guilt over his heart attack she could understand. But what else have you done?

Hearing voices coming from the living room, she doubled back to speak to Ned. Coming closer, she realised that the voices were low and urgent and she took a couple more paces, wondering whether it was a bad time to interrupt. Hearing Ned's grumbling tone, she hoped that he was already chewing Hannah's ear about Caroline, but his voice became clearer as she neared the door.

'We can't keep pretending this isn't happening, Mum. Sooner or later we're going to have to do something about it, and the worse it gets the harder it's going to be to keep it a secret. And Caroline isn't going to keep her mouth shut forever, she's made that very clear. Once that happens, we won't just be losing our livelihood but our good name as well. We'll be laughing stocks of the whole community, and I'm sorry, I don't think this is going to pass. Think how Dad will feel if that happens. What he's been through already is bad enough, but this? This could bloody well kill him!'

Chapter 17

Flora knew she wouldn't get a wink of sleep. She had crept away after hearing Ned's words last night, tiptoeing back down the hallway with her heart thumping in her chest. She had retaken her seat at the table and pretended to draw for a while until Ned came back into the kitchen acting as if nothing had happened. Shortly afterwards, he had announced that he was heading up to bed. She followed him after a few minutes, lying awake beside him, everything she wanted to say locked tight inside her as the clock ticked through the hours until morning.

When Ned woke to milk the cows, she'd taken the coward's way out and feigned sleep until he'd left the room. What would she have said to him? He was keeping something important from her and surely if he trusted her she would have been part of the conversation last night? Instead, *she* was one of the people from whom they were keeping the secret and that was what hurt most of all. They were supposed to be a couple, a team supporting one another through the good times and the bad, but last night she had felt excluded. After everything that she had done to help with Fraser, she had never felt less like a part of the family. It made her silently question whether Ned really loved her at all.

And then there was Caroline, the perfect blue-eyed blonde who Flora had never taken to and had chastised herself for feeling jealous of. But after last night she finally realised how much Caroline had insinuated herself into their lives. How she was always around, laying tiny barbs with her words, faking friendship and pretending to be caring when, in fact, she was anything but. Flora had no idea what hold Caroline had over Ned and his family, but something certainly wasn't right. She gave a shiver when she thought how calculating Caroline's behaviour had been last night.

Flora swung her legs over the side of the bed and sat up. She had two choices: she could either confront Ned and demand to know what was going on, or she could pretend that nothing was happening. Except, it wasn't really a choice; from what Ned had said, time was not a luxury they had.

It was, however, still early and she doubted whether Hannah would be up yet, preferring to stay by Fraser's side, which meant that she would have a little time on her own to gather her thoughts. Probably not much time, but it was better than nothing. She pulled on some clothes and went quietly downstairs and into the kitchen.

'I'll take you out in a minute, boy,' she whispered, running a hand along the soft fur of Brodie's back as she passed him on her way to grab a glass of water. The study was the obvious place to start looking, but first there was somewhere else she wanted to check, and she kicked herself for not having followed her instinct before. She crept past the door to the dining room, which was still closed, and went into the living room.

The mugs from the night before were still on the blanket box and she put them on the floor before lifting the lid to peer at all the things she had moved there a few days ago – more specifically, the thing which had been hidden inside a roll of tablecloth. Just what was it that someone had wanted to conceal?

She lifted out the piles of fabric and dumped them unceremoniously on the floor, pulling them apart until she found what she was looking for. She pulled the folder onto her lap, turning it around until it was the right way up and she could inspect the contents.

The first page was a bill, over-stamped with a banner of red ink which declared it to be a final warning. Flora blanched when she saw the amount. It was dated a month ago, just a few days before she had come to the farm, in fact. The second piece of paper was also a bill, as was the third. The fourth was a solicitor's letter and the fifth... Flora let the papers fall to her lap, her stomach churning with anxiety. There must have been twenty-odd invoices in the file and between them they spelled out the fact that the farm was in debt to the tune of something approaching forty thousand pounds.

She had to force herself to look through the rest of the papers, not because she wanted to, but because now that she knew the farm was in so much debt, she needed to know why. There must be some clue that would explain what had happened. The farm accounts were kept on the computer in the study and yet these invoices had been separated from the others. Why was that?

She checked the dates again and realised that they spanned a period of a few months from before Christmas last year. It was now February. What was evident though was that these were bills for routine items, run-of-the-mill things that the farm would need on a regular basis; they had not been incurred through some huge unforeseen calamity that necessitated the purchase of new and expensive equipment, for example. In a way this was far worse, because it meant that the farm was simply not holding its head above water.

She glanced up towards the living room door and then back down at the folder in her hands. It had been hidden among a pile of tablecloths, in the dining room... Somehow this didn't strike her as something that Ned would do; the dining room was Hannah's domain, and if she had hidden the invoices then she must know the full extent of the problem. But who else knew? Did Ned? Or Fraser? Had the stress of being in so much debt been a contributing factor in his heart attack? She thought back to the conversation she had overheard the night before, trying to recall the actual words spoken.

After a few more moments she gathered together the invoices and placed them back in the folder but, instead of putting them back in the blanket box, she simply piled everything else back in and got to her feet. Pausing at the living room door, she stole another glance down the hallway and walked calmly in the other direction, slipping into the study where she put the folder down on the large desk and pulled the door behind her as she left. Almost closed, but not quite.

Five minutes later she was back again, carrying a box of her art supplies and, after nudging the door open with her hip, plonked it on the desk. This time when she left, she made sure the door was firmly closed behind her. Then she went back through to the kitchen, opened the back door so that Brodie could go out for a wee and stood with the reassuring solidness of the wood behind her, gasping in lungful after lungful of the sweet morning air.

Her head was spinning. Half an hour ago she had woken up wanting answers. Now that she had them, or some of them at least, she wasn't so sure she wanted them at all. Nor was she sure if she was brave enough to find out all the rest of the pieces of the jigsaw, and what they would mean. A few weeks ago, she had come to the farm in love, excited, and hopeful for a new future. Now, though, it felt like the rug was being pulled out from under her, and the dreams she had were slipping further and further away. The tentative grasp she'd thought she'd had on life at the farm had proved itself to be nothing more than an illusion, and as for her relationships, perhaps they were the biggest illusion of them all. The trouble was, you couldn't demand honesty from people when you weren't being entirely honest yourself…

She gave a wan smile as Brodie came back into view, his tail waving gently as he spotted her. It looked set to be another beautiful day, but this early, still a little cool. Given a choice she would happily go back to bed and sleep for the rest of the day, but if she was to have a future at all, if any of them were, she needed to get to the bottom of this mystery, and soon.

With her head so distracted, Flora really hadn't thought she would be able to draw at all but, surprisingly, after about ten minutes of thinking she would have to give up, she suddenly found the flow and the calm that came with it. So it was not until a good couple of hours later that she became aware of voices in the hallway, and footsteps getting closer.

It was Ned who appeared, his head bobbing around the door, not really expecting to see her, and almost doing a double take when he did. The look of surprise on his face was quickly replaced by a grin.

'Blimey, I thought I'd lost you for a minute. Mum's just making a brew, would you like one?'

'Oooh, yes please. Sorry, I got carried away and forgot the time.' She checked her watch as if to corroborate her statement. 'I'm gasping for a cuppa actually.' She dropped her paintbrush into the glass of water on the desk, now a murky shade of brown, and tipped her head to one side, surveying her work. 'I'm rather pleased with that,' she said. 'Here, have a look.'

She waited while he came around the desk to stand behind her. 'What are you doing in here anyway?' he asked casually.

'Hmmm?'

He bent to kiss the top of her head. 'I just wondered why you were in here. Wouldn't you have more room in the kitchen?' He reached over her shoulder and laid a finger on the edge of the painting. 'God, that's gorgeous.'

'Thank you,' she said. 'One of Grace's bees.' She picked up the painting, carefully holding it out in front of her to view it from a different angle. 'Sorry, what did you ask me?'

Ned smiled. 'Nothing really. I just wondered why you were hiding away in here, when you'd have more room to spread out in the kitchen.'

Flora pulled a face as she turned to look up at him. 'I thought I'd give your mum and dad a bit of space. And also, if I'm in the kitchen, I have to constantly clear away my things whenever it's meal time. I can leave my stuff out in here, no one seems to use this room much.' She grinned. 'It's been great actually, I've got masses done. I'm ready for a break now though.'

She studied Ned's face. He looked tired, even though she was pretty sure he had slept. 'Are you stopping for a proper rest?' she asked. 'You look as if you could do with one.'

He ran a hand through his hair. 'Just… you know. Dad and everything… It's been a bit mental.'

Flora nodded. 'Hasn't it just… and quite possibly going to get more mental before it's finished.' He frowned at her, confused, but she carried on before he had a chance to ask his question. 'Actually, can we have our tea in here?' she asked. 'Only there's something I wanted to ask you about and I'd rather your mum… you know, I don't want to hurt her feelings.' She kept her face bright and open.

Ned looked slightly anxious but he agreed. 'I think Mum might take her tea with Dad anyway. I'm not sure he's allowed out of her sight just yet.'

'Ah… an astute observation,' she said. 'Understandable, but…'

Ned looked at her for a moment and she could see the worry written deep into his grey eyes. 'I think I'd be the same,' he said. 'If it were you. I'd never want to leave your side.'

Flora swallowed. Oh God, this was going to be even more difficult than she thought it was going to be. How could she do this to him, now, with everything else that was going on? Except that this *was* one of the things that was going on, and if she didn't do something about it, who knew where it might end.

She raised a hand and stroked the side of his face. 'I'd be happy with that,' she said, feeling a lump rise in her throat. 'Now go and fetch my tea before I die of thirst…' She gave a cheeky grin as Ned rolled his eyes.

'Yes, ma'am,' he said.

She sat back in her chair once he'd gone, her eyes closed, breathing deeply. This would be so much easier if she didn't love him quite so much. He was big, awkward, far too much man to fit inside his body, so that his arms and legs did strange things at times, but all that did was just endear him to her even more. Everything he did was born out of the best of intentions, even if at times his actions went wide of the mark. But then he didn't profess to have all the answers and, she was well aware, neither did she.

He was back before she had time to properly prepare what she was going to say. But then there was no right way; she had realised that while wrestling with her thoughts that morning. She just needed to bring up the subject and see where it went, but that was easier said than done.

Ned put down two mugs on the table and a plate with two slices of cake which he held in his other hand. He drew up a chair in front of the desk, the opposite side to her, and then he sat down, his elbow propped up, his chin in his hand. He gazed up at her, an overtly adoring look on his face. 'I'm all yours,' he said, looking for all the world like a lovesick puppy.

She sat back slightly. 'Ned, don't,' she said gently. 'This is serious.'

'Are you all right?' he asked, immediately sitting up and searching her face.

She smiled and reached out a hand. 'I'm fine, honestly. But I wanted to talk to you. About Caroline,' she added.

A look of alarm raced across his face. 'I know she can be a bit of a pain but—'

She cut him off. 'I think we both know it's more than that,' she said, taking a deep breath. 'I've had trouble figuring her out ever since I arrived,' she started. 'And at first I thought it was just me… feeling a bit jealous or something because she always looks so perfect, and she has an amazing figure, and I don't.' She held up her hand. 'No, let me finish. It always seemed on the outside as if she was being friendly, taking me out riding, introducing me to her friends, helping me out, but somehow… every time she did, I felt as if she were trying to make a point, or was laughing at me.'

'Look, I know she wasn't very complimentary about your painting yesterday and you're right, I—'

'It wasn't that, Ned.' She gave him a very direct look. 'I'm certainly not upset by a comment about my work from someone who doesn't have an artistic bone in their body, or any appreciation of the beauty of nature. Nor am I upset about the fact that she's always bloody round here, or that she never has a hair out of place and most of the time I look like I've been dragged through a hedge backwards, because, actually, I'm comfortable with how I look. I like the clothes I wear, and the way my hair never knows what it's doing from one minute to the next. They're me, Ned, that's who I am, and I can't pretend to be anything else, nor do I want to. With me, what you see is what you get and, as soon as I realised that, I understood what has really been bugging me about Caroline, which is that sense I've had that she's been playing some sort of game.'

She stopped for a moment to draw in another breath and to quieten her voice which was beginning to rise. 'And so, when I overheard you talking in the living room with your mum last night about some hold over you that Caroline seems to have, it started to ring my warning bells.'

She lifted her sketchbook from the side of the desk as if tidying her things. The folder full of invoices was underneath, and now in plain sight.

'And then I found these,' she said, and patted the folder. 'What's going on, Ned?'

She watched as the colour drained slowly from his face.

'Where did you find those? Did Mum...?' He looked about, as if the answer might be found in the room, although he didn't try and deny all knowledge of their existence, she noticed.

'No, your mum didn't leave them here. I found them where she'd hidden them when I moved the things from the sideboard so that Fraser could use it. A simple mistake; it should never have happened, and I'd be none the wiser now if I hadn't...' She trailed off, giving him a chance to explain. She raised her eyebrows, but still nothing. 'And of course, knowing that they were private, I didn't look at them, simply ferried them to their new home. Because I thought that obviously if they were important, as your future wife, you would tell me all about them.'

Ned looked like his world was about to end. All his breath left his body in one ragged rush and he sagged in his chair.

'Please don't hate me, Flora,' he said. 'Please, please don't hate me. I couldn't bear it if you left. You're the only thing that's good in any of this.'

He looked up, his eyes suddenly full of tears.

Flora leaned forward. 'Ned, I never said anything about leaving.' She reached forward, desperate to take his hand, but he left it, unmoving in his lap. 'And I could never hate you.'

'You don't understand,' he said, refusing to meet her eyes.

'Then tell me, Ned,' she urged.

There was silence for several seconds, no words, no movement; nothing to break the wall that was threatening to rise between them.

'I can't,' he said finally. 'Because when I tell you about the mess I've got myself into, you'll never speak to me again…'

Chapter 18

There was a wild rushing noise in Flora's head. She looked at the folder beside her on the desk, a can of worms that suddenly promised to contain far more than she had ever anticipated. Her heart was thumping in her chest; she was scared now because, however much Ned thought was at stake here, he didn't know the half of it. How on earth had they got to this point?

The study door was still open, and on shaking legs she went to close it before pulling her chair around the desk to sit beside Ned. She took his hands in hers and kissed them.

'I love you,' she whispered, praying that it was enough, and then she prepared herself to have her heart broken.

A slow tear tracked its way down Ned's cheek. 'I don't even know when it started,' he began quietly. 'A few years ago now… Our equipment was too old and we had to refit the milking parlour to keep up with regulations. The dairies were demanding more and more but paying less and less, but we had no choice if we wanted to keep going. I don't think we ever fully recovered from that. From then on things just snowballed. We were constantly on the back foot, trying to do the right thing by our cows but losing out financially because of it. That's still the case…' He shuddered. 'I'd rather sell the whole herd than resort to dairy's "dirty secret" even though it's the only way to claw back any money. Or rather, to stop any more of it flowing down the drain.'

Flora tilted her head. Debt she understood, but dirty secrets?

'When you think about it, it's kind of ironic that you're a vegetarian. I'm marrying a girl who doesn't like killing things and yet it's by doing what we believe to be the right thing that we've got into so much trouble…'

'Now you've completely lost me,' she said. 'Sorry, Ned, but what are you talking about?'

'Killing male calves as soon as they're born.'

She shook her head. She really didn't want to get into an argument about the ethics of eating meat. That wasn't what this was about. But then she realised what Ned had said. Her head snapped up.

'You do *what*…?'

Ned was quick to jump in. 'No, *we* don't… it's something we swore we would never do, but it's becoming common practice again. We're a dairy farm, Flora, think about it. Cows only give milk when they've had young, so we breed from them, but it's only the female calves that are useful to us. The male calves are raised and sold on later, but they're not bred for their meat and so we get very little for them. In fact, it costs us more to rear them than we get back when we sell them.'

'So you're saying that other farmers…' She trailed off, making a cutting motion across her throat. 'As soon as they're born?'

Ned nodded. Flora felt physically sick. 'And it's this that has put the farm in debt?'

'Partly, yes. It's certainly what's kept us in debt. It's a vicious cycle.'

Flora looked at his bowed head and twirled the ends of her hair through her fingers. She didn't want to give Ned a hard time, though; he wore his shame as if the word was written through him like a stick of rock.

'But what I don't understand is why, if you were in debt, you didn't do something about it? Couldn't the bank help you out or something, just until you got back on your feet?'

There was silence for a moment and she could see Ned's jaw working.

'Oh God, you did, didn't you? That's what this is about, you owe money to the bank…'

But Ned shook his head violently. 'I wish we did,' he said bitterly. 'It would have been so much simpler.' He hung his head again. 'What I did was just plain stupid. I kid myself sometimes that it was because we were desperate, and I was scared, worried about the effect the stress of being in debt was having on Dad, but actually I was just incredibly stupid, and naive… and so I took the easy way out. If I'd have stopped for a minute to think about Caroline's offer, I'd have seen it for what it was – part of her game plan – and now of course, all the things I should have thought about are coming back to haunt us.'

Flora's stomach gave a lurch. She had almost forgotten that her talking about Caroline was how the conversation had started, and now here she was again.

'Caroline?' She could feel the dread beginning to bloom in the pit of her stomach. 'Ah, I see,' she said quietly. 'She lent you the money, didn't she? What did she do, ask Daddy?'

There was no reply.

The pieces of the jigsaw were beginning to come together. 'So, Caroline lends you the money, or rather, her father does, and now what? What could they possibly want in return…?' She stared at Ned, her brain racing ahead. And then it came to her. Of course, it was obvious. 'We're sitting right in the middle of what he wants, aren't we? More land to add to his empire…' And then another thought occurred to her. 'Oh my God… Fraser doesn't know about the loan, does he?'

Ned's shoulders dropped even lower. 'No,' he said quietly. 'And I know we should have told him, but somehow I thought I could resolve it all without him ever knowing. Which just goes to show how pathetic I really am. That's why those invoices were hidden. They were never entered into the accounts, but paid using the money that Caroline's father lent us. Dad knows we're still struggling but he doesn't know the half of it.'

'Oh, Ned…'

He held up his hands. 'I know,' he said. 'I know; you don't need to tell me. But at the time it made perfect sense. I could see the effect that all of this was having on Dad's health and I honestly thought that by keeping it to ourselves, Mum and I were at least saving him that anguish. Except that now of course he's more poorly than ever, and I can't bear to think what it might do to him when he does find out.'

'But you are going to have to tell him, Ned.' Flora looked at the beaten expression on his face. 'Because even though every fibre of my being is telling me that under no account must Caroline be allowed to gain anything from this situation, the fact of the matter is that you now owe her father a considerable amount of money. And given that you have no way of being able to pay them back in the foreseeable future, in effect they already own a good portion of your land…' Her mind was freewheeling.

'But there must be a way to resolve all of this,' she said resolutely. 'And I'm damned if I'm going to let them win, so we're just going to have to bloody well find out what it is.'

As soon as she said it, the vision she'd had for the farm came back in a flash, a dream that up until now she'd thought was just a wild flight of fancy brought on by an overexcitable imagination. But could it really be the way out of all this? She sat up straight, needing to think.

'Flora?' Her sudden movement brought Ned out of his own reverie. 'Are you okay?'

She stared at him. 'Yes,' she said. 'I think I am.' She shook her head. 'Oh, but you're going to think I'm completely mad…' She touched a hand to his face, pressing her thumb to his tears. 'I've had an idea, not just now, it came to me a few days ago and I dismissed it, but now…' She lifted her head and shut her eyes, trying to capture the images that she'd seen so vividly from Grace's garden. 'Actually, it wasn't an idea, more like a vision,' she added, feeling a swell of excitement rise within her.

'I think you'd better tell me,' said Ned, a frown wrinkling his brow.

'Flowers,' she said, opening her eyes and turning to him. 'I saw rows and rows of flowers, in the field between our garden and the bottom of Grace's. It was where I walked the very first morning I was here. Oh, I knew it was special, Ned.' A sudden welling of emotion threatened to overcome her.

'Flowers?' he queried. 'What kind of flowers?'

'Every kind,' she breathed. 'We were growing them. It was that day I went over to visit Grace, when I took my prints for her to see,' she added. 'We talked about art and she took me into her garden, and then after we'd looked at the bees, she told me never to give up being creative and as I looked out at the view…' She stopped, aware that she was talking in one long sentence, hardly drawing breath. 'I had a vision of the field, you couldn't really call it anything else, Ned. It felt like it was real, like it was our future…' She lifted her hands from her lap and then let them fall again in a helpless gesture.

He took her fingers. 'Then what did you see?'

'Well, nothing, it was just the flowers, but I knew they were ours and that we'd planted them.' She looked up into his face, blushing from the absurdity of what she'd just said.

To give him his due, Ned didn't laugh. Instead he entwined his fingers tighter with hers. 'So what did it mean?' he asked.

'I've been buying flowers from wholesale florists for a huge chunk of my life, Ned, but I've never before thought of becoming one. But that's what we were, I'm sure of it; a flower farm.'

He sat back, holding her look. 'I rather like flowers,' he said eventually. 'Did I ever tell you that?' He swiped a hand across his face, grimacing, drawing in a deep breath before visibly pulling himself together. 'And if it hadn't been for that one single spur-of-the-moment visit to your shop with your beautiful flowers, I would never have met you.' He kissed the back of her hand. 'And on that day my life blossomed into something I never ever thought I'd have. I am such an idiot, Flora,' he said. 'And what I hate more than anything is that I can't give you the kind of life I want to, the kind of life you deserve.'

'Oh, Ned…' She leant forward to kiss him. 'You are an idiot… but only because I'd be happy with any kind of life, just as long as I get to spend it by your side.'

She looked up into his gentle face, still full of anxiety, and realised just how true her words were, how much she loved him. Ned couldn't know it, of course, but she knew exactly how he was feeling. And time had taught her that, however hard it was, there was always a way around debt. She might have learnt that the hard way but she had learnt it, and now it meant that they could sort this out together because, as long as they had each other, nothing else really mattered.

'Ned, there's something—'

He pulled her into a kiss that silenced her words and left her in no doubt how he was feeling.

'I don't know what I'd do without you,' he said, his fingers still stroking the side of her face. 'I tell you what a monumental mess I've made of things and you calmly come up with a brilliant idea. You should be angry at me or something... I don't know...' And then his face split wide into the lopsided grin she would never tire of seeing. 'Do you really think your idea would work?' he asked. 'Here, I mean. Could we actually start a business selling flowers?'

'Well, there's really only one way to find out,' she replied.

Ned eyed the two mugs that were still on the desk where he had put them what felt to Flora like a lifetime ago. Their contents were stone cold. 'Shall I go and make some more tea?' he asked.

*

An hour later Ned had reluctantly returned to work, but, before he did, between them they had filled the air with an excited babble and Flora had filled two pages of her notebook with scribbled ideas, thoughts, and a vague to-do list that seemed both thrilling and insurmountable at the same time.

It was a reversal of what she'd been doing for years, thinking as a florist buying from a wholesaler, whereas now she needed to think as a wholesaler selling to a florist. Her thought processes were working backwards. She knew flowers. She knew when they were in season, at their best, lead times for ordering, the key celebrations throughout the year traditionally marked with flowers, and which flowers were popular for each. Now, she had to think about how long those flowers took to grow, when they would need to be planted, what conditions they would need, and who would be buying them from her. How, how, how... She underscored the word several times in her notebook. Her list of questions was getting longer by the minute, but that was okay, because Flora knew where she could find the answers.

She practically ran up the stairs and yanked open the bottom drawer of the big chest beside the window. She had stashed all her old books there, never thinking for one minute that she would need them again, but loath to throw them away. It had been a huge part of her life, and one that she thought had died. Perhaps, after all, it had simply been sleeping. She hugged the thought to her as she lifted out the topmost book. It was her bible; her florist's guide to flowers, growers, and associations. And within its pages would be the starting places for all the help she needed.

Ducking her head into the kitchen, she was relieved to see that Hannah was nowhere in sight. With the door to the dining room closed it was likely that she and Fraser were taking an afternoon nap, and so, grabbing a slice of cake from the tin, Flora returned to the study and switched on the computer. Ned had given her the password and with any luck she would have a few hours of uninterrupted research.

The first thing she did was google a list of florists in the local area, and then a list of hotels; big posh places, the type that made a huge fuss over weddings. Ten minutes and a phone call later and she had an appointment with the wedding planner at The Castle, or rather Ravenswick Hall as she must remember to call it. Tomorrow morning at ten sharp, by which time she would need to know exactly what they were offering.

Chapter 19

Ravenswick Hall was only a fifteen-minute drive away, but Flora made sure she got there twenty minutes early. As a prospective bride looking for a wedding venue she would have wanted to do a little research on her own, but as a prospective supplier it was even more important.

The hotel's website had given her a fair idea of what to expect. The building was its obvious selling point, looking like something out of a Walt Disney film and set in lush parkland. A majestic, sweeping drive led up to a grand entrance complete with stone portico atop a flight of steps which would provide the most wonderful posing place for photographs. No flowers though, Flora noticed, as she passed through.

Inside, the entrance hall was a sumptuous mix of polished wood and marble, with huge chandeliers hanging from an impressively high ceiling, but whether original to the building or by some clever alteration, the space was divided into a series of smaller areas and was cosy and intimate. The reception desk was ahead of her to the right, but Flora ignored it and walked through into a series of three interconnecting lounge rooms. She counted a total of four arrangements of flowers, which, including the two at either end of the reception desk, made six in total.

She sat for a moment in a window seat, trying to collect herself. She probably wouldn't get the opportunity to talk in any detail today, but she might, if luck was on her side, get a further appointment. She caught the eye of a businessman sitting a little distance away enjoying a cup of coffee. He seemed determined to extract every ounce of creamy froth from his cappuccino by swiping his finger around the inside of the mug and transferring its contents to his mouth. She smiled as she caught his eye, and dipped her head as she acknowledged his embarrassment. She would have done exactly the same.

The sun was shining at least and, after a few more moments, Flora got up and walked to the reception desk to find out if the bright spring morning had put the wedding planner in an amenable mood.

She had been standing waiting for a few moments when she became aware that there were anxious voices coming from behind the desk. An impossibly tall, thin young woman had appeared and was deep in conversation with the receptionist, who inclined her head towards Flora on more than one occasion. The tall woman had glossy chestnut hair pulled high into a ponytail that added at least another three inches to her height. It swung as she gestured, mesmerising Flora to such an extent that she scarcely realised that the woman was now coming towards her.

'Flora?' she asked, hand outstretched, a broad smile welcoming her to the hotel.

'I am so sorry to keep you waiting, and indeed I must apologise. I know you were expecting to see Michelle today, but I'll be perfectly honest, the poor girl is suffering from the most horrendous morning sickness and I had to send her home ten minutes ago. She's in no fit state, I'm afraid, but we mustn't let you down. I'm Kate, the Events, Business and Hospitality Manager. I hope that's okay?'

Flora couldn't believe her luck.

'Shall we go and make ourselves comfortable to begin with and I can answer some of your questions. I've organised some coffee... or tea if you prefer?'

'No, coffee's lovely, thank you,' replied Flora, following Kate's sashaying walk through the lobby.

They reached the same area of the lounge where Flora had previously been sitting. 'Is here okay for you?' asked Kate, indicating a seat. 'It's such a beautiful morning, and the view from here – well, you can see for yourself how special it is.'

Flora sat down, breathing deeply. Kate looked entirely relaxed and Flora tried to mirror her pose, praying that her knee wouldn't start jiggling, which it often did when she was nervous.

A tray of refreshments appeared the minute she sat down, but instead of busying herself with the coffee, Kate sat back and studied Flora.

She leant forward. 'Can I just say how much I love your dress,' she said. 'I'm probably not supposed to, but it's gorgeous. And your boots. I love my job, Flora, but honestly I have to wear suits all week, and it practically kills me. Oh, for some colour!'

Flora's mouth dropped open. It was the last thing she expected and she didn't know whether Kate was telling the truth or just very good at her job. She decided to go for the former. It would make what she had to say so much easier.

'Thank you!' She smiled in return. 'Actually, I thought about wearing something today that was a little tamer, a little less... me,' she said, 'but then I decided, what the heck. How I'm going to wear a wedding dress that's just one colour, and white at that, is beyond me...'

The two women smiled at one another.

'So when are you planning on getting married, Flora?' She indicated the coffee pot and Flora nodded.

'We haven't actually set a date yet,' she admitted. 'Is that a problem?'

'Not at all... Milk and sugar?'

'Just milk, thank you.'

'You need to take your time and have a good look around before you commit to a venue,' added Kate. 'It absolutely must be perfect for you, and I'm so pleased that you've decided to have a look at what Ravenswick can offer. May I ask how you know about us?'

'Oh, word of mouth, of course.'

There was a satisfied smile as Kate passed Flora a cup.

'Now, I hope you have a million questions for me to answer, because I'd much rather answer those than talk at you for an hour. You can get a huge amount of information from our website, but I find that's not usually the things that most brides want to know.'

Flora was beginning to feel a little bit guilty. Kate was far too nice and she really would have to fess up soon, otherwise she would end up not saying anything.

'Is everything all right?'

Damn, thought Flora, she was perceptive too.

It was no good, she was going to have to come out with it. She'd probably be shown the door in two minutes but it was worth a shot.

'Yes, fine,' began Flora. 'Except perhaps that I haven't been entirely open with you. I am getting married,' she added quickly, 'so I'm not here under false pretences, just that I'm here for another reason as well.'

Kate took a reflective sip of her coffee, but she couldn't hide the beginnings of a smile at the corner of her mouth. 'Then perhaps it's time for me to admit that I'm not being entirely honest either.'

Flora's cup rattled in its saucer. 'You hate my dress?' she suggested, the beginnings of a blush rising up her neck.

To her enormous relief, Kate grinned. 'No, I *love* it, I really do. But I have to confess to knowing who you are. I twigged as soon as I saw your name. Flora Dunbar… there can't be too many people around here with the same name.'

Oh, God, what had she done now? Her face must be scarlet.

'But you don't need to worry,' continued Kate. 'Because now I'm just as intrigued as you are. I really didn't expect to see you here – knowing Hannah, I'd have thought that the wedding would be up at the farm?'

'You know *Hannah*?' Flora's cheeks were getting hotter by the minute.

'Yes, and Fraser and Ned of course…' Kate laughed out loud. 'I'm Caroline's cousin.'

'But…' Flora opened her mouth to say something and then thought better of it. This really wasn't going the way she had planned; she might as well go home now.

'And, it's okay,' continued Kate, 'I'm on Caroline's mother's side. We're the black sheep of the family. So you won't have heard about us, we're *never* mentioned…' She was grinning from ear to ear.

Light dawned. 'Ah…' said Flora. 'Well, that makes sense. This place came up in conversation while I was out riding with Caroline the other day, and nothing was said about you. Now I get it.'

'You went riding?' Kate faltered.

'Oh, don't worry,' said Flora quickly. 'I am *never* going again.' She gave a shudder. 'You might, however, like to know that this is still considered *the* place to get married around here.' She paused. 'But you're right, I don't think the wedding is going to be here, sorry… Hannah has asked us to consider having it at the farm and—' She suddenly stopped, realising that what she was about to say might be news to Kate.

'It's okay,' came a quick reassurance. 'I know about Fraser… Tough times for you guys?'

Flora nodded. 'And I'm honestly not sure when the wedding is even going to happen. Things are a bit up in the air at the moment.'

Kate's smile was sympathetic. 'I did hear that Fraser's home though. Is he doing okay?'

'I think the expression is as well as can be expected, but getting better every day.'

Kate took another sip of her coffee. 'Good. And the wedding will be much better if you have the reception up at the farm. It will give you far more flexibility timewise than if you commit yourself to a date with us.' She wrinkled her nose. 'We *are* popular, Flora, and I'm afraid it's got to the point where we have to charge a cancellation fee if things don't go ahead. I'd be very happy to show you around, of course I would, but I'd hate for you to get caught out. Besides, with Fraser's illness, I think a reception at home might be the best bet, don't you?'

Flora hadn't really thought about it like that, in fact she hadn't really thought about it at all, but Kate was quite right. Hope Corner Farm had always been at the centre of the Jamiesons' world, now more than ever since Fraser's illness. Flora had almost forgotten why she was there, but a fresh wave of resolve was flooding through her. The farm must not be allowed to go under. She couldn't bear the thought.

As if sensing her mood, Kate sat forward slightly, grinning. 'So that's me come clean,' she said. 'What was it that you needed to own up to?'

Flora cleared her throat. 'When I originally made the appointment to see Michelle, I really just wanted to meet with her in person, so that I might ask for a further meeting, to discuss a business proposition. I thought it would seem better than cold calling and…' Flora dipped her head. 'Well, I don't have a huge amount of time and I didn't want to be turned down. I thought being face to face might help.'

'Well, that's completely intriguing,' replied Kate. 'Go on…'

'Oh…' Her response threw Flora for a minute. 'But now I don't know, perhaps it's you I need see after all.' All the lines that she had rehearsed in her head had gone completely from her mind. 'Would we be able to put something in the diary?'

'We *could*…' replied Kate, drawing out the last word for about four seconds.

Here it comes, thought Flora, the 'but'.

'But… I'm not sure why I would want to do that.'

'No, no, of course,' muttered Flora, becoming flustered. 'I've sprung it on you, I know, and…'

Kate's face split into a wide smile. 'Flora?' she said, waiting until she had her full attention. 'I only meant that I don't want to put something in the diary when you're sitting right in front of me now, that doesn't make sense at all.'

'But you must be busy?'

'I am. But I came to meet you prepared to give you a tour and the whole Ravenswick singing and dancing wedding routine. You'd be surprised how long some brides-to-be want to talk. They can go on for days… So we've got at least an hour yet, will that give you enough time?' She settled her cup back into its saucer and pushed it onto the table. 'Besides, you said it was a business proposition. You've got my interest well and truly piqued.'

Flora hadn't brought anything with her and now she wished she had, because at home she had a portfolio of her work as a florist, the details of charges she would have made for wedding flowers, together with all the notes that she had recently made. She took a deep breath. She would have to wing it.

'I used to be a florist,' she explained. 'I had my own business in Birmingham for over ten years and during that time provided the flowers for a considerable number of weddings. Unfortunately I don't have my portfolio with me, so you'll have to take my word for how fabulous I was.' She risked a cheeky grin.

Kate laughed. 'Of course! That goes without saying.'

'And now I would like to grow flowers at Hope Corner on a commercial scale and offer them for sale. In fact, I'd like to become Ravenswick's preferred supplier.'

Kate's eyebrows nearly shot off the top of her head, but she was still smiling.

'Well, I wasn't expecting that,' she said, tilting her head a moment and studying Flora. 'Although, I can see perfectly how appropriate that would be for you. What a lovely idea.'

She thought for a little longer. 'Are we just talking weddings here? Only we've never advocated any one supplier over another to our brides in the past. Michelle obviously gets asked, and from time to time might volunteer an opinion or pass on a recommendation from someone, but endorsement can be a tricky business, it can backfire horribly. And I'll be honest, Flora, the majority of brides these days seem to want to make their own minds up about things. I am interested though, I can't deny that, but what would be the incentive for us? Or our clients for that matter?'

'I wasn't just thinking weddings, no. It's big business, but the model I'm offering would work equally well for other family occasions, parties, funerals, even corporate functions.'

Kate lifted the coffee pot and, satisfied by its weight, began to refill the cups. 'I think we need another, don't you? Go on, I'm listening.'

Flora was just beginning to get into her stride. 'Using wedding flowers as an example for a moment, the normal arrangement would be for the bride and groom to engage the services of a florist to provide bouquets, buttonholes, floral decorations for the church, reception venue, the cars, et cetera. In order to do that the florist would have to order in whatever was required from a wholesaler – a wholesaler who sells onto the florist for a profit – and then in turn that florist sells on her services to the bride and groom, also for a profit. Two lots of mark-up and a hefty price tag for the happy couple.' She looked up to check that Kate was still with her.

'I think I'm following…'

'With flowers from Hope Corner Farm, though, the hotel would be buying the flowers on behalf of their customer, who would still get the same bespoke service from the florist. But you'd be cutting out the middle man and buying the flowers direct from the grower herself, at a substantial saving. How much of that you choose to pass on to your clients is of course entirely up to you.'

There was silence as Kate weighed up what she'd just heard. 'And we'd have to guarantee to buy from you, would we?'

'No, not at all. Anyone who books a wedding package with you would still be free to make their own arrangements for their flowers, but I'd like to think that the cheaper cost of our service would be a great incentive for many. And you might find that as you'll be making a profit from it too you'll be happy to promote the service…' She looked up and caught Kate's eye.

'We might…' she replied, amused.

'And we really would offer a bespoke service. Brides could choose whatever they wanted, in fact…' Flora was thinking on her feet now. 'We're only just down the road from you here, and I'd envisage the farm being open to visitors. People could even come and see the flowers growing before making their choice.'

Kate was staring into space and, apart from one brief nod, she remained that way for long enough that Flora was beginning to get very nervous. And then with one quick shake of her head, which sent her ponytail flying, she looked directly at Flora, her eyes twinkling.

'Why has no one thought of doing this before?' she asked. 'I think it's a brilliant idea!'

Flora only just managed to keep from squealing out loud. She allowed her hope to surge, but just for a moment; it was good news but nothing had been agreed as yet. There was, however, one final incentive she had up her sleeve. She returned Kate's smile.

'I also noticed that in your reception and lounge areas alone you have six large floral arrangements. If we were to become your suppliers I would be able to provide whatever flowers you need at a substantially cheaper price than you're paying now.'

'And you know that for a fact, do you?' Kate's eyes were twinkling.

Flora held her look. 'I would guarantee it,' she said without hesitation. The smile had dropped from her face as she willed her words to be successful.

Kate might be Caroline's cousin, an admirer of Flora's taste in clothes, and a welcoming, very approachable person, but she was also a businesswoman and it was this part of her that Flora was talking to now.

There was a slow nod of the head and an appraising glance.

'You're absolutely determined about this, aren't you?'

'I am. Not only because I'm passionate about flowers and on a personal level can't think of doing anything nicer, but also because…' She broke off, wondering just how honest she needed to be. 'It's the right thing for us to be doing. Fraser's heart attack has given us all cause to think about the future.' She wasn't sure she could physically say anything else.

Kate was quiet, sipping her coffee reflectively while Flora tried to keep her knee from jiggling and a confident smile on her face. Whatever was going through Kate's head, she would hear about it soon enough.

'I can imagine that last statement is merely the tip of the iceberg,' she said, after a moment, giving Flora a sympathetic smile. 'I've met Fraser a few times, and Hannah of course. I liked them, they're good people, and farming isn't an easy life. If your ideas are a step towards making a better life for you all then I really think I should try to help.'

She gave Flora a searching look, the corners of her mouth crinkling as she broke into a smile. 'Of course, it helps enormously that I think this could be an amazing opportunity for the hotel as well. I really like your ideas, Flora, I like them a lot. So tell me where you are with everything?'

Flora couldn't believe how well the meeting had gone so far, but there was nothing she could do now but be honest. To make out that her venture had gone any further than the tentative planning stage would be suicide. And then she thought of the greenhouse full of seedlings back at the farm and she smiled to herself. Had she unwittingly known back then that she was literally sowing the seeds of their future?

'I have pages and pages of notes, Kate, and not much else at the moment, but – and it's a big but – by the summer we could have a field full of flowers.' She pulled a face. 'Correction, we *will* have a field full of flowers, but I'd be much happier growing them knowing that I had at least one place to sell them to. As this is our first season, though, the only things we won't have are some of the early bulb-grown flowers and biennials, but there are ways around these things.'

Kate nodded. 'Right. Well, from my point of view I need to have a chat with the General Manager, and then, with what I hope is that formality out of the way, I think you and I need to meet again to discuss things in greater detail. There will be much I'll need to look at from the hotel's point of view as well, but perhaps, as this would be a new venture for both of us, we should work on it together?'

'Oh my God, thank you!' gushed Flora; she just couldn't help herself, and it took all her self-control not to throw her arms around Kate as well.

Kate matched her smile, but held up a hand. 'But only on the condition that you tell me where you bought your dress from.'

'Deal!'

'I think it is,' agreed Kate, and the two of them grinned at one another.

Flora scrabbled at her feet for her bag. Her head was whirling with not only excitement, but the list of things she needed to do.

'I can't thank you enough, Kate,' she said. 'But I must let you get on, I've taken more than enough of your time.' She thrust out her hand. 'It's been lovely meeting you.'

'It's been lovely meeting you too. I wasn't expecting this, I'll be honest, but I'm so glad you came by. And I'm so pleased to see that Ned has finally managed to evade Caroline's clutches. Do you know, she even came waltzing in here one time demanding to see me and pretty much telling me she expected to get their wedding reception for next to nothing because of our family connection. I can't tell you how happy I was when Ned called things off with her. I'm sorry, that makes me sound awful, doesn't it, but I'm so glad he's finally found someone like you.'

Chapter 20

Flora wasn't quite sure how she made it through reception and out of the door, but somehow she managed to nod and smile and say goodbye to Kate, holding her head high and promising to be in touch soon.

Now, though, she was safe in the privacy of her car, staring out of the windscreen at nothing with her heart beating wildly. She felt sick.

How had she not known that Ned and Caroline had once been engaged? Why had no one told her? More to the point, why hadn't Ned told her?

She felt utterly stupid. No wonder Caroline had been laughing at her behind her back. She tried to think rationally – after all, she'd had relationships in the past, it would have been perfectly normal for Ned to do the same. In fact, when Hannah had mentioned a previous girlfriend the day she told Flora about moving into the cottage, Flora had thought nothing of it. So why hadn't Ned told her? Unless…

No – she tried to cast the thought from her mind, but it was already there, worming its way in, burrowing deeper and deeper into her brain until she could think of nothing else. What if the reason Ned hadn't told her was because there was still something between them? He might have called off their engagement, but perhaps they still had feelings for one another. After all, every time she turned around it seemed as if Caroline appeared…

Moments ago, she had been ecstatic, hope soaring, filled with determination for her new venture and all that it could bring them as a family… but now… now, she didn't know what she was. The minutes stretched out as Flora gulped in lungfuls of air trying to calm herself. She fished in her pocket for a tissue and gave her nose a good blow, sifting back through the conversations of the last day or so.

Ned had been utterly distraught as he revealed the circumstances of the debt the farm was in. He had been ashamed, worried about his father, angry at Caroline's actions, but perhaps, more than anything, upset because he thought he had failed Flora. That didn't seem to be the behaviour of someone who had set out to mislead her, or – worse – was telling her outright lies, but even a virtual stranger had assumed that she would know about Caroline and Ned, and yet she didn't. So who was the stranger now?

No, Ned loved her, Flora knew he did, but there was no way she could go back to the farm, not straight away. She needed some time to put distance between how she was feeling and everything that would be waiting for her back home. Because she had plans to make, costings to prepare, forecasts; the list was endless. And she couldn't attempt any of it in her current frame of mind. She needed to regain the feelings she'd had only moments before Kate inadvertently let slip about Ned and Caroline, because that was what she needed to hang onto. It had still been a wonderful meeting, one in which she'd suddenly seen the possibility of everything she dreamed coming true. And then it came to her. She knew exactly who would be able to help.

*

'I'll put the kettle on,' Grace said, as soon as she opened the door and saw Flora standing there. Flora followed her straight into the kitchen.

'I've got some brilliant news for you about the paintings,' she continued, filling the kettle at the sink. 'And some not so brilliant news, but I think you'd better go first. You look fit to burst.'

Flora plonked herself down on a seat at Grace's breakfast bar. 'I'm sorry, Grace. I shouldn't even be here but…'

'Explanations are not necessary, Flora. I gave you an open invitation, and I meant it. Now, biscuits… yes?'

'Why did no one tell me that Ned and Caroline were engaged before?'

Grace stopped dead, her hand halfway to a cupboard above her head. She turned around, but the look on her face told Flora all she needed to know.

'So you knew I hadn't been told… I thought as much. Am I the only person around here that *doesn't* know?'

'Before I answer that,' replied Grace softly, 'may I ask where you heard this information from? And before you protest that it doesn't matter, it does, and you will hear why in a moment.'

Her expression was sympathetic but quite firm, and Flora realised that this was why she was here. Grace was as straightforward as they came.

'I've been up to Ravenswick Hall this morning,' she explained. 'And I met with a lovely woman called Kate, who, it turns out, is Caroline's cousin. But I expect you know that too?'

Grace nodded.

'And she only mentioned it in passing, without realising that she'd put her foot in it because, of course, she expected me to know, which is why I'm wondering how come I don't.'

'I see,' said Grace, quietly. 'Well that was unfortunate, yes, but actually doesn't change anything, at least not from where I'm standing.' She took down the biscuit tin and slid it across to Flora. 'Jammie Dodgers,' she said. 'Take several.' She busied herself with the tea things before continuing. 'I sincerely hope you're going to tell me in a minute what you were doing up at The Castle and why you were talking to Kate. But the reason why I asked who had told you about the engagement was that I had Ned up here a couple of days ago, agonising over the fact that he hadn't told you about it straight away, but that now, in his words, telling you would just look "really dodgy"?'

Flora gave a wistful smile. That was so like Ned, exactly the way he would put it.

She thought back to their conversation yesterday, trying to recall the detail as shame coloured her cheeks. Now that she thought about it, Ned had looked immediately alarmed as soon as Caroline's name was mentioned, but then she had demanded to know about the invoices and things had snowballed from there...

Grace nodded at the expression on her face. 'Obviously I advised him to talk to you as soon as possible, and am I right in thinking he might have tried to tell you?'

Flora groaned. 'Yes, I think he might have, but I... well, I changed the subject and, well, we never really got back to talking about Caroline and him. Oh, now I feel dreadful.'

'Well, you shouldn't. I can only imagine how much of a shock it was hearing that little gem from someone else. You need to talk to Ned, Flora, but I can honestly tell you that it was never his intention to deceive you. More a matter of trying to protect you, coupled with appallingly bad timing.'

And Flora could see precisely how this had happened, because hadn't she tried to tell Ned yesterday about her own situation, and got sidetracked? It was easily done when everyone was so busy and there were always more important things to attend to.

'You two haven't had the easiest of starts,' continued Grace, 'what with Fraser's heart attack and the situation with the farm. But you're on the same side, don't forget, and I've never seen Ned so besotted with anyone as you. He might not always show it… Hannah isn't a particularly demonstrative person, as you may have discovered, and hearts are not generally worn on sleeves in the Jamieson household, but it's how he feels, just the same.'

Flora nodded, feeling overwhelming relief at Grace's words. After all, she had no reason to deceive Flora. Well, if she'd felt stupid before, she certainly felt more foolish now. But then something else occurred to her.

'Just now you said *the situation with the farm*… What did you mean?'

Grace had turned to pour water into two mugs. She paused for a second or two, and then faced Flora again, clearly weighing something up.

'I know about the debt,' said Flora, immediately seeing the look of relief on Grace's face. 'Is that what you meant?'

There was a sombre nod. 'I did. And, I might add, something else that Ned has been berating himself for, not that it's his fault by any stretch of the imagination. It's no one's fault actually and he might not have handled it particularly well, but it's easy to be critical when it's someone else's life you're passing judgement on.'

Flora nodded. The time had passed for blame and judgement. It was what they did next that counted. And she should know that, just as well as Ned.

'I've known Ned since he was a child,' added Grace. 'And there are times in any child's life when a conversation needs to be had with someone, anyone, who is not your parent. And so it was the case with Ned.' She smiled at the memory. 'When he needed to confess to a guilty secret, a bit of naughtiness that was playing on his conscience, usually because he'd kicked a ball through a window and sworn blind he hadn't, it was me he came to. And I guess, somewhere over the years, that child grew up into the man you know and love, but my door has always been open.'

She smiled fondly at Flora. 'And now it's always open to you too, Flora. Always remember that. And also remember that, here in the country, our houses may not always be that close geographically speaking, but we're a tight-knit community, which often means that everyone knows everyone else's business and, if you're not careful, secrets don't remain secrets for very long. There have been things in my life that I haven't wished to be in the public domain and Ned and his parents have kept my counsel over the years. I do the same for them and that's really all there is to it.'

Flora grinned at her. 'Is that last statement code for "don't tell Caroline"?'

Grace handed her a mug of tea. 'Well spotted.' She gestured towards the biscuit tin. 'Now, tell me everything about your meeting up at The Castle with Kate, I'm dying to know.'

*

It wasn't until Flora pushed open the door to the farmhouse some while later that she realised she had never asked what the brilliant news was that Grace had to share. Or the not so brilliant news either.

Chapter 21

'I want to get as much worked out as we can before we say anything to your parents,' said Flora. 'Kate's response was amazing but that isn't going to be enough to keep us in business.'

It was the afternoon of the next day and she and Ned were hidden away in the study. It was the only place they could be sure they wouldn't be interrupted.

Ned grinned at her. 'See, I knew you were smart. I don't mind admitting I'm not looking forward to that conversation one little bit.'

Flora looked down at her notebook and bit her lip. 'Do you really think they're going to hate the idea?'

'I think there's a massive difference between dairy farming and flower farming, that's all I'm saying. *I'm* finding it hard to get my head around.'

'Which is why I'm grateful for all your questions,' replied Flora. 'I need to know what the answers are, otherwise I might as well give up now.'

Ned snuggled closer to her. 'Right, come on then, let's recap over what you've got so far.'

'So, for starters, I've drawn up a list of hotels in the area. Now, I don't think we should approach anyone other than The Castle for wedding business, because I want *them* to think they're getting a deal no one else has. But *I* also want the cachet of having them as our exclusive client. That will say a lot to prospective brides everywhere. With any luck they'll be begging to have us provide their flowers. I do think we should still approach the other hotels though, just for floral arrangements and the like.' Flora turned a page. 'Then there are the florists. Quite a number within a reasonable distance, but I've checked the distances to the other wholesalers and it's comparable. There's no reason why they shouldn't use us, and I think, if we can be open to the public and trade customers all day and every day as far as possible; people might enjoy coming to see what we have growing.'

'Provided we have something growing.'

Flora tutted. 'Yes, I'm coming to that.' She consulted her list. 'Now, as far as other avenues for trade go, we'll need a website obviously but I've contacted my previous company and, really, that's quite a minor detail. I'd link everything with my Etsy site and social media and, although we won't be able to deliver orders for flowers nationally for a while, I really think it's something we should aim towards. And I also think we should emphasise that our flowers will be locally grown, traditional British varieties.'

Ned was staring at her open-mouthed.

'I need to look into the logistics of this a little more but we could also offer an area for Pick Your Own flowers and even run a flower box scheme, a bit like fruit and veg boxes... possibly even hijack an existing company and use them to deliver for us. Being able to offer added value is always appealing.'

'I'd never have thought of half these things.'

'I wanted to do all this when I still had Daisy Doolittles but there was just me and it was too much on my own.' She flicked her finger gently against the tip of Ned's nose. 'Now there's all of us.'

'There are,' agreed Ned firmly. 'Although with everything you've got planned I'm not sure just the four of us are going to be enough. We might need a whole army!' He caught hold of her fingers, bringing them to his lips to kiss. 'It was tough enough before even when Dad was fit. I know he'll be back up to speed soon but how we'll see to the cows plus everything you've got planned, I don't know. We'd better get in training.'

Flora stared at the wide smile on his face, feeling a ripple of confusion at his words. Her own smile began to falter.

'Yes, but we won't need to do both, will we?' she said, wondering what Ned was thinking.

He frowned. 'Won't we? Why?'

Her stomach began to twist with unease. 'Because we'll be running a flower farm, Ned…' Oh God… The penny dropped and she realised with horror that he had completely misunderstood her. 'Ned, this isn't a business to run alongside the dairy farming. It's instead of it…'

'What?' She could see the light dawning on his face, his body straightening in shock, drawing away from her. 'You mean… We'd need to sell the cows, not milk them any more?' He swallowed. 'No! No way, Flora. We can't do that. Jesus, what were you *thinking*?'

A flicker of anger began to curl around Flora's heart at Ned's flat rejection. What did he think she meant? And for goodness' sake, the least he could do was hear her out, but his mouth was set.

'Well, thanks, Ned. I thought I was thinking of a way that could get the farm out of debt, or have you forgotten about that?'

'No, of course I haven't,' he flashed back. 'Don't be ridiculous. But I didn't think you meant for us to give up the family business…' He broke off, inhaling. 'It's a shock, that's all.'

Flora tried to soften her own words. 'I realise that, Ned, but I've done the sums and the only way you can repay the debt to Caroline's father quickly is to sell the land.'

He rolled his eyes. 'Can we please leave Caroline out of this for a minute? It's got nothing to do with her.'

'Ned, it's got *everything* to do with her. You owe her father forty thousand pounds and you told me that what he wanted was our land. So let him have it, we don't need it all.'

'No.'

Flora shook her head. 'Then what else do you suggest?' She was becoming more and more exasperated by the minute. 'Sell the land, and clear the debt, Ned. It's quite simple. Put an end to this once and for all.'

Ned opened his mouth, and then closed it again, anguish flooding his face. He gave a small groan. And then he shut his eyes tight, his jaw clenching. When he opened them again, he looked at Flora, just for a second, before turning his gaze away.

'It's not that simple,' he said quietly.

Flora felt her stomach turn to ice. 'Why not?' she said slowly. 'Ned... Why is it not that simple?'

'Because Caroline... Oh Christ...'

But Flora knew what was coming next, somehow it couldn't be anything else. 'So Caroline's father lends you the money, hoping that what he'll end up with is a prime chunk of land. Which just leaves Caroline, Ned. What could possibly be in it for her...?' Breathing suddenly felt like she was trying to draw in lungfuls of treacle. She gulped. 'Are you...?' A stinging rush of tears. 'Are you having an affair?'

'God, no!' Ned's face contorted with emotion. 'I would never—'

Flora scrambled to her feet, her thoughts darting in all directions. 'Then what, Ned?' She so desperately wanted to believe him.

She watched him closely for a moment, holding his look, until his gaze flickered and he looked away. His eyes closed again and he swallowed, his lips parted as he sucked in breath.

'Me,' he said, so quietly it was scarcely more than a sigh. And then he opened his eyes. 'She wants me.'

He held her look this time, eyes wide open, like a rabbit caught in the headlights. He had no idea how to make any of this right, and was pleading for her help. Did that make it better? Or worse…?

She had no idea what to say next. And neither did he.

They looked at one another for a moment, suddenly strangers.

'And is she going to get you?' Flora asked, her fingernails digging into the palm of her hands.

'No!' The reply was instantaneous, Ned's voice harsh, his eyes wild and scared, pleading with her to believe him. She wanted to, but there was something else, some other thought nudging the edge of her mind that she couldn't yet translate.

'You have to believe me, Flora,' Ned finally managed. 'I'm not good with words,' he continued. 'But this place is all I've ever known. I love how I know every inch of the land around here, the way the sun catches the hill in the morning, which patch of grass always gets the first frost, and how sweet the cows' breath smells in the springtime. I can't lose this place, Flora, and I thought at one time I'd do anything to keep the farm…' He rubbed a hand over his eyes. 'Only now I've found out that sometimes the price is simply too high. I don't want Caroline, I never have, not even when we…'

Flora raised her eyebrows. 'Even when we *what*, Ned? Got *engaged*?'

His hands were lifeless in his lap and he stared at them now, swallowing hard before he could speak. 'I wanted to tell you, Flora. But it all went wrong, right from your very first day, when you came into the kitchen and found Caroline there. It was so awkward, I couldn't say anything at the time and, apart from that, I was worried what *Caroline* would say. Then Mum upset you and it was such a tough couple of days I didn't want to make things any worse. After that, with Dad so poorly, I couldn't seem to find the right time to tell you and later on, well, it just would have looked suspicious.' He looked up at her. 'I should have told you, I realise that, but...' He hung his head. 'I'm sorry, Flora. Something else I made a complete hash of.'

She thought back to Grace's words of the day before. What Ned had said certainly seemed to ring true.

He was staring straight ahead, lost in the past. 'I could never be with Caroline,' he said. 'She is shallow, grasping and incredibly selfish. The only thing she loves is herself.' He gave a hollow laugh. 'She pretends to love her horses, but even those are cared for by someone else...'

Flora thought back to the day at the stable and the 'lowly' stable lad to whom she hadn't even been introduced as if he were a nothing, a nobody. She sat back down, nodding. Caroline was almost certainly arrogant, but then so were a lot of people. She was about to say something else when Ned interrupted her.

'The only thing she loves about her horses is the access to the right kind of social life; riding around and gossiping with a load of tacky, fake wannabes whose only aim in life is to bag a rich husband who can keep them in the manner to which they've become accustomed...'

Flora let out a breath. 'Blimey, Ned, that's a bit harsh. I haven't exactly taken to her myself, but she's not that bad, surely?' She looked at the disgust on his face. 'You really don't like her, do you?'

'No, I don't.' Ned's voice was suddenly clear. 'I tolerate her because our families are friends, and to alienate her would only make things worse, but even though I know what she's like, I'm so bloody stupid I've walked straight into her web.'

Flora's eyes widened. 'Okay,' she said. '*Now* you're making her out to be some sort of bunny-boiler crazy person. You *should* have told me about your engagement, but I guess I can live with that. Just don't take it too far, Ned.'

He was silent for far too long. 'You're not getting it,' he said quietly. 'I grew up with Caroline, we had a relationship which I broke off, but even then… you've seen how it is, Flora, she's *always* here. She won't let me go. Everywhere I turn there she is, and it's been going on for so long that no one really notices any more. When Caroline first offered to lend us the money, I thought it was just a generous gesture, I never thought there would be quite so many strings attached. But that's precisely how she wanted it. Knowing how anxious I was about Dad and losing the farm, she wanted a hold over me that would pretty much guarantee I would do anything she said. But that was all before you arrived, Flora, before I fell in love with you. So now you're here, and she can see her plans falling to pieces, it's like she's pulling out all the stops. She's determined to have the farm, Flora, and me with it. She's made my life a misery over the last few weeks, making suggestive comments, that kind of thing, but I'm scared to say anything because until we pay the loan off we're on really dangerous ground. If they demand the money back straight away, we could lose the farm, Flora. And I don't know what to do. I'm terrified of what Caroline is capable of, and what that might mean for us.'

She thought about his words. How Caroline had made herself out to be Flora's friend, and yet she had done things that no true friend would ever do. And Ned was right, she was always at the farm, always popping up by his side, asking him questions, just like she was on the day when Fraser had his heart attack and Ned had looked so agitated. Clearly there had been things going on behind Flora's back, but she'd been so preoccupied with her own anxieties about fitting in that she couldn't even see what was happening. And Ned, doing his best to protect her, hadn't said anything either…

And what she *could* see was how Caroline thought she had the perfect plan. To generously bail Ned and the farm out of trouble. To make herself indispensable to them, Little Miss Sweetness and Light, and then bag herself a man and a chunk of prime land into the bargain. Flora had to hand it to her, it was a pretty much flawless plan until she turned up. But Flora was not about to let Caroline get away with anything; she'd be damned if she would.

Ned looked up at her as her mouth tightened. 'I told you you'd hate me,' he said.

She looked at his weary face. He was an idiot at times, that much was true. But a well-meaning one, and a sudden surge of anger flooded through her.

'Do you know what makes me *really* mad in all of this?'

Ned opened his mouth to answer but Flora carried on, all the anger she felt towards Caroline suddenly rushing to the surface.

'That Caroline has even used Fraser's heart attack to try and further her own aims and that really is low, even for her. I'm getting heartily sick of her telling us we're going to fail every minute of the day, although now of course I understand why it's been "poor Fraser this", and "poor Fraser that", or "Do you think you'll have to sell the farm?"' She mimicked Caroline's cut-glass accent, which was just as fake as the woman herself. 'Sounding all innocent, when she's nothing of the sort. Innocent, my arse… Well, I'm sorry, but it's obvious that she'd like nothing more than for your dad to become the frail old man she's all too eager to tell us that he *has* become. And Fraser has done nothing to deserve this. He's a hard-working, loving man. Bluff and a bit scary at times, but a good man all the same, and one who is now hurting very badly and terrified of what his life has become.'

Her voice rose steadily as she spoke, her thoughts gathering pace as they began to tumble from her mouth. 'That's why we need to sell the land, Ned. We need to do something that gives Fraser back his life, but not the old one that was all about debt and failure, but something new, something with promise. In fact, what angers me most about Caroline's involvement in all of this is not what she's threatened you with, or the fact that she hates me – we're young and fit and can stand up for ourselves – but Fraser can't. There are more important things in life than holding onto a lost dream of how this bloody farm used to be, and Fraser's health is one of them. And if it isn't, then somewhere along the line someone's got their priorities very wrong indeed.' Flora sat back, eyes flashing.

There was silence for a moment as Ned held her look. 'I see,' he said finally. 'And that someone would be me, would it?'

Flora looked up, startled. Shit. That wasn't what she meant at all, but somehow, in her rush to get her point across, and with the anger she felt towards Caroline spilling over, it hadn't come out quite the way she had meant it to.

'No, God, Ned, I'm sorry. I didn't mean *you*... I just meant in general, I—'

Two blooms of colour had appeared on his cheeks. 'Well, that's easy for you to say when it's not your livelihood at stake. When you don't have to worry about earning money to put food on the table. Have you any idea what it costs to run this place?'

She stared at him. 'Who says I don't? Jesus, Ned, credit me with some intelligence. Have I not just proven how much a part of this family I am? Or maybe not… Thanks a million, Ned. I think you've just made it very clear how you view me. And I am not your mother…' she hissed. 'That old-fashioned nonsense about it being the man's responsibility to earn a living is bullshit as far as I'm concerned. I'm just as capable of earning money, but I'd rather do it here, working alongside you, than somewhere else.'

He glared at her. 'That wasn't actually what I meant…'

'Then what?'

'I *meant* that when you've got a nice little stash of money safely tucked away you can afford to think things like money don't matter.' And then he stopped, a startled expression crossing his face as if someone else had just said the words.

'Of course money matters, don't be so bloody ridiculous…' She glared back at him. 'Anyway, who says I've got a pot of money?'

He didn't answer and a suspiciously guilty look crept over his face.

'Ned? Who says I've got a pot of money?' Her demand was met with a stony expression. 'Oh… of course, *Caroline*. I might have guessed. She just happened to drop that thought into conversation, did she? Another little seed she planted inside your head.'

He ignored her statement, but she could see the guilt written across his face. 'It's obvious, isn't it? You sold your business, Flora. Or had you forgotten that?' He sucked in air through his teeth. 'Jeez, it was bloody killing me, the thought of having to ask you whether you might be prepared to use that money to pay off the loan. Thinking that I'd failed you too, even though I hoped you'd see it as part of an investment in our future life together. Well, now you've made it perfectly clear where *you* stand by denying the very fact that it exists—'

'I don't *have* any money,' she broke in, holding his look defiantly. 'If I *had*, I would have given it to you without you even having to ask. I would have *offered* it. Do you really think that little of me?' She practically spat the last words.

The little voice in her head was screaming at her to shut up, but she took no notice, so wound up that she was incapable of stopping. She could see the chance of saving themselves slipping further and further away from her, but somehow she seemed powerless to alter the course she was on. And then Ned opened his mouth and she felt the precipice under their feet.

'So where did it go then? I might have been a bit naive in the past, but I'm not stupid. You had a business, Flora, with a flat attached to it, that you *owned*. And I know your business wasn't exactly flourishing but even by the time you'd paid back any mortgage or debt, there must have been something. So what happened to it?'

A wave of heat washed over her. 'I can't tell you,' she said softly, feeling the life drain out of her. 'So please don't ask me.'

She felt physically sick. How could she possibly tell him now what she'd done? She'd accused him of keeping secrets in the past but she was no better than he was.

She could feel Ned's eyes boring into the top of her head as she sank back into her chair.

'So you *did* have money from the sale,' he argued. 'Caroline was right…' He stopped, realising what he'd said but in his anger unable to stop himself. 'And what about the other money too, from the sale of your paintings? More money that I'm not supposed to know about. Makes me wonder what other secrets you've been keeping,' he said, the disgust in his voice plain to hear.

She stared at him in confusion. What money from the sale of the paintings? And then she remembered Grace's words from the day before. She'd said she had good news about the paintings and some not so good news. So Grace must have sold them and somehow Caroline must have found out that she had asked Grace to keep her earnings a secret between the two of them. And of course she had hotfooted it to tell Ned straight away.

'I think you need to make your mind up, Ned, about who you believe; Caroline or me. You tell me how much you despise Caroline and yet you're quite happy to listen to her lies. Why are you doing that to yourself? Why are you doing it to me?'

His face softened for a moment but then he pinned her with a look.

'Just tell me, Flora. Have you kept the money a secret from me?'

How could she possibly answer that? She had done just what he had accused her of, but it wasn't what he thought. She was damned either way.

He took her silence as his answer.

'And you accused me,' he said bitterly.

His words were like knives, but she deserved them. She should have told Ned what she'd done right from the start, but she'd had a hard time admitting it to herself. Her future was just opening up in front of her – a glorious, magical, whirlwind romance that she could never have dreamed of. She'd been scared that if she told Ned what she'd done, it would have killed them stone dead, and so she had kept it to herself and, if there was ever a moment for coming clean, it had long since passed. And now her secret had destroyed them anyway because she would have offered the money if she'd had it, of course she would... and now Ned had practically accused her of hiding it so that she didn't have to give it to him.

She could feel herself filling with anger at Ned, at his attitude, and even though it was she who was in the wrong, she also acknowledged that a part of her wasn't prepared to let it go for some reason. And then, suddenly, as she tried to reason with herself why that was, the thought which had been evading her throughout their conversation skewered her brain like a white-hot spike. The bottom of her stomach dropped away in shock and her hand travelled to her mouth unbidden.

'Oh, my God,' she said slowly, staring at Ned with wide eyes. 'How could I have been so stupid?' She shook her head. 'How long did it take you to think up *your* plan, Ned? I mean, it can't have been all that long, because my shop was on the market when you first came in…'

'What…?'

'And I even remember thinking to myself how things like this didn't happen to people like me. That men didn't just come into my shop to tell me how beautiful I was, or go on to wine and dine me, buy me presents and tell me that they just can't get me out of their minds…'

Her eyes bored into his. 'And the reason that doesn't happen other than in soppy films is because it wasn't true, was it? You didn't think any of those things at all, you just wanted someone to get you off the hook with Caroline. To be the love of your life so that she would see how impossible her plan was… maybe even give it up. The fact that I would potentially arrive with a pot of money as well was even better – God, I bet you couldn't believe your luck.'

Ned stood up, throwing himself backwards and away from her as a gale of sarcastic laughter exploded from his lips.

'Me?' he accused her. 'That's what *I'm* supposed to have done? What about you?' He licked his lips as a dribble of spittle rolled down his chin. 'You say you had no money, no business… and therefore no home… My God, Flora, it would be funny if it wasn't so bloody insulting. Not only have you accused me of being false, but *you* actually are. You didn't come here because you loved me at all. You came here because I was your meal ticket. Admit it. Coming here has given you a roof over your head.'

He broke off only to gather breath, but she had got to her own feet now and pointed a finger at his chest.

'Well that just goes to show how little you know me, or how little you think of me. Don't you dare accuse me of that. Not after all I've done. Running around after you all, back and forth to the hospital, caring for Fraser like he was my own dad. How could I have done that if I didn't love you?' She was close to tears, her anger rapidly fading, as a wrenching sadness threatened to overwhelm her. 'Just tell me the truth, Ned. Tell me that it didn't honestly occur to you how useful I could be…'

She looked up into his face, longing to see the denial there, hoping that even after all they had done to each other he could still find it within himself to protest his innocence and pull her to him. But although he opened his mouth to speak, he hesitated for a fraction of a second. Just long enough for the truth to climb inside. And even through her pain Flora could see the irony of it. Ned was a good man, he was basically an honest man not given to lying, and now his hesitation had given him away.

'I thought so,' she said as a single tear broke free and rolled down her cheek. And then she left the room.

Chapter 22

For the first twenty minutes or so Flora walked blindly; she didn't care where she was going, she just wanted to be away from the house. It wasn't until she reached the stile at the far end of the field that she realised she was heading for Grace's house, or rather her garden. She wanted to sit on the slope below the beehives and let the peace she'd found there seep inside her before she could even contemplate thinking about what had just happened.

She'd pushed past Hannah as she walked through the kitchen on her way out, evading her concerned questions, but aware that her anxious face was following her movements. She stopped only to collect a coat from the scullery and pull on her boots and, although Hannah had come to the door after her, Flora hadn't even turned around before she walked out. Hannah wasn't daft; Flora and Ned hadn't exactly shouted at one another, but the walls were thin and their dispute had been heated. Flora knew that she would have heard enough to figure out what their argument had been about. She just prayed that, with the dining room door closed, Fraser hadn't heard a thing. If she were really lucky, he might even have been asleep. She scrubbed the thought from her mind; her luck seemed to have well and truly run out.

She reached the gate at the bottom of Grace's garden and looked up at the steep slope ahead of her. On other days it might have seemed a little daunting, but Flora was not in the mood to let anything stand in her way and she picked up her pace, powering up the incline until she reached the point where she wanted to be. She sank to the ground, not caring about the cold and damp, and then brought her knees to her chest, wrapped her arms around them, and dropped her head.

She gazed out across the fields she had just walked, the farm spread out and perfectly framed in front of her, just like a photograph. Which was of course the very reason she had walked here in the first place; she wanted to see how far she had come. Not today, but from that first day when she had arrived with all her dreams of a new future packed in her suitcase, thinking that the house at Hope Corner would be the place to see them come true. Now those thoughts seemed foolish... or did they?

Her breathing had slowed with her march across the fields, risen after her ferocious ascent of the hill, and now began to settle again as the soft breeze of a fine spring day nudged her gently. It was mild under the shelter of the trees and the sun, still tentative, had found a little warmth. And as she breathed out her worries, she breathed back in the stillness she had been longing for.

The trouble was that she could still see the future mapped out. The solution to the farm's problems that had been staring her in the face was now literally right in front of her, and she thought back to the day not long ago when she had caught her first glimpse of it. She had seen flowers everywhere, standing in rows and rows against a cloudless sky, their heads swaying gently in a benign breeze, and it had felt possible. It had seemed like something which could actually happen here, not a hare-brained scheme, but part of a new life which she and Ned could forge together. And everything she had learned and planned over the last couple of days had proven that to be the case.

Less than two weeks ago she and Hannah had sown tray after tray of flower seeds and, even though she hadn't really been aware of the farm's problems at the time, had she somehow known what the solution could be? Common sense told her that it couldn't possibly be the case, but the wheel of Flora's life often turned according to her intuition, and she had never doubted it before.

The year just gone had been her last as a florist. She'd been struggling for a while and, although the loan had helped in the short term, she'd known she was fooling herself, pretending that business would pick up and get back to how it had been before. And then had come the day when her world had fallen apart and it had taken less than a week for her to figure out what she must do. After that, it had all seemed so simple. Her own need for change had coincided with the door to her shop opening and Ned walking in. It didn't alter anything, not really...

So had what he accused her of been true? Had she taken advantage of him, however unwittingly, to make the new life for herself that she desperately needed? But whichever way she thought about it, she was certain that wasn't the way it had happened. Having a partner simply hadn't figured as an immediate part of her future and the intensity of feeling that swept over her whenever she was with Ned had taken her completely by surprise. She had blossomed when she met him, become fully awake to all the possibility that lay within her. But, more than that, she had been accepted for who she was and loved – she had thought – for all her silly notions, and ridiculous clothes that other people thought made her weird. When Ned had proposed, her initial reaction had been panic, until she'd realised that it wasn't panic at all, but excitement, a feeling that up until that time she'd had little experience of. Flora could fill with joy at the drop of a hat, but real excitement was what had carried her forward right up until this day.

She unclasped her hands and laid a palm on the grass beside her, feeling the energy of the young green shoots between her fingers, their size belying a strength that could split concrete. A solitary bee buzzed an early bunch of clover and she looked up the slope behind her towards the hive. If ever there was a testament to the power of working together then that was it. And how sweet the reward...

She was certain that the conclusions she had come to over her own business could be made to work here; the farm needed to cut its losses, a radical change instead of an energy-draining struggle. Hope Corner Farm needed to become small, to sell off its land and keep only what it needed, using the money raised to clear its debt and become its own powerful force for the future. They had everything they needed here, they always had, but it broke her heart to think that this probably now no longer included her.

She would give anything to be able to stay and work alongside Ned day by day, sharing their lives, their good days, their bad days, weathering it all inside the shelter of their love. But sometimes, however much you wanted them to, things just didn't turn out. She stared out across the fields, at the house, at the windows, as if with X-ray eyes she could see the very place that Ned would have taken himself to lick his wounds.

Flora knew he was hurting. The look on his face as she left would stay with her for a very long time. And she knew he loved her, it wasn't that. But somehow they had moved past caring and their relationship had become a test of faith, of trust in each other, and in that regard they had both failed. The very foundation of their love had been shown to have been built on shifting sands, not solid ground as it ought to have been. And, as a result, everything they had piled on top of it had slipped at the first sign of pressure.

She sat for a few more moments, letting the rays of the low sun warm her face, and then she slowly got to her feet and began the walk back to the farm.

It was even warmer in the greenhouse and Flora ran a light finger across the surface of the soil in one of the seed trays she and Hannah had planted. Then she picked up a watering can that sat underneath one of the benches and, half filling it from the outside tap just across the yard, returned to tend to her young charges. It was the least she could do.

As the soil darkened from the water, she peered closer, wondering at first whether it was a trick of the light, but no, there were definite green shoots. Only tiny, but pushing their way up towards the light nonetheless. She dropped the watering can, righting it quickly before all the water was lost, but her vision was blurred by the sudden tears that burst from her, leaving her gasping. It really was too cruel. But Flora couldn't stop herself now, and the tears continued to flow as she stood, chest heaving, weeping at the sight of hundreds of tiny seedlings that she would never see grow.

It was quiet in the house when she finally got back. Quiet and too still, as if something indefinable had left. It made moving through the house awkward as if she no longer had any right to be there. In a way she was grateful; better to simply slip quietly away now and avoid any unpleasantness. At least this way she would spare Ned any more upset. Resolutely avoiding Brodie's eye as she passed, she walked through into the hallway on her way upstairs to pack a bag. Enough for just a couple of nights, until she was settled with her sister and could arrange for the rest of her things to be sent on.

And she almost made it. She had one hand on the newel post, but then—

'Flora?'

She turned back, only now noticing that the dining room door was open. Fraser sat in his chair, a book in his lap.

Straightening herself up, she dragged a smile onto her face.

'Hi, Fraser. Is everything okay, do you need something?'

There was no sign of Hannah.

'You've been out,' he said. 'It looks like a beautiful day.'

She nodded. 'It is. Quite warm.'

He tutted and at once she could see the frustration on his face.

'And if I have to stay sitting in this chair any longer, I shall go stark staring raving mad.' He picked up the book and then tossed it dismissively onto the low table by his side. 'I haven't read a book in years. Not something I'm especially proud of, but then when have I ever had time to read a book? I'm always outside, and if I don't get out, right now, I'm very afraid I shall be sitting in this chair forever.'

Flora looked around, fully expecting to see Hannah appear.

'She's gone for a lie-down. Upstairs,' said Fraser. 'So I was wondering… whether I could ask you to accompany me on what might turn out to be the world's shortest walk. Even if I can just lean up against the side of the house, panting, it will be something.'

'But I'm not sure…'

'I'm supposed to be walking every day. Doctors' orders. Five minutes today, or longer if I can manage it.'

Flora didn't know what to do. Surely this was Hannah's territory? And what if Fraser overdid things or, worse, got into difficulty while they were out? And of course that was without the fact that she had just been bawling her eyes out and was planning on leaving.

Fraser was still looking up at her. 'Please, Flora. The thought of the whole afternoon and evening ahead of me is almost unbearable.'

It was hard to refuse him. 'But do you feel all right?'

There was a long pause, which made Flora realise the question wasn't one which required an answer. But, bless him, Fraser drew himself up, looked her in the eye and inhaled a breath.

'No,' he said. 'I feel like shit. But as I'm going to feel like that pretty much anywhere, I'm happy for it to be outside.'

Despite herself, Flora smiled. She knew exactly what he meant.

She looked around the room. 'Have you got some shoes somewhere?'

'Somewhere. But seeing as putting them on will feel like running a marathon, slippers it is.'

'Well, a coat then? Hannah will kill me if you get cold.'

'Since when have I ever worn a coat?'

'Since around the time you asked me to accompany you on a walk.'

He held her look. 'You bloody women are all the same, bossy as hell,' he said, but he was smiling.

'So how do we do this?' she asked, wondering what help he needed.

'Even slower than slowly…' came the gruff reply as he began to inch forward in his seat.

Flora hovered, not knowing whether she should be supporting him or not, but she winced as he got to his feet, obviously in pain. She put out a tentative hand, which to her surprise he took, giving it a squeeze.

'I don't know how we do this either,' he said. 'So that makes two of us.' He looked her square in the face. 'I guess we'll just have to figure it out together.'

The breath caught in her throat. There was something in his eyes she couldn't quite fathom, a message she couldn't quite decipher, but one that she was meant to see.

He dropped her hand, motioning that she should walk on ahead and, after what seemed like at least twenty minutes had passed, they reached the back door. He was already out of breath.

'Don't ever have a heart attack, Flora,' he panted. 'I really don't recommend them.'

It was all she could do to nod, let alone reply as another rush of tears threatened to engulf her. It was hateful seeing Fraser like this, but at least his heart was hopefully on the mend; hers was broken beyond repair.

'We'll walk to the edge of the garden,' he added. 'And that way I can do laps as I improve. It will give me something to aim for each day. I need to get better, and sitting on my backside being waited on hand and foot isn't going to help. I'm counting on you, Flora. I need some of your determination to get me going.'

She helped him on with his jacket. 'Me?' She almost laughed. 'I think you've got me confused with someone else,' she said.

He stopped suddenly and she thought she had hurt him as she tried to ease his arms into his coat. The thought of what had been done to his breastbone was at the forefront of her mind.

'Oh, I don't think so,' he said, clear as a bell. 'You're the best thing that's ever happened to this place. We needed shaking up. Waking up, actually.'

He waited while she opened the door and then, holding onto the door frame, he lowered first one leg over the step and then the other until he was on the path.

'I've been doing a lot of thinking over the last few days, not something I'm all that familiar with as it happens and I'm not proud of that either. But you have to do something when you can't bloody sleep and, funnily enough, having nearly kept my appointment with the Grim Reaper, there's been one or two things going around my head...'

'Oh, Fraser...'

'And one of the things that's been going around my head is this place, not surprisingly.' He stopped and turned his face towards the sun. 'Ah, that's a slice of heaven, isn't it?'

Without waiting for a reply he took another step forward. 'Which is why I've also been thinking about you... and Ned... and why I really don't want to see you go, Flora.'

She stared at him, mouth open.

'You *were* leaving, weren't you? Anyone who creeps through the house like you did just now is after a quiet getaway.'

If anything, her mouth dropped open even more.

'Aren't you going to ask me how I knew?'

'No,' she said weakly. It was pointless to try and deny that she'd been about to leave. 'Because if you know, that must mean you know other... things... as well. Fraser, I'm so sorry, I—'

'Have no need to apologise, lass, I'm not cross with you. Neither am I psychopathic...' He frowned.

It took a moment for her to work out what he meant, then she laughed. 'Er, I think you might mean either psychic, or telepathic,' offered Flora, a grin crossing her face.

He lifted his hand. 'Aye, that's the one... Anyways, it was really quite easy. But only if you know that the chimney in the dining room and the one in the study are connected. And conversations that take place in either room can sometimes be heard as clear as if you're standing in the same room. Not all the time, of course, I think it has to do with certain weather conditions, the direction of the wind maybe. I dunno, but aye, I heard it all...'

Flora groaned, her ears beginning to burn in shame. 'Shit.' There was a long pause while the conversation replayed itself in her head.

Fraser hadn't just heard her argument with Ned, he would have heard everything, and that included what had happened to the farm, how much debt they were in, and the fact that it had been kept from him. 'So…'

'Aye, lass,' was all Fraser said.

She hung her head. 'You weren't supposed to find out like that. I would have told you, I think Ned would have, or Hannah… once things were more… settled. I'm really sorry, Fraser…' And then she stopped as she remembered why Fraser hadn't been told. 'Jesus, are you okay?'

'Well, I'm still standing…'

They had walked a few steps out into the garden and Fraser indicated that they should keep walking.

'And as Caroline's visit of a couple of days ago and our subsequent chat set me thinking anyway, you could say you've done me favour today. I had been wondering quite how to bring the subject up…' There was even a wry smile.

She looked across sharply, and to her amazement, Fraser nodded.

'Of course Caroline told me about the loan,' said Fraser simply. 'People like her can't help themselves and she couldn't possibly keep something so juicy as that from me. All said and done in my best interests of course, she was very keen to tell me that, and all—'

Flora's anger surged. 'How dare she tell you! Doesn't she know what that could have done to you?'

Fraser held out a reassuring arm. 'Actually, in a way it was the best possible time to tell me. I'm not saying it didn't start my heart fluttering, 'cause it did, but I reckon now maybe it's strong enough to take it. Besides, I've faced my terror, Flora, faced it and stared it down. I don't think Caroline could tell me anything that was going to hurt any more than what I've already been through in the past few weeks.' He paused, gathering himself before taking another step.

'You could, though,' he added.

Flora frowned and was about to ask him what he meant when Fraser suddenly let out a breath. 'Sheesh, it's like learning to walk again. I think I did a better job when I was a wee lad.'

'Then let's stop a while. I can get a stool for you to sit on if you want, just for a minute. You're talking as well, which doesn't help.'

But Fraser resolutely shook his head. 'No. To the fence, that's what we agreed, and that's where I'm going.'

Flora pulled a face, but she couldn't argue. They took a couple more steps in silence, but then she cleared her throat. 'What did you mean, Fraser? That I could hurt you?'

He was quick to answer. 'Not intentionally, lass, I know that, and I also know you have to do what's right for you. Sometimes, though, we don't always know what that is. We think we do, but time has an uncanny ability to prove us wrong...' He trailed off to search her face, his pale eyes lit by the afternoon sun. 'Will you stay, Flora? Please. I don't want to beg, but I will if I have to.' He held a hand to his chest. 'All this stress... it's not good for me...' But the corners of his lips were twitching.

'Fraser, that's not fair!'

'What?' he replied, a sudden grin brightening his face.

She shook her head, smiling in return. 'You know what.'

He walked on ahead and, as she watched him, each step requiring almost superhuman effort, she realised how much this must have been costing him, and yet he had done it anyway, for her as much as for him. And then she realised how inordinately fond she had grown of him over the last few weeks.

'But what about the farm? And everything else?'

'That's what I meant when I said we need waking up. That's what you've done for us, Flora, and I'm sure, if you put your mind to it,

you can come up with something that will help us get through this.'
He winked at her. 'That's if you haven't already.'

She stared at him. How could he possibly know?

'I've had a heart attack, Flora, not been struck deaf and blind. I know
you've been up to something the last couple of days.' He broke off,
smiling. 'And of course there's the fact that I also heard everything you'd
been planning earlier. Plus, I saw you just now,' he added. 'Marching
out across the fields. You don't half go when you want to, I wasn't sure
whether it made me feel determined or just plain pathetic...'

He put out a hand to stop her from interrupting. 'But I knew
where you were headed and, although I couldn't see you after a while,
I guessed you'd be sitting somewhere pondering on this place, and Ned
of course. Deciding what you were going to do...' He scratched his
head. 'And then you came a marching back in exactly the same way,
determined, like. And I know you were thinking about leaving, but I
also know that you can't get this place out of your head, can you? Nor
everything you'd planned for it. I know you can see it would work.
And I also know that, despite everything that's happened, you'd still
love the chance to make it so... Or did I get that wrong?'

Flora couldn't help smiling. 'You're a very wise man, Fraser,' she said.

'Aye, and a knackered one.' They had come to rest at the boundary
fence between the garden and field beyond. 'So am I right?'

'We'll see.'

'Right,' replied Fraser, blowing out a puff of air from his lips. 'Well,
that's me done then, well and truly. Now before we go back, there's
just one more thing I need to tell you.'

Flora braced herself.

'Because while you've been very patient watching me shuffle about
the garden like an old man twice my age, I'm aware that there was a

lot more to your conversation with Ned earlier than just this place. Now, I don't profess to find talking about emotions all that easy, and I'm also very aware that this is a private matter between the two of you, but I couldn't let you go today without saying this…' He shifted his weight a little, supporting himself on the fence post and waving away her concern.

'I've loved Hannah since the minute I clapped eyes on her, and never stopped neither. I know she's a fusspot and a martyr to the regimen of housekeeping, but she's looked after me and loved me for more years than I should probably be able to remember. Despite the fact that most people think she rules the place, she has never tried to influence what I think, and more than that she's the one who always gave me the courage to be the person I wanted to be. People are like flowers, Flora, they are every shade of every colour, and some colours you will like and others you won't. Love is about acceptance, about knowing who a person is, the good and the bad, and loving them anyway. Not in spite of it, but because of it.

'Life's too short to be with someone who doesn't set you free, Flora. You need someone who doesn't seek to change you but is happy for you to be anything you want to be just as long as they can be by your side whilst you're doing it. Someone who makes you feel more alive than anyone else. So, you need to ask yourself if Ned does that for you. If he doesn't, then you already have your answer, but if he does, then do whatever you have to do to keep him. Don't let him go just because he's an idiot, Flora. We're all capable of that. Love makes idiots of us all…'

Chapter 23

And so the next day dawned and Flora stayed. She and Ned were courteous and civil with one another and, after he had left to milk the cows, despite the earliness of the hour, she was summoned by Fraser to accompany him on another walk. And all the while they walked, she tried not to think about the look on Ned's face, or the way his hair curled around the nape of his neck, or the way his legs had a habit of walking on ahead of him before his body was quite ready.

Back inside the house, Fraser bid Hannah to make a large pot of tea and then the three of them sat at the kitchen table, an expectant air settling between them.

'Right you are then, lass. I reckon you had better tell us what this is all about, and if I were you I'd start at the beginning and not stop until you get to the end.'

And so, fixed with Fraser's fierce stare, Flora did just that. And when she was done, she went on to tell them about her ideas for the farm and all the information she had found. Fraser may have been surprised by her ideas, Hannah certainly was, but neither laughed and, bit by bit, Fraser began to ask questions. And then more followed, and Flora found she had answers to them all. By the time she had finished talking, over two hours later, Fraser's face was split wide with a smile.

'Aye, lass,' he said. 'I reckon that might do it.'

Nearing lunchtime, Flora returned from the garden, her arms laden with bunches of daffodils, to find that Fraser had called a family meeting. Or at least that's what it looked like. Three solemn faces met her as she walked into the kitchen, stopping her in her tracks.

Fraser patted the chair beside his.

'Come and sit down, Flora,' he said. 'You look worn out.'

She gave a wan smile. 'I should put these in water,' she replied; the last thing she wanted to do was sit down.

'Will they die in the next twenty minutes if you don't?'

She paused. Fraser was getting altogether too good at reading her.

'It's just that I've been having a good long think about the things you said this morning and it struck me that now might be a good time to discuss this with all of us, as a family. Now that Ned's here,' he added, as if Flora couldn't already see him.

'But you don't need me here to do that,' countered Flora.

'No,' said Fraser slowly. 'I don't…' He broke off, looking her straight in the eye. 'Or do I…? Because this is the part I'm having real problems with, Flora. You see, you *are* a part of this family, and if anyone needed any more proof of that then they just have to think about your ideas on how to save the farm, or they can just watch you leave, and I can explain what I think we should do…' He smiled.

'You're leaving?' Ned's startled retort was loud in the quiet room. He got to his feet.

Flora shot Fraser a glance. 'Well, I…' The truth was that she hadn't really decided yet and was just about to say so when, to her surprise, Fraser got to his feet as well, pulling himself up by the table.

'Sit down, Ned,' he said. His voice wasn't loud but Ned dropped to his seat as if he'd been shot, his face a mixture of shock and sheepish indignation.

'I should think so too,' he added. 'I'm not sure how you can possibly act surprised when you've not even asked her to stay, have you?' He gently lowered himself back into his own chair before turning to look at Flora. 'You too, lass. Come on, sit down.'

Flora did as she was asked, laying the yellow blooms on the table.

'And in case you were wondering,' continued Fraser, his voice shot through with the effort that standing had cost him. 'You're right to feel ashamed, Ned, but that's the kind of stupid thing that happens when you're in love and can't think straight. Besides, this isn't about laying the blame at anyone's door, for anything... I asked Flora to stay, in fact, I practically begged her to and I don't mind admitting it. We've all been guilty of stupidity and a certain... blindness to circumstance – well, all except Flora. Which is why I really don't want to dwell on how we've behaved in the past; it's the future that will count.' He shifted slightly in his chair. 'Besides, I don't have the breath for it.'

He held a palm to his chest and cleared his throat. 'Now, before I ask Flora to say what she needs to, I'd just like to make it clear that I do know everything about this whole sorry mess we've got ourselves into, and I do mean *everything*... So if you've any notion about trying to deny any part of it, Ned, save *your* breath.'

Ned's eyes were fixed front and centre although Flora could see the effort it required to keep them that way. Even so, he still managed to look incredibly guilty. Hannah, on the other hand, stared first at Ned and then at Fraser as if she had never seen them before. She opened her mouth to speak and then closed it again.

Flora didn't know whether to laugh or cry. Fraser was by far the frailest in the room – stringing several sentences together was leaving him panting – and yet if he had asked any of them to do one hundred star jumps, stark naked, they would have. Even Brodie was sitting to attention.

Fraser jerked his thumb at Flora.

'Off you go, lass,' he said, sitting back in his chair.

She had no idea where to begin but a deep breath seemed called for at the very least. She tucked her hair behind her ears and wriggled in her chair.

'I haven't been entirely honest, Ned,' she began, avoiding his eyes. 'And there are some things I need to say first about my life before I came to Hope Corner. Things that you don't know.' She dropped her hands into her lap. 'I've been accused of coming here under false pretences, but I didn't, I—'

'Flora, wait—'

Fraser put out his hand. 'Let the girl speak, Ned, you'll get your chance.'

Flora gathered herself again. 'I didn't come here under false pretences, but neither can I pretend that it wasn't the most serendipitous timing on your part, Ned. You came into my life at a time when I had reached a crossroads and, from where I was standing, there was only one route available to me. I hadn't even bothered to look at the other roads because frankly any idiot could see that they weren't viable options. But then you came along, Ned, and suddenly my whole world was filled with possibility, the roads became endless, stretching out on all sides…'

She held his look for a second, but it was all she could manage. 'And so I accepted your offer to travel those paths and I understand full well how that might appear dishonest, but in my book that's just the universe doing its thing, in all its wonderful glory…'

Her head was suddenly filled with an image of Ned standing in her shop on the very first day she had met him, the sun glinting off his coppery hair, his mad freckles a dark smudge across his otherwise pale skin. At the time, she had felt a sudden jolt as if fate were shouting her name and begging her to pay attention. The fact that she had seen the same response mirrored in Ned's eyes had been an even bigger surprise. She choked back her tears.

'I've always trusted my intuition,' she continued. 'I still do. I can't help it if that makes me weird, or kooky, it's just me… who I am.' She shrugged. 'And I'm not about to change, sorry.'

She bit her lip and carried on while she still could. 'So even though things haven't worked out here, I still believe that I came with honest intentions and moreover that everything that happened in my life beforehand has somehow given me the means to find a way forward for the farm… and I couldn't leave without explaining. I think I owe you that much.'

Ned leaned forward, his forearms resting on the table. 'What happened, Flora?'

'My business failed,' she said simply. 'In a nutshell, that's what happened. And I've agonised over the reasons why, but actually I think it had just had its time. Nearly ten years all told, and brilliant years for the most part. I met some amazing people, and my little shop was my world through each and every season, marked out by the flowers that came and went as our little planet circled the sun. But times change and, where once there had been a place for me and my flowers and people were happy to buy them, that changed too, for all sorts of reasons.'

She sat up a little straighter and cleared her throat. 'And then my brother-in-law offered me a loan, just to tide me over… and I thought, like you did, that this was the answer to all my problems. And it was, for a little while, before everything came crashing down and I realised I'd made the biggest mistake of my life.'

'Oh, Flora…' said Ned, staring at her with a mixture of surprise and wariness, wondering what was coming next. But then his expression changed slightly and he lifted his head a little. 'Go on,' he said. 'Why was it a mistake?'

'Because my sister discovered that her husband was a compulsive gambler and had mortgaged their house to the hilt, run up a huge amount of debt and stolen money from his company as well. Money which he then lent to me.'

Ned groaned. 'Oh, Christ,' he said, and Flora knew it was as much for what had happened as it was the realisation of just how similar their situations actually were. 'And that's why you sold the shop…' he said.

'Yes. That's why I sold the shop. How could I keep the money knowing that it had been swindled from honest people? I had to pay it back. And because of me, Rowena has been left with virtually nothing; she lost everything she had and what little remained she had to sell to pay back her husband's debt. Even though I didn't know he had stolen the money he lent me, I was stupid and deluded thinking that a loan would solve everything. I knew it was too easy, that there was something about it that didn't seem quite right, but I didn't ask any questions, I didn't check, I just took the easy way out and grabbed the money. I was one of the reasons why my sister was left with nothing, and in the end no better than a common thief. How could I possibly keep my shop, knowing that?'

She stared at him, feeling the flush of anger and shame that filled her rising up to colour her cheeks as she dared him not to agree with her.

'And that's why you didn't tell anyone? Oh, Flora… you're not a thief, you're—'

He was about to continue when the door burst open and Caroline walked in.

'Morning!' she sang. 'And how is everyone today? Oh, Fraser, you're up…'

She chattered on for a few moments, completely oblivious to the fact that no one was answering, but then realisation dawned and she suddenly stopped.

'Oh, have I come at a bad time?'

'Well, yes, dear,' said Hannah. 'Perhaps if you—'

But Flora had had enough. All the hurt and anger and upset of the last few days rose up in a surge that would not be denied. And what the hell did it matter what she said anyway? She had nothing to lose.

'Actually, Caroline, you've come at the perfect time because there's a few things I want to say to you.' She got to her feet. 'Firstly… don't you think it's rude not to knock? You might be a friend of the family, although frankly I doubt that, but in any case you just waltz in here as if you own the place. Well, you don't, not yet, and if I have anything to do with it, you won't, ever. So next time you come around, give some thought to the fact that Fraser is still recovering from his operation and, as his bedroom is now downstairs, for all you know he might be wandering around in his underpants. And even if he isn't, he mightn't want you just bursting in when you feel like it.'

Flora broke off, her heart beginning to thump in her chest, but she was only just getting started. Ignoring the two red spots that had appeared in Caroline's cheeks, she carried on.

'Secondly, I know all about the loan that you made to the farm, a loan made so generously that you're now wielding it over everyone here like a big stick. That's not generosity, that's bully-boy tactics, so don't come in here pretending friendship when you wouldn't know the meaning of the word if someone wrapped it up and baked it in a pie for you.'

She shook her head. That didn't sound quite right but she rushed on regardless. 'And how *dare* you suggest that Fraser isn't up to running the farm? Poor Fraser this, and poor Fraser that. Well, let me tell you, this man has more courage and determination in his little finger than you have in your entire bloody jodhpur-clad body. You have *never* had to fight for anything, Caroline, least of all your life, so until you're qualified to make such judgements, I suggest you keep your mouth shut.'

'Well, really...' Up until that moment, Caroline's face had registered only the shock she was feeling. Now, though, her mouth twisted into an ugly sneer as she found her voice.

'How dare I?' she spluttered. 'How dare *you* more like. What on earth made you think you could talk to me like that? Don't you know who I am? I'm probably the oldest and closest friend Ned has and our families go back even further. I have always been welcome in this house and I would never do anything to hurt them... whereas *you*...' She drew herself up, flicking her hair back over her shoulder. 'You're nothing but a little gold-digger. Don't think I haven't worked out why you really came here.' She gave Ned a triumphant smile. 'I don't have to dig for gold, Flora, I already have plenty of it.'

Flora suddenly felt icy calm as she lifted her chin and stared into Caroline's cold blue eyes. 'No, you don't, Caroline, you have money, and there's nothing golden about that. Not when you use it to create a world where you're better than everyone else.' She placed her hands palm down on the table and leant forward as if to emphasise her words.

'Now... why don't you take your manipulative, butter-wouldn't-melt airs and graces and leave. And take your grubby money with you too, no one here has any need of it.'

Caroline's mouth dropped open as she looked first at Ned and then Fraser and Hannah in turn. There was complete silence and Flora daren't even breathe.

'Well, aren't you going to do something?' She was looking back at Ned now. 'Are you just going to sit there and let her talk to me like that?'

The seconds ticked by. It was all Flora could do to stand still and not flee the room. She looked at Caroline's red flustered face, an ugly expression overriding her normal studied pose. She had finally lost her very practised but artificial poise and a part of Flora was pleased. Even if it meant that she had now blown any chance of remaining at the farm, at least she had stood up for the things she believed in. It almost made it worthwhile. Almost… She daren't even look at Ned but then a movement caught the corner of her eye as, very slowly, he got to his feet. And she braced herself for his response.

'No, Caroline,' he said. 'I'm going to stand up and let her talk to you like that, because Flora is right. She's been right about a lot of things, and she has more honesty and integrity than you will ever have. I can't believe it's taken me so long to stand up to you myself. You've tried to manipulate me into a corner and you've used my fear over losing the farm and worry over my dad to do it. Well, not any more. I am incredibly stupid, I've got two left feet, a body and a brain that doesn't always know what it's doing, but one thing I do know is right from wrong. So, yes, I *am* stupid, but not stupid enough to believe your lies and lose the one thing that means more to me in this world than anything else. I love Flora and she's the best thing that's ever happened to this place. We don't need your money, Caroline, and as for what we've already borrowed, we'll repay it.'

A slow smile spread across his face. 'And you can tell whatever stories you like to all your cronies, I really don't care. About you, or your money… Flora was right when she said that you had never been a friend to us and all I can say is that I'm utterly astounded it's taken me so long to realise it. Or to realise that everything – or rather everyone – I do truly care about is right here in this room, and they were here long before you came in.'

It was Flora's turn to look astounded. Had she really heard that right? Her heart was pounding but she still couldn't look at Ned in case she had got it wrong. She risked a glance at Fraser, only to find that he was smiling at her, a broad smile that lit up his face and chased away the tiredness from it.

'That's my boy,' he said. 'And Flora, why don't you go ahead and tell Caroline why we won't be needing any more of their money?'

Flora caught his eye and with a surge of affection beamed back. 'We're going to open a flower farm,' she said.

Ned's mouth split wide into a grin. 'Yes, we are,' he said, turning back to look at his mum and dad. He let the words roll around his head for a few minutes and then, 'Bloody hell... we're actually going to open a flower farm!' He looked straight at Flora, his eyes filled with the same look she had seen on the very first day she had met him, a look that made her feel like there was no one else in the room.

'You don't seem too sure, Ned,' said Caroline, unwilling to give up.

'Oh I am,' he replied, beaming. 'I've never been more sure of anything. Because if Flora says that's what we're going to do, then that's what we're going to do. And do you know why, Caroline?' he asked. 'Because I gave nothing to Flora when she came here, apart from the chance to be by my side. I threw her in at the deep end, knowing the farm was in trouble, but still she swam, for the simple reason that she loves this place. She's shown more care for all of us here in the last couple of months than you have in your entire life.'

He gave a curt nod. 'I'm well aware that we still owe your father a great deal of money, but we will be taking some proper advice first thing in the morning and it will be repaid. You'll be hearing from us, as they say.' He was already moving towards Flora. 'Oh, and Caroline, please shut the door on your way out.'

It had been the last thing she was expecting, but seconds later the door slammed behind Caroline and Flora was caught up in Ned's arms as he whirled her round and round until she was giddy. They stumbled to a halt, still laughing.

'Oh my God, you were brilliant!' said Ned, his eyes lit with excitement. 'I don't believe it. Why the hell didn't any of us stand up to Caroline before?'

'That's a very good question,' came Fraser's voice from the table. 'And one of the many things I've been thinking about the last few days.' He held a hand to his chest. 'Yesterday, I told Flora that we needed waking up and what I meant is that we needed shaking from the roles we've all assumed over the years. Roles that have become so entrenched that we've followed their rules blindly, without even considering what they might mean for us. It's no one's fault, but it's taken Flora to make me realise how blinkered to life we've all become.'

Flora smiled at him fondly. 'That's very kind of you, Fraser, but do you not think that staring death in the face might have had something to do with it?'

He pulled a face. 'Certainly not…' he replied, his eyes twinkling. 'Although, that does remind me that I wanted to ask you something.' He paused, looking up her with the look that she was beginning to recognise. The one that said he knew exactly what she was about.

'Go on then,' she said, a little warily.

'Because I got to thinking about when I *was* staring death in the face. I obviously didn't think about it at the time, but these things come back to you and… well, it seemed to me that you were altogether more clued up about what was going on with me than you should have been. And I wondered why that was…'

Flora sighed. There really was no getting anything past Fraser. But then, as she looked up into his knowing eyes, she suddenly realised that it was okay. Her fear had gone. She had faced it just like Fraser had and they had both come through it.

'I was thirteen when my dad died,' she began. 'I was with him when he had his heart attack; we were out in the garden raking up leaves and he suddenly got sick and keeled over. He hadn't been feeling well all day but thought that the fresh air would do him good.' She gave a sad smile as Ned pulled her wordlessly into his arms. 'All but one of his arteries were blocked and so he was scheduled to have a bypass, Fraser, just like you. It took place on a Monday, two weeks after my birthday, but he died on the operating table, another massive heart attack. There was nothing they could do…'

Hannah's hand went to her mouth. 'Oh, my dear…'

Ned's lips bent to her hair, his arms wrapping her in a cocoon. 'Oh, Flora, why didn't you tell me? Why didn't we know?'

'No one asked me,' she said simply. 'And I couldn't say – it would have been too much. I couldn't bear the thought that it would happen all over again.'

'Aye,' said Fraser, softly. 'I thought as much. It was the way you looked at me, lass, like you knew every thought that was in my head. And I reckon you've had plenty of years where you've thought about little else. But it helped, Flora. I want you to know that.'

Flora loosened herself from Ned's embrace and stood in front of Fraser. 'May I?' she asked, holding out her arms and, as he nodded, she gave him the gentlest of hugs.

'You're going to be okay,' she said. 'I know that too.'

'Aye,' he said. 'I reckon I am.' He cleared his throat, as he blushed slightly.

'Got something in your eye, Dad?' asked Ned, grinning. 'But I reckon we're all going to be okay. What do you think, Mum?'

Hannah was sitting upright in her chair, staring into space and twiddling the ends of her hair. She looked down at her brown jumper as if seeing it for the first time, and then she looked up at Flora, a gentle smile softening her face.

'I think you're absolutely right. And I never thought I'd hear myself say this, but it is definitely time for things to change,' she said. And then she got to her feet. 'I'll put the kettle on, shall I? We have some more plans to make and I always think better with a cup of tea in my hand.'

She got halfway across the room before she stopped and turned back around. '*Fraser, wandering around in his underpants*... Oh, God, that's funny...' Her peal of laughter rang out around the room.

Fraser snorted and then clutched his chest. 'Oh, don't make me laugh, it hurts...'

Chapter 24

Flora couldn't stop looking at Ned. Or kissing him.

'And you're really sure you think it's a good idea? I mean, just because I love flowers doesn't mean that everyone else has to.'

They were still sitting at the table and Ned still had hold of her hands. 'Just answer me one thing… Will I still have to get up at the crack of dawn when we're a flower farm?'

Flora grinned. 'Oh yes, and worse, you'll be bent over double in a field for most of the time. Come wind, rain or shine.'

'Excellent…' But he was still smiling. 'It's going to take a while,' he said. 'I'm not sure I can get my head around it all just for the moment…'

'Aye,' said Fraser. 'But you won't have to, son. Not all in one go anyway. The cows will still be here for a while to come yet until we can start to make the changes that Flora has in mind. We just won't be breeding from them any more, which will reduce our overheads straight away. We'll sell what land we can, pay off our debts and then the rest of the dairy business can go in time. I can't deny that I'll be sorry to say goodbye to the old girls but it's time to do something different, and we'll not get a better opportunity than this.'

Hannah reached out to take Fraser's hand. 'I'm sorry,' she said. 'I thought by trying to keep everything the same that I was helping…'

'And there's nothing wrong with that, love. You've kept us all going, is what you've done, and thing is, before all this happened with my bloody heart, I'd have probably wanted a helping of "the same" for breakfast, lunch and dinner…' He winked at Flora. 'Trouble is, I've had to learn a lot over the last couple of weeks, and much to my surprise, being an old duffer and whatnot, I've found I rather like learning stuff. And I think I'd like to carry on doing it.'

He smiled fondly at Hannah. 'Normal doesn't have the same appeal it once did,' he said. 'How can it, when nothing about what's happened is normal? But that's okay. I don't just want to settle for normal. I've been given an opportunity to take a step back and look at my life and maybe that's something not a lot of people get…'

Flora reached out and took Hannah's hand too. 'And we're going to need your help, Hannah. I know about flowers, but you, you know about planting, and you know everyone around here too, and we're going to need that, to get word out about what we're doing.'

Fraser nodded. 'Flora's going to get in touch with an association that helps people with start-up businesses like this, and they run courses too, but I bet you already know half of what they'd have to say.'

'And you're so good at being organised,' added Flora. 'And teaching people new skills; you'll have us all licked into shape in no time.'

Hannah blushed. 'Now you're just trying to flatter me,' she said, but Flora could tell from the warmth in her eyes that she didn't mind one little bit.

'I don't profess to have all the answers, but I have started to work out a lot of the detail, and the start-up costs are relatively minimal… The main focus will need to be on preparing the field ready for plant-ing. We've already started on seed sowing, but we need more, sown in two-week intervals so we get a continual supply of flowers throughout the summer and into autumn. We'll need more greenhouse space for when the seedlings are pricked out, and then once they've grown on they'll be ready to start planting out in about six weeks. We need to get cracking.'

Ned nodded. 'But the loan, Flora, our debt… what are we going to do about that? How can we be talking about start-up costs when we don't even have the money to pay our way now…'

Flora shot Fraser a glance. 'You give Caroline and her father what they want…' She held up a hand. 'Only you don't think of it like that…'

'I don't want to give them anything!' Ned shot back. 'After all they've—'

'I know,' said Flora, her voice as soothing as she could make it. 'Which is why we all need to reframe our way of thinking…'

'Go on…' replied Ned.

'I can see as much, if not more than any of you, a million reasons why we shouldn't give in to Caroline because her family traded on years of goodwill and a so-called friendship that was anything but. They've used you and the farm's misfortune to their own gain, but now it's time for you to do the same. Sell them the land they want… play them at their own game. They'll buy it from you, rather than on the open market, because it's a damn sight easier and, importantly, quicker than going through agents and paying fees, et cetera. Exactly the same reason why, in fact, you didn't go to the bank and get a loan in the first place, rather than borrow from a friend. It's exactly the reason I did it too. I'm not saying do it without drawing up a proper legal agreement and getting a professional valuation for the land first, but they'll still bite your hand off because it will suit them to do so.'

'But, they still win,' said Ned, scratching his head.

'No,' said Flora. 'They don't. Or maybe they do in their heads, but as we're not going to be concerned with them what does it matter? What matters is how *we* think about it. We've been missing the point, so desperate not to sell to Caroline's family that in effect we've cut off our noses to spite our face. If selling the land is the best thing to do, then it's still the best thing to do whoever we sell it to. Try to stop thinking about it as letting Caroline and her father win, try thinking that doing this gives us want *we* want. Isn't that what matters?'

A slow smile crept over Ned's face. 'Is there anything you haven't worked out?'

'Oh, masses of stuff,' admitted Flora. 'But I've made a start, and maybe that's all we need? I thought we might do the rest, together…'

Ned grinned and threw his hands up in the air. 'Flora Dunbar, you are completely and utterly bonkers, and although I know there should be umpteen blooming reasons why this is such a crazy idea we shouldn't even contemplate doing it, for the life of me I can't think what they are. I am an idiot, but I do love you, Flora, even though I've behaved appallingly badly.'

He lowered his head, aware of a sudden prickling in the room.

But Flora wasn't the only one who had learnt a lot over the last few days. 'You might be an idiot, but you're *my* idiot,' she said as she leant forward to claim another kiss, a much longer and slower kiss this time.

'Ahem.' Fraser cleared his throat.

Hannah flapped her hand at him. 'Oh, go on with you, don't stop them. I think it's lovely.'

'I didn't say it wasn't lovely,' replied Fraser. 'But all this excitement's not good for my heart.'

And whereas once Hannah would have fussed or looked alarmed, now she merely smiled. 'Well, your heart had better get used to it, Fraser,' she said. 'I think there's going to be a lot of it around…'

Flora beamed at her. 'Oh, yes, especially once we get around to planning the *wedding*,' she said. 'Although I think we might have the wedding flowers covered, don't you…?' She broke off, blushing a little. 'I've been thinking about it, Hannah, and I know we haven't had a chance to speak about it yet, Ned, but there's nothing I'd like more than to have the wedding here. Would that still be all right?'

Hannah's hands clasped together in delight. 'Oh, I'm going to need such a big notebook,' she said, thrilled.

'That's settled then,' said Ned firmly, and then he turned so that he was looking straight at her. 'There is just one more thing,' he said. 'I just want you to know why I didn't marry Caroline. It's important to me that you know why, Flora, because Caroline has never cared about the farm, not like you do. She's seen it as her birthright, something she's entitled to, not something that has to be earned. I've never seen her tip her head to the wind to feel it dance around her like you do, or stop in her tracks, her breath taken away by the sun lighting up the fields. And if we married this place would have ceased to exist, swallowed by the desire to own things, to accumulate wealth and then sit back on one's laurels, enjoying the rewards. I don't want that. I want to have earned what I have, to know when enough is enough. When I'm old and grey I'll retire knowing that I have lived a life of integrity and truth beside the woman I love.'

'Well said, lad, well said,' muttered Fraser, sniffing a little.

Ned gave Flora a look out of the corner of his eye. 'Of course I didn't fancy her either…'

'Ouch…'

'And that's why things have been so wonderful since you've come. You want to be a part of things here, a proper part, by doing whatever it takes. Farming's a hard life, but it's a good life, and I can see that you understand that. And what you've done for us here is more proof of that than I will ever need.'

Hannah cleared her throat, already looking to get things organised. 'There will need to be economies of course,' she said. 'We'll need to grow more of our own vegetables, and meat is far too expensive and really not all that good for you. And I know we will be busy and so things will need to be less… rigid than they have been. I might even concede to buy the bread from the shop in future.'

'Oh, no,' said Flora, blushing a deep red as a sheepish expression crossed her face. 'Would now be a good time to confess that I actually like making bread! Apart from being incredibly satisfying to make, and making me feel like a proper domestic goddess, it tastes so much better than anything you can buy in the shops.'

Hannah laughed. An honest-to-goodness gale of laughter that rang out around the kitchen.

'Never mind that,' said Ned. 'What are we going to call ourselves… Hope Farm Flowers…? That's a bit boring…'

'Ah, no, Flora's come up with something much better than that, haven't you, lass?' said Fraser. 'Go on, tell 'em what it is…'

Flora grinned. Her conversation with Ned of several weeks ago when he had first mentioned the place where the farm stood had stuck in her memory. It was perfect for all sorts of reasons.

'Well, it's just a suggestion, but it seemed fitting somehow. I don't mind though; we can call it something else if you want.'

Ned rolled his eyes. 'For God's sake, woman, spit it out. What are we going to be called?'

'I was thinking… Hope Blooms, you know on account of where we are, Hope Corner?'

There was a glint in Ned's eye. 'Aye, I know where we are right enough…' He looked out the window before turning back and pulling her to him.

'Aye, Hope Blooms,' he said, smiling. 'Indeed it does…'

Epilogue

'Is everything all right, dear?' asked Hannah, coming across the garden.

Flora turned. 'Yes, fine. But I seem to have lost Ned for a minute.' She grinned. 'Although I probably ought not to admit that…'

Hannah tutted, shaking her head in amusement. 'Don't worry, he hasn't gone far, I just saw him heading over to the house,' she replied. 'He said he needed to check on something.'

'Oh…' Flora glanced in the direction of the garden and then looked back towards the house. 'I might just check and see if he's okay,' she said.

'What now?' asked Hannah, frowning slightly.

'I won't be long, honestly…' She grinned again, already beginning to move away before Hannah could argue.

It was hot out in the yard, away from the shade of the trees and out in the full sun. Flora squinted up at the sky. The weather had been perfect for weeks, but goodness, today was a scorcher. She'd be glad to get back inside the relative cool of the kitchen; her dress was far too thick for the heat and even though her hair was pinned up she was beginning to feel rather wilted. She was almost at the house when she noticed a figure standing by the gate at the far end of the yard. A young woman, looking somewhat lost.

'Hello!' Flora called, waving an arm. 'Do you need any help?'

The young woman looked up in puzzlement as Flora approached. 'Probably,' she admitted, staring at Flora's dress. 'Sorry, I think I must be intruding.'

Flora waved away her concern. 'Not at all. What can I do for you?'

'Well, I was given some directions to somewhere called Hope Blooms, but I'm not sure if I'm in the right place or not? I'm not terribly good at following instructions.'

'You're better than you think,' Flora replied, grinning. 'Apologies, but we haven't got around to getting our sign up yet... or rather, we nearly did but I ordered it over the telephone and when it arrived it said Hope Balloons. Honestly, whoever heard of a flower farm called Hope Balloons?'

The young woman smiled nervously. 'So I am in the right place then?'

'You certainly are. And I'm Flora.' She held out her hand over the top of the gate.

'Melissa,' said the young woman. 'Are you sure I haven't come at an inconvenient time? Only the lady at The Castle said you could come here to see the flowers for yourself.'

Oh, Kate, you star, thought Flora.

'Mind you, that was a couple of days ago,' she continued. 'But I haven't had a chance to get over here since then, I had to take the car in to the garage on my day off.'

'No problem, you're here now. Come on in and we can have a chat. I was headed inside as it happens anyway. I'm melting in this heat.'

She opened the gate and led Melissa into the yard. 'So when are you getting married?' she asked. 'Next year?'

There was a long pause, so much so that Flora turned to check if Melissa was all right. She had stopped, an anguished expression on her face.

'No, in September… in fact, that's the problem, I don't know if you can even help us at all but Kate mentioned you were a new florist and might not be so booked up. Mine has just let me down, some massive mix-up or other, and now…' She broke off, looking like she was about to cry. 'Now, I've got no flowers for my wedding at all.'

Flora gave her a sympathetic smile. 'Well, we can't let that happen, and don't worry, I'm a new grower, not a new florist, so I can definitely help. Come on, let's go and have a quick chat.'

Melissa looked doubtful. 'Are you really sure that's okay?'

'Positive,' replied Flora, hoping that it was.

It was much cooler in the kitchen and Flora sat Melissa down, grabbing her notebook that resided more or less permanently on the table.

'Shall I take a few details first of all, and then we can discuss what you originally had in mind? I don't have any of my books with me just now, but I expect as you had already booked your florist that you know what you want anyway.' She glanced out of the window. 'And there are a few things I can show you today…' She couldn't stop the enormous grin from spreading over her face. 'So, first things first, let me make a note of your full name and take a contact number.'

Several minutes later and Flora had all the information she needed. 'Does that all sound okay?' she asked. 'And come back next week like we discussed, I'll be a little more organised then and we can really make some plans for you. But the most important thing for you is not to worry, we've got plenty of time.' She was relieved to see that Melissa was looking much happier.

'I can't believe that you've even seen me today,' replied Melissa. 'It's really incredibly kind of you.'

'Well, your wedding day should be the one day when everything feels right in the world, shouldn't it?' She smiled across the table. 'Would you like to come and have a look at our flowers now?'

They were just about to leave the kitchen when Flora heard footsteps from behind her.

'Flora!'

She whirled around to see Ned standing by the door into the hallway, clutching a fistful of papers. He was about to speak again when he realised that there was a third person in the room.

'Ned! I wondered where you'd got to…' Flora crossed the kitchen to plant a kiss firmly on his lips, taking hold of his arm. 'Come and say hello to Melissa. I found her by the gate and we're just about to go and have a look at the flowers…' She gave him a very direct look. 'She's getting married in September and has very sadly been let down by her florist, so of course I said that we'd be happy to help…'

Ned picked up her cue. 'But that's outrageous, we can't have that.' He held out his hand. 'I'm Ned,' he added. 'Shall we?' He walked past them both and chivalrously held open the door. 'After you, ladies.'

Flora smiled reassuringly at Melissa, who was looking more and more bemused by the minute. 'All will be revealed, I promise.'

Picking their way through the garden, it took a few minutes to arrive at the gate into the field that Flora had first stood at all those months ago. She couldn't even have dreamed what had happened since, but standing here now, a young bride-to-be by her side, was more perfect than she thought possible. She opened her arms expansively, directing Melissa towards the view.

'Welcome to our flower garden,' she said.

The shocked intake of breath beside her was response enough and Flora fell silent for a moment, giving Melissa time to take everything in. It was just like her vision, the one she'd had standing on the slopes of Grace's garden, the one that pulled her through the dark days that followed. And now there *were* row after row of flowers growing in the field, flowers of every colour, shape and size, holding their heads towards the sky and drinking in the sun.

She felt Ned's hand slip into hers as her eyes began to well with the happiest of tears, and she leaned back into him. 'What have you got there?' she whispered, touching a hand to the papers he still held.

'Emails,' he whispered back. 'I'm sorry, I couldn't help myself, I had to go and check… But this is just a few of them, Flora… Three requests for wedding information and seven orders… We've done it, Flora, we've bloody done it!' His voice was still hushed but he couldn't keep the excitement from it.

Flora turned back to Melissa. 'I'm sorry I can't take you down into the field today but, as you can see, I'm not exactly dressed for it. Perhaps when you come back?' And she looked down at her dress, a single sheath of shimmering white which fell from her shoulder to the floor, decorated with rows of daisies at the neckline, the cuffs and the hem. 'But if you'd like to see them, I'd be very happy to show you some wedding flowers I just happen to have made earlier.'

And she turned to face the other direction, towards the huge marquee that covered most of the lawn behind them, spilling out of which came the sound of laughter, and music, and love.

Melissa's eyes lit up. 'You mean, in there?' she asked.

Flora nodded. 'No time like the present…'

Ned came to stand beside her. 'I suppose we *had* better get back to the wedding, hadn't we?'

Flora looked down at the shining band of gold on her left hand. 'Yes,' she agreed, 'I suppose we better had.'

Ned grinned. 'Come on then, Mrs Jamieson, or there'll be no champagne left...'

A letter from Emma

Hello, and thank you so much for choosing to read *The House at Hope Corner*, I do hope you enjoyed it. But of course it really wouldn't be fair to leave Ned, Flora, Hannah and Fraser for too long, and so I hope you'll join me for a new linked story later in the summer. This story will also feature a much-loved character from a previous book, someone whose story I've been wanting to tell for a very long time... I really hope you'd like to stay updated on what's coming next, so please do sign up to my newsletter here and you'll be the first to know!

www.bookouture.com/emma-davies

Having readers take the time to get in touch really does make my day, and if you'd like to contact me then I'd love to hear from you. The easiest way to do this is by finding me on Twitter and Facebook, or you could also pop by my website where you can read about my love of Pringles among other things...

I hope to see you again very soon, and in the meantime, if you've enjoyed your visit to *The House at Hope Corner*, I would really appreciate a few minutes of your time to leave a review or post on social media. Every single review makes a massive difference and is very much appreciated!

Until next time,
Love, Emma x

 @EmDaviesAuthor

emmadaviesauthor

www.emmadaviesauthor.com

Acknowledgements

I've always had a love of nature, never happier than when wandering in woodland, the sun on my face and the wind in my hair, but over the last year or so I've read many books and articles on beekeeping, or tending as I like to call it. No one *keeps* bees… but if we're very lucky we might get to share in the lives of these amazing creatures. It seemed natural therefore to write a story where bees had a supporting role and, although I can't remember when I first had the idea to write about a flower farm, it's been in my mind for quite some time. Putting these two elements together was a natural conclusion. To this end I am indebted to Clare Ashcroft of The Flower Farm in Lancashire (*www.theflowerfarm.co.uk*) for her advice on planting schedules and all things flowery. I would also like to thank Helen Jukes for her wonderful book, *A Honeybee Heart Has Five Openings*, and Alys Fowler and Steve Benbow for the delightful *Letters to a Beekeeper*.

Finally, huge thanks, as always, go to the wonderful team that are Bookouture, for giving me the opportunity to write for them again and for making sure that, when I do, I enjoy every minute.

Lightning Source UK Ltd.
Milton Keynes UK
UKHW010604111219
355129UK00001B/137/P